Swamp Team 3

by Jana DeLeon

Chapter One

"You are not shaving your face!" Ida Belle glared down at me, hands on her hips. "Jesus, I'm no girlie woman and even I know that shaving just makes more hair grow. Your upper lip is not the place you want to be sporting more hair."

I sighed and slumped lower in my kitchen chair, horribly regretting my decision to tell Ida Belle and Gertie about my dinner date that night with Carter. The two of them had descended on me shortly after breakfast, certain that I needed help presenting myself as a normal girl. It's not that I disagreed with them. I just didn't think they were going to offer much of an improvement to the process.

Now I sat captive in my own kitchen with pink polish on my toenails and wearing some oily lotion stuff on my face that Ida Belle said was hydrating my skin and had to sit until it dried. It was all I could do not to lift the tablecloth and wipe my entire face with it from scalp to neck.

"Sorry," Gertie said, "but this wax is taking forever to heat." She poked a wooden spoon into a pot of yellow sticky stuff and frowned.

"Is a couple of hairs above my lip really worthy of this much effort?" I asked.

"Yes," they both replied at once.

I sighed again.

"It's either the wax or I tweeze them," Ida Belle said. "I'm not exactly a finesse sort of gal, so the wax is probably the better option."

"I could do it," Gertie offered.

"No!" Ida Belle and I both responded. Despite constant nagging, Gertie hadn't had her glasses updated in years. If she got a hold of me with tweezers, I was as likely to end up missing a lip as the hair.

"Well, you don't have to yell about it," Gertie said.

I stared out the kitchen window at the perfectly beautiful Louisiana day. The sun was shining, and a cool breeze blew across the bayou, gently rocking my hammock. My recently acquired roommate, a black cat named Merlin, was taking full advantage of the weather, stretched out in a patch of sunlight near the azalea bushes.

After sharing space with Merlin, I'd decided that if I believed in reincarnation, I'd want to come back as a cat. Cats were surly and not required to participate in anything, but managed to convince humans to provide everything they needed. It was the perfect existence for someone like me, who found everyone and everything as suspicious as cats did.

"Can't we do this later?" I asked. "It's only ten a.m. and Carter's not picking me up until seven."

"The wax will burn a bit," Gertie said. "You'll need time for the redness to go away."

"Burn?" I sat upright in my chair. "Nobody said anything about burning."

"It doesn't burn." Ida Belle shot a disapproving look at Gertie. "It just stings a little. It's not like she's going to throw a pot of boiling water on you or anything."

I rolled my eyes. "Am I supposed to thank you?"

"Sarcasm is neither warranted nor appreciated," Ida Belle said.

"I appreciate it." Gertie smiled. "I've always thought sarcastic people were clever."

Ida Belle stared at Gertie, one eyebrow raised. "You don't think I'm clever."

Gertie waved a hand in dismissal. "That's because I know better."

I barely managed to hold in a laugh at Ida Belle's dismayed expression. Served her right for putting me through this, and all over eating food. It seemed like an awful lot of effort for a meal, and given that I'd once crawled two miles in the sand in hundred-degree heat to eat a cactus, that was saying something.

"Well," Ida Belle said. "You and I should head upstairs to pick out an outfit. Maybe while we're gone, Gertie can figure out how to work the stove."

Ida Belle stalked out of the kitchen. I jumped up from my chair as Gertie shot her a dirty look. I hoped my hasty departure didn't make it appear as if I were taking sides, but if the choice was looking at clothes versus having scalding wax applied to my face, looking at clothes was going to win every time. With any luck, that wax would remain a cold, hard lump and those five hairs, or whatever, would go on to live healthy and prosperous lives.

I followed Ida Belle upstairs to my bedroom where she flung open the closet and sighed. "This won't take long. Haven't you bought anything new since you've been here?"

"Yes, but I burned it all after wearing it to Number Two."

When I'd first arrived in Sinful, Ida Belle and Gertie had roped me into their search for a missing friend. The search extended to an island in the swamp the locals appropriately called Number Two. The entire place smelled worse than a sewer.

Ida Belle had pointed out that if Ahmad, the arms dealer who had a price on my head, ever tracked me to Sinful, Number

Two would be the perfect hiding spot. I'd already decided that even if the hounds of hell were chasing me, I wasn't going within a mile of that island again. Ever.

"I'm not talking about hunting gear," Ida Belle went on. "I mean regular clothes…you know, the kind a girl might wear. Sundresses, maybe a skirt and blouse."

"In my defense, I just passed the three-week mark here. I know it probably seems to you that I've been here a lifetime. It definitely feels that way to me. But it hasn't even been a month since I was forced into a nail salon, had hair extensions glued on, and was shoved onto a bus bound for Sinful wearing a suit and high heels, and with instructions to act like a girl. I'm an assassin. We usually don't wear sundresses."

She gave me a sympathetic look. "I know this is hard for you. I spent years in Vietnam playing the part of the defenseless little woman, kowtowing to foolish men so that they were careless around me. If I'd ever let on that I was more clever than them, I couldn't have been successful at my work."

"You were a spy," I argued. "It was your *job* to infiltrate without discovery. What I'm doing isn't work. It's just eating dinner with a guy." I still couldn't bring myself to say the word "date."

Ida Belle nodded. "You could look at it that way, or you could look at it as playing the role you were assigned by your boss. You may not be on a mission here, but you're more or less still on the job. I would argue that infiltrating without discovery is exactly what your orders are this time."

"So you're saying my boss ordered me to act like a silly woman…running after men."

"You're hardly 'running after' Carter. He asked you out to dinner. You said yes. In a place the size of Sinful, you'd draw far more attention if you turned him down. Besides, it's a completely normal thing for two young, attractive people to go to dinner."

I looked at myself in the mirror on the inside of the closet door. I'd never seen myself as attractive. Deadly, certainly. But attractive was a label I assigned to other women. Mostly women who didn't kill people for a living. Female assassins were few and tended to be a fairly tough bunch.

"You don't see it, do you?" Ida Belle asked.

I jerked my head around. "What?"

"You have no idea that you're beautiful."

I shook my head, silently ordering the blush that was creeping up my neck to disappear. "No way. I mean, I guess I'm not awful, but beautiful describes someone else entirely."

"Like your mom?"

I felt my heart tug a bit, as it always did when I thought about my mom, whom I'd lost way too young. "She was beautiful. And that's not just me saying that. Everyone who knew her said so."

"And don't those same people say you look like her?"

I glanced once more at my reflection and blew out a breath. I understood the point Ida Belle was trying to make, and I'd be lying if I didn't admit that I'd been surprised by my own reflection more than once since I'd arrived in Sinful. With the long blond extensions, street clothes, and a dash of lip gloss, I looked a lot like my mom—the way I remembered her. But it wasn't something I was ready to dwell on. Thoughts of my mother always led to thoughts of my father, and nothing beautiful lay in that path.

"Yeah, I guess they do," I said finally, hoping Ida Belle would let the whole thing drop.

She gave me a satisfied nod and turned back to face the clothes. "He said casual, right? I think the blue sundress is perfect for a casual summer dinner, and it goes well with your eyes." She reached for the sundress.

"Fire!"

I froze for a moment as Gertie's voice resounded throughout the house, then bolted out of the bedroom and down the stairs, Ida Belle on my heels. The scene in the kitchen was confusing and frightening. A skillet on the back burner of the stove, containing the remnants of bacon grease from my breakfast, had flames shooting up a good six inches from the bottom. Gertie, who was clearly panicked, was flipping the dials on the stove, as if that was somehow going to extinguish the fire.

I ran for the sink and snagged a pitcher, but Ida Belle grabbed my arm. "You can't put out a grease fire with water," she said. "You need flour."

"I don't bake!" I yelled. "Throw it out the back door."

Gertie grabbed a dishrag as I leaped across the kitchen to the back door. I flung the door open and launched to the side as Gertie hurtled toward me with the pot of wax.

"Not the wax!" I screamed, but it was too late to stop forward progress.

Gertie had already revved up her fastball and hurled the entire pot of wax when she was halfway across the kitchen. I cringed and I'll admit it, cowered behind the door, expecting her to miss the opening entirely and splatter the whole mess across the kitchen. But for a change, luck was on my side. The pot went sailing past me and out the door.

Ida Belle had managed to find an old bag of flour and was poised to toss the whole mess on the burning pan. As I dashed over to help, I heard someone yell outside. Ida Belle, who was already midway through her toss, flinched. Half the flour fell on the burning skillet. The other half flew directly in my face, where it promptly clung to the oily, undried lotion.

"Oh no," Gertie said.

I spun around just in time to see Deputy Carter LeBlanc, my dinner date, stomp into my kitchen, hot wax splashed across the center of his T-shirt. I gave a silent prayer of thanks that Gertie's aim hadn't been any higher…or lower.

"What the hell is going on here?" Carter glared at Gertie and I thought for a moment he was going to start yelling again, but then his vision shifted and he caught sight of me. His eyes widened and his jaw dropped, but not in a good way.

Then it occurred to me I probably looked like Casper the Friendly Ghost, which likely wasn't at all what he had in mind when he'd asked me to dinner.

"Gertie started a fire," I explained.

Gertie put her hands on her hips. "Oh sure. Go ahead and blame me like always."

"Ida Belle and I were upstairs," I said. "The skillet did not catch fire on its own."

"You don't know that," Gertie argued.

"Oh for Christ's sake," Ida Belle interjected. "You turned on three burners. If you'd get new glasses and wear them, it would probably improve the lives of everyone in Sinful."

"I don't need new glasses." Gertie stalked outside, I assumed to retrieve the flying wax pot.

Carter, who had finally managed to close his mouth, stared at me for several seconds, then his lower lip started to quiver. Finally, he couldn't hold it in any longer and the grin he'd been fighting against crept out.

"Just an FYI, I'm not much for the Gothic look," he said. "I prefer my women with a little color to their skin."

I ripped the tablecloth off the kitchen table and dragged it across my entire face, top to bottom, then stared in dismay when I saw next to no flour on the cloth. "First of all, I am not *your* woman, so what you prefer isn't relevant. Second, all of this is your fault for asking me to dinner in the first place."

He continued standing there with that shit-eating grin. "Well, it's probably cost me a perfectly good T-shirt, but so far, the invitation is scoring high on the entertainment scale."

"Get out." I dropped the tablecloth and pushed him toward the back door. "It will probably take a sandblaster or an exorcist to get this crap off my face. So unless you want me looking like this at dinner, I need to get to work on it now."

I slammed the door behind him and locked it for good measure. A second later, the banging started.

"Hey, let me in," Gertie yelled. "I need to pee. I promise I won't set anything else on fire."

I looked over at Ida Belle. "I suppose you want to tweeze me now?"

Ida Belle shook her head. "After this, anything is an improvement."

I sighed. That pretty much summed up my entire stay in Sinful.

It took two hours, exfoliating scrub, and a putty knife to get the flour off my face. By that point, Ida Belle and Gertie felt so guilty about the botched day of beauty that no one mentioned wax or tweezers again. At least that's what I thought. On closer inspection, it appeared the offending hairs had gone away with the scraping of the flour.

Once I had ditched the corpse look, I sent both of them packing and went upstairs for both a shower and a bath—a shower to wash the flour out of my hair and a bath to work the knots out of my back and neck. Then I went outside to the hammock, where I promptly fell asleep, Merlin splayed across my stomach. I had set my watch to go off thirty minutes before

Carter was set to pick me up. Anything I couldn't do in thirty minutes wasn't going to happen regardless.

Based on Carter's appreciative expression when I opened the door that evening, thirty minutes was more than sufficient. Quite literally more than, as I'd used twenty minutes of it to get ready and the other ten figuring out where to strap my pistol under the thin, clingy dress. I'd finally given up and selected the most girlie and least efficient option, my purse. During my entire professional career, I'd never once encountered a criminal who waited on a woman to remove her firearm from her purse, but then I hoped odds of my needing to use it tonight were low.

Carter gave me the once-over and smiled. "I see you're back from the undead."

"The whole vampire look is last year," I said as I stepped outside and locked the door. "How's your T-shirt?"

"Waxed so well I could probably surf on it, and currently standing upright in my garbage can."

"You should send Gertie a bill. I'm thinking about a lawsuit for pain and suffering. Mostly the suffering part."

He grinned and opened the passenger door to his truck. "If I recall correctly, I've repeatedly told you that the two of them are trouble."

I waited as he walked around and slid into the driver's seat. "I never disagreed with the trouble part. But since they're not the evil, mean-spirited kind of trouble, I decided to ignore you."

He started the truck and shook his head. "Continue to do so at your own peril."

"I probably will." I stared out the windshield as we drove out of my neighborhood and toward Main Street, trying to come up with something to ask or say that didn't prompt Carter to ask about my past. I was a professional liar, but not a very creative one. A spur-of-the-moment lie rolled past my lips like a breath mint. An entire past of lies would probably choke me.

When he turned onto Main Street, I let out a quiet sigh of relief. Other people would be at the restaurant. I could always ask Carter to tell me about them. That would be neutral enough. But instead of pulling into one of the Main Street parking spaces, Carter drove straight through town and pulled onto the highway.

"Where are we going?" I asked, already afraid I knew the answer.

"New Orleans. Tomorrow is my day off, and I still haven't figured out if you're doing any work at all, so I thought we could venture out for something besides Francine's."

My palms went clammy and my pulse ticked up a notch. If I'd been locked in that truck cab with two enemy assassins and a pit viper, I would have been more comfortable. The thought of hours of round-trip conversation, plus dinner, was something I wasn't mentally or emotionally prepared for. I didn't like team sports and had only started watching television a couple of weeks ago. I didn't even have enough material to cover the main course.

But if I waited for him to start a conversation, he might open with "tell me about yourself." Faking a heart attack would be easier than making up details that would pass inspection by a cop. Good Lord, how had I gotten myself into this mess? This was all Ida Belle and Gertie's fault, insisting that dating made me look more normal. Maybe that worked for other people, but they should have known better with me.

"So how long did you serve in the Marine Corps?" I asked, then cringed.

My initial thought was that the military was something I could discuss intelligently and pass off as having friends who'd served, but now, I realized I'd just asked him something personal about his past. According to Gertie, that gave Carter permission to do the same with me. With my first question, I'd already managed to screw up the entire evening.

"Twelve years," he replied. "When I went in at eighteen, things were pretty quiet. The first Gulf War was over, per se, and the second hadn't fired up yet."

"How many tours in Iraq did you do?"

"Four, but most days it felt like forty."

"I can't imagine," I said, even though I knew exactly what he was saying. Every mission I'd done seemed to play out in only two speeds—lightning fast and reverse. The actual takedown was usually only a matter of seconds. But the research and placement time leading up to that one shot could take months, even years.

"I don't think I could fathom it either if I hadn't been there," he said. "When I was a kid, some of the high school guys enlisted and served in the first Gulf War. I talked to several of them before enlisting myself. I heard the stories, and they tried to explain what it felt like, but words couldn't do it justice. It wasn't until my first tour that I understood exactly how insignificant their descriptions had been compared to the reality."

"What was your specialty?"

"Nothing at first. I didn't have a college education and no particular skill set, so I went over as infantry. Got promoted to rifleman after a while. I was good at it, so I stayed there."

Red lights began flashing in my mind. Riflemen were excellent shots but often also served as scouts. If Carter was a scout, he would be specifically trained to recognize other military personnel by movement and reaction, not just uniform. Which meant that if he ever saw me in action, he'd know I wasn't the librarian, Sandy-Sue Morrow, I was pretending to be.

The overwhelming feeling that agreeing to this dinner had been the biggest mistake I'd made since arriving in Sinful was something I could no longer ignore. With every bit of information I discovered about Carter, the possibility of him discovering my true identity ticked up several notches. When things were calm, I barely managed to portray an innocuous civilian. When things heated up—and they always seemed to—it was next to impossible to stop myself from my natural reactions to a threat.

Carter's cell phone rang and he checked the display and frowned. "What part of 'night off' did you miss in my instructions?"

I heard a high-pitched female voice. It sounded somewhat familiar, but I couldn't place it exactly.

"What?" Carter's voice hardened. "When? Yeah, tell Sheriff Lee I'm on my way."

I stiffened as I realized the voice was Myrtle Thibodeaux, the night dispatcher for the sheriff's department and one of Ida Belle and Gertie's cohorts in the Sinful Ladies Society, a group of older single women who controlled a good part of what happened in Sinful.

He dropped his cell phone on the seat and gave me an apologetic look as he took the next exit off the highway. "I'm really sorry about this, but I've got to get back to Sinful."

"What's wrong?"

"There's a house fire that I need to check on, and I figure you're going to want to come with me."

I sucked in a breath. "Gertie?"

"That would make a hell of a lot more sense, but no. The fire is at Ally's."

Chapter Two

"Is Ally all right?" I asked, my voice increasing in octave and in volume.

"Yeah," Carter said. "She inhaled a bit of smoke, but the paramedics said she's going to be fine. Still, I figured you'd want to make sure."

"Yes, of course. Thanks." I clutched the door handle as Carter made a U-turn with minimal decrease in speed, then got back on the highway and pressed his accelerator to the floorboard.

Ally was a waitress at Francine's but was working on opening her own bakery. We met when I first arrived in town, and I'd found her honesty and kindness a breath of fresh air. She'd quickly become the first female friend I'd ever had in my age group. Unlike Ida Belle and Gertie, Ally had no idea that I wasn't the real Sandy-Sue Morrow, and that's the way I intended to keep things. It was safer for both of us that way.

"How did the fire start?" I asked. The combined thoughts of Ally's daily baking and Gertie's grease fire all ran together, creating a viable reason for the tragedy.

"They're not sure yet. Hopefully the firemen will know more by the time we get there."

"I hope it's not all gone." I couldn't even imagine losing everything I owned in a matter of minutes.

Carter looked over at me and nodded. "Me, too."

The fire was nothing more than a smoke trail leading into the clouds once we arrived, and I was relieved to see the house still standing. The firemen appeared to be congregated around one corner at the back of the house. I saw Ally on the sidewalk, talking with a large woman in workout clothes, who held a leash with one of those small, yappy dogs on the other end. As I jumped out of the truck, the woman gave Ally a quick hug and headed across the street, I assumed to her home.

Ally glanced over as I hurried up and her face crumpled as she launched into me, throwing her arms around my neck.

"I can't believe it," she said, her voice raspy.

I lifted my arms to encircle her, feeling more awkward at that moment than I had in Carter's truck.

"I've never been so scared," she said.

I gave her a squeeze. "All that matters is that you're safe," I said.

She sniffed and released me, taking a tiny step backward. Her eyes were red and a single tear rolled down her cheek. My entire life, I'd never wished more than at that moment that my mom had lived longer. A normal woman would have been able to handle this without even thinking about it. A woman who'd been raised by a father who was a cross between James Bond and Rambo didn't stand a chance of understanding normal emotions.

"What happened?" I asked.

She wiped the tear off her cheek and shook her head. "I don't know. I'd been testing a new layer cake recipe and the layers needed to cool, so I headed upstairs for a shower. I had just turned off the water when the smoke detectors went off. I swear I almost had a heart attack right there. It took me a couple of seconds to even register what the noise was."

I nodded. I'd had a few of those unexpected jolts of noise since I'd arrived in Sinful, but at least since mine had happened when I was sleeping, I hadn't had to stop and consider clothes.

"I didn't take time to dry off," Ally continued. "Just pulled on yoga pants and a T-shirt and ran downstairs. I could see fire creeping toward the stairwell, and the smoke was already billowing up to the second floor. I didn't even think to grab a wet towel to cover my mouth. Stupid."

"You're not stupid. Your house was on fire. Flight is a perfectly reasonable response."

She gave me a grateful look. "I probably shouldn't have taken the time to dress."

"In this case, I don't think a handful of seconds made a huge difference, although it would have been much more dramatic if you'd run out of your front door naked. That's probably one people around here don't see all that often."

"You'd be surprised."

Ida Belle's voice sounded behind me and I spun around to see her and Gertie standing there.

"Are you okay?" Gertie asked Ally. "Shouldn't you be sitting? Someone bring her a chair, for Christ's sake! What's wrong with you people?"

I grinned as Gertie clenched Ally's arm and studied her as if her medical prognosis were written on her forehead. Ida Belle rolled her eyes at all the dramatics.

"I'm fine," Ally assured her. "Just a little raspy from the smoke."

Gertie frowned, clearly not believing her assessment, and yelled again. "Where's the damn chair?"

A cute young fireman walked up with a plastic lawn chair and placed it next to Ally, casting nervous glances at Gertie as he moved away.

Six foot two, muscular, midtwenties. No perceivable flaws. Threat level medium if unarmed.

He headed back toward a group of firemen standing near the front of the house, so I turned my attention back to Ally.

Ally took Gertie's hands in hers and looked her straight in the eyes. "I swear to you, I'm fine."

Ida Belle flopped into the chair. "Then you won't mind if I sit down. All this drama looks like it might take a while, and my bunions are killing me."

Gertie frowned down at her. "You should have those removed."

"Tell you what," Ida Belle said. "I'll have them removed when you get new glasses."

"Anyway," I interrupted, not about to listen to that age-old argument again. "So what do you think happened?"

Ally shook her head. "I have no idea. I shut everything down in the kitchen before I went to shower. Mrs. Parker, the lady I was talking to when you drove up, was walking her dog and saw smoke coming out of the window. She called the fire department right before the smoke detectors went off."

"You don't have a smoke detector in the kitchen?" Gertie asked.

Ally gave her a sheepish look. "I disabled it. I set it off so many times trying new recipes that I was afraid my neighbors would have me arrested for disturbing the peace."

"So it probably started in the kitchen," I said.

"I guess." Ally frowned. "But I don't see how. I *know* I turned everything off before I went upstairs. I've been paranoid about that sort of thing ever since my dad caught our pergola on fire while barbecuing when I was a kid."

"I remember that," Ida Belle said. "Flames shot up a good twenty feet in the air."

Ally nodded. "That's because dad's first mistake was painting it with lacquer instead of varnish. I'm pretty sure Momma was still complaining about it at his funeral."

"Having known your mother her entire life," Ida Belle said, "I'm sure you're right."

"But if you turned everything off," I asked, "then how could it have started?"

"Gas leak?" Gertie asked.

"Something still has to ignite the gas," I said.

Ally shook her head. "I would have noticed the smell of gas."

I looked over at the house and saw Carter standing on the front porch, talking to the fireman who'd brought over the lawn chair. He shook the man's hand, then came down the sidewalk toward us. He nodded at Gertie and Ida Belle, then focused on Ally.

"The firemen have assured me that the house looks worse than it really is, but it's not safe for you to stay there. It will take hours for the smoke to die down completely and there's no way to secure the house well enough for you to live in until things cool down. Even then, I wouldn't recommend it until the worst of the ash and soot has been cleaned."

Ally's eyes widened. "Oh, wow. How long will that take?"

"I'm not sure," Carter said. "A lot depends on how quickly your insurance company moves and whether a cleaning crew is available. There are specialized crews for this sort of work."

Ally stared at the house and bit her lip. "What about everything inside? I mean, if you can't secure it…"

"Once it cools down, David Leger, the fireman I was just talking to, offered to cover the damage to the exterior walls with plywood. That should help you avoid any potential tragedies from the nosy among us."

Ida Belle looked over at David and narrowed her eyes. "Is that Edith Leger's grandson?"

Carter nodded. "He just moved here from Lake Charles last week when the job opened up."

"Doesn't look at all like his grandfather," Ida Belle said. "Gilbert was a total toad."

Gertie shook her head in dismay. "Well, really."

Ida Belle waved a hand at her. "Don't go acting all pious. You faked mono for an entire six weeks to get out of being partnered with him for square dancing in gym class."

"That was because I don't like to dance," Gertie argued.

"You have an entire shelf of DVDs on break dancing," Ida Belle said. "I have no idea why, since the only thing you're likely to break is a hip."

"Ladies," Carter interrupted. "All discussions of toads and break dancing aside, our biggest concern at the moment is that Ally stay somewhere safe."

Ally nodded, still looking a bit dazed by everything. It would probably take some time before the full weight of what had happened hit her. "Can I go in to get my purse and some clothes?" she asked.

Carter nodded. "The stairwell is stable, but I'd still prefer one of the firemen go with you." He whistled and motioned to David. "Can you please escort Ally upstairs so that she can pack some clothes?"

"Of course," David said.

Ally gave him a huge smile, and I saw a blush creep up his neck as they headed toward the house. Carter stared after them and frowned.

"You gonna tell us what's eating at you?" Ida Belle asked. "Or are you just going to stand there staring?"

Carter turned back to face us, a worried look on his face.

"Telling the three of you this goes against all my better judgment, but I need your help."

A feeling of dread came over me as Ida Belle jumped up from the chair to stand beside me. "What's wrong?" I asked.

Carter took a step closer to us and leaned in. "The chief said it looked like the fire was deliberate."

"What?"

"No way!"

"That's impossible!"

Carter glanced around and motioned for us to quiet down. "They're going to send an arson investigator to be certain. But until I can sort all this out, I need to know that Ally is somewhere safe and not back in that house."

I felt the blood rush from my face. "You think someone tried to kill her?"

"Lord help," Gertie mumbled and dropped into the lawn chair, her face as pale as the white lace on her collar.

"I don't know what to think yet," Carter said. "But I can do my job better if I don't have to worry about Ally."

"She can stay with me," I said.

"Are you sure?" Ida Belle said. "Gertie and I are better prepared to handle guests."

I knew exactly what Ida Belle was implying. Because Ally didn't know anything about the real me, her living with me opened up opportunities for discovery. But it was a risk I was willing to take. While I didn't doubt for a moment that Ida Belle and Gertie would defend Ally to the death, neither was as qualified or as paranoid as I was. If Carter wanted her safe, then the best place for her to be was with me.

"I'm sure," I said. "It will be like a long girls' weekend." I'd heard that phrase on one of the sitcoms I'd watched the night before. I still had no idea what a "girls' weekend" entailed, but the women on the show had acted all excited about it.

"You just want her for her baked goods," Ida Belle said and gave me a barely imperceptible nod.

"Naturally," I said.

Carter smiled. "I'll probably have to drop by often and check on her."

I looked over at the house as Ally stepped outside and smiled at David before hurrying toward us.

"Here she comes," I said. "I don't think we should say anything about this to her until we know something for sure."

"I agree," Carter said.

Ida Belle and Gertie both nodded and everyone tried to force a normal expression as Ally walked up.

"I'm sure I've forgotten something," Ally said, clearly flustered. "I can't even think straight."

"Anything important," Carter said, "let me know and I'll get you an escort back inside."

"And anything else," Ida Belle chimed in, "you can get at the General Store."

"You're right," Ally said. "I've got work clothes for a couple of days and anything else can wait." She reached into her purse and pulled out her cell phone. "I didn't even think to check this thing and make sure the smoke didn't damage it. I need to call Aunt Celia and let her know I'll be staying with her for a bit."

"No," I said and put my hand on her arm. "You can stay with me."

Ally's expression softened. "Oh, Fortune, that's so nice of you, but I don't want to put you out. Aunt Celia's family. Putting family out is totally acceptable."

"You wouldn't be putting me out," I said. "And besides, staying with Celia is more likely to put you out than her."

"True that," Gertie said.

Ally bit her lower lip and looked back and forth from Gertie to me. "Okay, if you insist."

"I insist."

Ally smiled. "I really appreciate this."

I felt a blush creep up my neck. "You could probably repay me with some blueberry muffins."

She laughed. "I'll have to check your kitchen for equipment first. I think Marge liked cooking as much as you."

"I'll put together some supplies from my house," Ida Belle said.

I stared at her.

She put her hands on her hips. "What? I like blueberry muffins, too. And mine never turn out as good as Ally's."

I was momentarily confused by Ida Belle's comment, because her blueberry muffins were every bit as good as Ally's, but then I saw Ally's expression and realized Ida Belle's compliment was meant to shift her thinking away from her house and make her feel better.

Ally laughed. "You guys are going to make me blush."

"You're going to make me hungry," Carter said.

"Oh no!" Ally said. "You had to cancel your date."

"Dinner," I corrected. "We were having dinner. Not dating."

Carter gave me an amused look. "No worries," he said to Ally. "We'll reschedule our *dinner*. And I have leftover chicken potpie at home."

"You cook?" I asked.

He raised one eyebrow. "Would you be interested in dating if I did?"

"I'd have to try your food first."

He shook his head. "Ladies," he said to Ida Belle and Gertie, "would you please give these two a ride home while I get back to work?"

"Of course," Gertie said.

"I'll talk to you later about rescheduling our *dinner*," Carter said to me, then gave me a sexy smile and a wink before sauntering off toward the firemen.

Gertie whistled. "If I were twenty years younger, I'd eat anything he put on the table."

Ida Belle snorted. "If you were twenty years younger, you'd still be old enough to be his mother."

Gertie stuck out her lip. "Would not."

"Are you sure?" Ida Belle asked.

Gertie frowned for a moment. "Whatever."

Ally grinned. "I'm going to have to agree with Gertie on this one. Even if he serves up a grilled cheese sandwich, you should go for it."

I sighed. "I suppose most of the single women in Sinful would launch on him over frozen pizza."

Ida Belle shook her head. "Most of the single women in Sinful would cook a twelve-course meal if they thought it would get them in his front door. But he hasn't seemed interested in any of them."

"Until you," Gertie said.

They all nodded.

"No pressure there, right?" I said. "Let's get going. I've been in girlie clothes and makeup way too long and as it turns out, for no good reason. I hear yoga pants and bare feet calling me. Not to mention the leftover pot roast from the stash Gertie brought me yesterday."

They all looked at one another, exchanging this know-it-all smile that made me want to scream, then Gertie pulled out her keys and they started walking toward her car. I shot one final look back at Carter. He stood next to the front porch, talking to

David, but as I looked over, he turned his head to look at me and smiled.

It made my whole body tingle.

Damn it.

Chapter Three

It took a couple of hours for things to get settled at my house. Despite the fact that the broken windowpane hadn't been fixed yet, Ally chose the bedroom across from mine, claiming she liked to awaken to the morning sun shining on her face. That sounded like torture to me, but then I hadn't exactly been able to sleep in since I'd arrived in Sinful, so I supposed in the big scheme of things it didn't matter.

We had the leftover pot roast while Ida Belle and Gertie rounded up some additional kitchen supplies, then we all had pound cake and coffee. It was close to 11:00 p.m. before I locked the front door, and Ally and I collapsed in the living room, each with a glass of wine.

"Are you sure this isn't going to be an imposition?" Ally said.

"I'm sure. Stop worrying about it."

"It's hard to. I've spent too much of my life trying to please other people—coworkers, my mom, Aunt Celia."

"Uh-huh. And how many times were you successful?"

Ally blinked. "Ha. Never."

"Then why bother?"

"I swear I'm going to stop. When I called Aunt Celia earlier to tell her about the fire and let her know I would be staying with you until the house was fit to live in again, she pitched a fit. Said it was her duty as family and a Christian to put me up, and I was basically disparaging her as a host, a family member, and a godly woman."

"That's a lot of insult just because you chose to sleep in someone else's house."

Ally sighed. "That's Aunt Celia."

"Which is exactly why you don't need to stay with her. Between trying to run everything about the house repairs and your life, she'd drive you crazy."

"So true. But enough about me. Tell me about your almost date…er, sorry, *dinner.*"

I shrugged. "Not much to tell. He picked me up, started driving, then he got the call about the fire and we came back."

She looked disappointed. "No smoldering glances, a quick feel of the rear—yours or his—a stolen kiss, anything?"

"He brushed my shoulder with his hand when he opened the truck door."

She slumped back in her chair. "We've got to work on your game."

I laughed. "I haven't exactly seen you rushing about with men. Isn't cleaning up your own doorstep one of those Christian things, too?"

"Touché. Although, if I could find a guy who did it for me, I could totally become walking sexy, at least around him."

The thought of Ally as a sex symbol made me smile. "You'd have to wear those really high, skinny heels that I see on television. I've never seen anyone 'walking sexy' in flip-flops."

She laughed. "Shuffling sexy?"

"Well, you were barefoot outside of your house and that cute fireman seemed to enjoy the view."

Ally's eye widened. "David? He was just being nice."

"If being nice makes him blush, then I guess you're right."

"He blushed?" Her brow wrinkled. "Do you really think he

might be interested?"

I shrugged. "Don't ask me. I'm the original anti-girlie-girl."

"Who's being hit on by the hottest guy in town."

"And I have no idea why."

Ally studied me for a moment, her expression puzzled. "You really don't know, do you? At first, I thought you were being modest, but that's not it at all. You really have no idea how attractive you are."

I felt a blush creep up my neck and was thankful that only a single lamp was on in the room. "It's not something I think about."

"But you did all those pageants," Ally said. "I guess I just figured you'd know everything about looks and putting yourself out there."

I hesitated for a moment before answering. The real Sandy-Sue Morrow had spent time on the beauty pageant circuit, and it was the hardest part of my cover to swallow. The lies were on the tip of my tongue, just waiting for me to queue them up, but I felt guilty continuing to lie to her. Then reality took over, reminding me that I didn't have a choice.

"That was really my mother's thing," I said, passing off my fake past. "I was never into it, and I think she probably exaggerated a good bit about my accomplishments."

Ally frowned. "That sucks on both counts. Why can't parents let kids do what they want and support them? Why do they have to make up stories to be important to their friends, or whatever?"

"Some parents are great," I said, faint memories of my mom running through my mind. "Others, not so much."

Like my father.

"I suppose you're right." Ally rose from her chair. "I'm going to head up to bed. I'm completely wiped out."

I nodded as she headed up the stairs, our conversation replaying in my mind.

It was the second time in a single day that someone had commented on my looks. Back in DC, where I was focused solely on my career, I didn't have to think about my parents. Now, it seemed as if they were on my mind every day.

I rose from my chair and turned off the lamp. I'd been given entirely too much to think about in the last couple of weeks. Sinful and its residents had found a way to make me take a hard look at my past, my present, and my future.

Unfortunately, I still didn't have answers for any of them.

I was in the middle of a dream where all my enemies had to dress like ballerinas when the bed started shaking. I bolted out of bed, grabbing my pistol, readying for fire by the time my feet hit the floor.

"Don't shoot. It's Ally."

I blinked and my eyes began to focus in the dim moonlight. Ally stood at the end of my bed, her hands in the air.

"Put your hands down," I said. "I'm not going to shoot you."

She dropped her hands to her sides and let out a breath. "You could have fooled me. Jeez Louise, you move fast."

"It's probably just adrenaline," I said, trying to brush it off. "What's wrong?"

"I heard something outside in the bushes right below my window."

"It's probably Merlin."

She shook her head. "He came in about an hour ago and curled up at the end of my bed. When I got up to check the noise, he took off downstairs."

I frowned. "I'll check it out."

I headed downstairs, Ally right behind me, then crossed the living room to the front door.

"You're not going out the back door?" Ally asked.

"I want to sneak up on them."

Her eyes widened. "Oh, I didn't think you were going outside. I thought maybe you'd just flip on the back porch light and scare them off or something."

"Then we wouldn't know who it was." I opened the front door. "Lock the door behind me. And stay inside. If you hear a scuffle, call the police."

"Shouldn't we just call the police now?"

"He'd be gone before they got here." I slipped out the door and pulled it shut behind me before she could formulate another argument.

I hurried down the front steps and around the side of the house to the back. With my luck, it would be another cat. Perhaps one that had seen Merlin con his way in and thought he could follow suit. Or even worse, a dog. I'd had Marge's old bloodhound, Bones, living with me for a bit when I first moved to Sinful, but he was so old he didn't do much besides sleep. A younger, more active dog would be far more work than I was interested in, especially with a cat already in residence. That sounded like a recipe for noise and broken things.

I inched up to the edge of the house and stopped, listening to the faint rustling of bushes in the still night air. Something was definitely back there, but I couldn't gauge size by the limited amount of noise. Figuring I may as well get it over with and get back to bed, I sprang around the corner and came face to face with a masked man.

I'm not sure who was more surprised, but he uttered a startled yelp before spinning around. I managed to grab his mask as he turned and his head yanked back. Got him, I thought, but then the mask ripped and he fled down the side of the house behind the bushes. I took off after him, clutching the torn mask, hell-bent on catching him and forcing him to talk. He jumped onto the back porch about ten feet ahead of me and I saw him reach down and lift something up from the floor and attempt to hurl it at me. Because he was running and twisting at the same time, he didn't come close to his target and the object went hurtling into the backyard.

A moment of confusion swept over me because I couldn't recall anything sitting on the back porch, but I got my answer a second later when I heard a high-pitched screech and a low-pitched yell. As I leaped onto the porch, Ally burst out the back door, pistol in hand. I tried to put on the brakes, but the forward motion of my leap made it impossible to stop before slamming into Ally. Her gun went off and I tackled her onto the porch.

I sprang up almost as quickly as I fell and started to reach my hand down to help Ally up when I was struck blind with a beam of light. I put one hand up, trying to make out the figure walking toward us, but I was afraid I already knew. Only one person existed in Sinful who would walk toward the fiasco on my porch rather than run away.

"I don't know which to be more pissed off about," Carter said as he stepped up to the porch, "the fact that you threw a cat on me or that you shot at me."

"Well, since I am innocent of either infraction," I said, "choose whichever you'd like."

He aimed the flashlight at the back wall of the house, casting a glow over the porch.

I dropped my hand from my forehead as Ally scrambled up from the porch. "She didn't shoot at you," Ally said. "I did. I mean, not on purpose. It was an accident."

She looked at me, then back at Carter. "I don't know anything about throwing a cat. Is that for real?"

Carter aimed the light at his head where we could see three fine scratches running up his forehead, tiny droplets of blood trickling from them.

"Oh," Ally said, then bit her lower lip. "Is the cat all right?"

"Based on the way he tore over my head and off toward the shed, I'd say the cat got the better end of all this."

Carter aimed the flashlight back at the house and glared. "Someone tell me what the hell is going on here!"

"I heard a noise," Ally said, "and woke Fortune up. She went out to check."

Carter fixed his gaze on me. "Just like that. Not even a thought about calling the police?"

Ally sucked in a breath, and I stepped down on her toes. "If I called the police every time a raccoon or cat or whatever makes a racket at my house, you'd run me out of town."

Carter stared. "So I'm supposed to believe the cat made enough noise to get you outside, then flew ten yards out of the bushes?"

"No," I said. "There was a guy in the bushes. When he saw me, he ran. He threw the cat. I think he was aiming for me, but he wasn't a very good shot."

Carter narrowed his eyes. "What guy?"

"I don't know. He was wearing a mask." I held up the remnants of the mask.

Carter reached up and took the mask from me, shining the light on it. "Good God Almighty, this is a beanie hat with holes cut in it."

I shrugged. "I guess he improvised. Probably not a big call for ski masks in Sinful."

Carter gave me an exasperated look. "The point is someone

took the time to create a makeshift mask in order to sneak around your house."

"Oh," I said. "Yeah, I guess I see the problem."

Carter shook his head and reached over to pick up Ally's pistol. "Is this yours?" he asked me.

"It's mine," Ally said.

He looked at her, one eyebrow raised.

"I swear," Ally said. "Fortune didn't even know I had it. I was listening at the back door, but when I heard all the racket, I was afraid someone was attacking her so I came out to help."

Carter sighed and handed her the pistol. "It will be a damn miracle if the two of you can live together without shooting anyone. Can you try? I mean, try really hard?"

"I didn't even fire my weapon," I said, feeling rather pleased with myself. "I suppose I could have shot the beanie-hat-ski-mask guy but I figured it might be a problem." I looked at Carter. "Should I have shot him?"

"No!" Carter yelled. "You're not supposed to shoot random people."

"Even if they're in my yard, wearing a fake ski mask?"

"Even if. You're supposed to call the police."

I shrugged. "Doesn't look like I had to. You were already here." I frowned. "Why were you already here?"

"If you must know, I was patrolling the bayou. I saw something moving in your backyard—probably your masked friend—so I docked my boat and headed up here to check it out."

"Okay," I said. It made sense, except for the part about patrolling the bayou. The entire time I'd been in Sinful, I hadn't ever heard of scheduled midnight bayou patrols by the sheriff's department. If Carter was on the bayou in the middle of the night, he was looking for something. He just wasn't about to tell me what.

Carter shoved the mask in his back pocket. "Get back inside and lock the doors. If you hear anything again, call the sheriff's department. I'm on call all night." He locked his gaze on me. "Under no circumstances are you to leave the house until after daylight. And no firearms." He looked over at Ally, then back at me. "Either of you."

"No problem," I said.

He didn't look remotely convinced, but he whirled around and stalked off toward the bayou. I waved Ally in the back door and locked it behind us.

"What the heck is going on?" Ally asked. "What was that guy doing behind your house, and wearing a mask? The whole thing is weird and creepy."

I watched as the running lights on Carter's boat came on and he backed away from the bank. "I don't know what's going on. But you can bet I'm going to find out."

Chapter Four

I awoke the next morning to the smell of warm blueberries. I threw back the covers and took a huge sniff, certain I'd died and gone to heaven. I'd been over the moon about the muffins before, but that was before I'd eaten them straight out of the oven. I may have to be committed before the morning was over.

Unwilling to delay greatness any longer, I pulled on yoga pants and headed downstairs. Ally placed a tray of huge, fragrant muffins on the stovetop as I stepped into the kitchen. Merlin was in the corner, lapping at a bowl of milk, and looking none the worse for the wear from his unscheduled flight into Carter's head.

Ally looked over at me and grinned. "I see the muffins got you out of bed."

I walked over to the stove and inhaled. "I didn't even stop to brush my hair. You're lucky I took the time to put on pants."

She laughed. "Well, grab some coffee and take a seat. All this cooking has made me hungry."

I filled a mug with coffee and sat down at my breakfast table as Ally slid two plates of muffins onto the table followed by a tub of butter and a knife. As I cut into the muffin, the fragrant steam rose from the center, amplifying the already incredible aroma in my kitchen. I dumped a hunk of butter in the center and pushed the sides back together, giving it a couple seconds to melt.

When I took the first bite, I closed my eyes and sighed. "This may be the best moment of my entire life."

Ally laughed. "I appreciate the compliment, but that is so incredibly sad. You need to get out more."

"Nope. Carter gave me strict orders to stay inside."

Ally rolled her eyes. "You know good and well you don't listen to a thing he says. And he only meant that for last night because of the creeper."

"Maybe." I took another bite of the muffin. Fresh-baked blueberry muffins, coffee already made…so far, this whole roommate thing was stellar.

Ally shook her head and took a bite of muffin. Her eyes widened. "Oh, maybe you're right. These may be my best yet."

I crammed the last of the muffin in my mouth and jumped up for another. "Definitely. What did you do differently?"

"Fresh blueberries. One of the local farmers stopped by yesterday with a truckload and I bought several freezer bags full. They were still sitting on the coffee table, so I stuffed one of them in my bag on the way out."

"I'm glad you did." I slid back into my chair. "Were you able to get back to sleep last night?"

"Finally. For a couple of hours, I swear I heard every noise in Sinful. Exhaustion must have caught up with me and then I slept like the dead. I can't believe I didn't wake up until eight o'clock. I almost never sleep past six."

I jerked my head toward the kitchen clock. "Jeez, it's after nine o'clock already."

"So what? Today is my day off, and you've got a whole summer off, sorta."

"I've been trying to sleep late since I arrived. I just haven't been overly successful. And I'm surprised Ida Belle and Gertie haven't already stormed the gates. Every time there's a whisper of a chance of my sleeping late, Gertie shows up with the chickens, banging on my door."

I'd barely gotten the words out when someone knocked on my front door.

"Speak of the devils," I said and headed to the living room to answer the door.

I flung open the door, still clutching half of my second muffin, but it wasn't Ida Belle and Gertie standing on my porch. It was Carter.

"Looks like I'm just in time," he said, staring at my muffin. "Or maybe too late? Please tell me I'm not too late."

I waved him inside and headed back to the kitchen. "Another ten minutes and I'd be giving you a different answer. But as it is, you're in luck."

Ally jumped up from the table as Carter walked in. "Oh, crap, I'm still wearing my robe."

"Hey," Carter said, "if you can cook in it, the robe is okay by me."

A blush ran up Ally's face. "I'll be right back. Help yourself."

"I intend to," Carter said as he pulled a muffin from the tray.

I poured him a cup of coffee and pointed to the butter as I sat back down. He slid into the seat Ally had vacated. I expected him to tear into the muffin as I had, but instead he glanced back, then leaned toward me.

"I just finished talking to the arson investigator."

I felt my pulse tick up a notch. I'd thought he was here to bitch at me some more about the creeper. I'd never considered that he'd have information on the fire so quickly. "That was fast."

"He came out first thing this morning. It didn't take him

long to find the source. The fire was definitely set, and it's no professional job. Someone poured gasoline on the back corner of her porch and tossed some up on the walls."

"That doesn't make sense. Why would anyone want to hurt Ally?"

Carter shook his head, his expression grim. "I don't know, but you can bet I intend to get to the bottom of this."

I heard the floor creak overhead and glanced up. "Do you have to tell her?"

"I don't see any way around it. Her insurance company is going to require the investigator's report before processing a claim."

"Crap. Have you had any other suspicious fires in Sinful lately?"

"No. The fire incidents we have here are mostly the usual illegal trash burning or accidents while working on boat motors. The last house fire was the homeowner's fault. The fool was barbecuing and when it started raining, he thought it would be a good idea to move the grill into his living room. He tripped and dumped the entire mess in the middle of his floor. Sent the house up in flames."

I stared. "Incredible." I blew out a breath. "I hate this."

"Look. I know you're trying to protect her, and I'd like to as well, but the reality is, if someone is trying to hurt her, Ally is the person in the best position to know who and why. And if she's on alert, she'll be more careful."

He was right, but that didn't make it suck any less. "What about footprints or any other evidence? I know a lot was probably destroyed by the fire and all the water spray, but you processed the crime scene, right?"

He narrowed his eyes at me and I saw the shift in his expression. Carter the man who asked me to dinner was long gone. Carter the cop was in full force. "I did and will do my job, as I always do. What I need you to do is keep an eye on Ally and stay out of my way."

"Of course," I said, and I thought I sounded pretty convincing, especially considering I had zero intention of complying.

Apparently, I wasn't as convincing as I thought.

Carter pointed his finger at me. "Do not get in the middle of this, Fortune. You've been lucky so far that your meddling hasn't resulted in a blown case or something far worse. And just in case you've conveniently forgotten what interfering in a police investigation can result in, I brought something for you."

He pulled a folded sheet of paper from his jeans pocket and handed it to me. I unfolded the paper and stared at it in disbelief.

"You're billing me for the sheriff department's toilet repair?" During my last adventures in investigating, I'd gotten into a bit of trouble with the toilet at the sheriff's department. I was of the opinion that I'd sustained more damage than the toilet, but apparently, I was wrong.

"You're the one who broke it," Carter said. "Just because I don't know what illegal or unethical thing you were up to at the time doesn't mean I don't know for certain that you shouldn't have been doing it. So from where I sit, the toilet was likely broken in the commission of a crime."

"Are you serious? The only crime I committed was stepping in gum." By God, that was my story and I was sticking to it.

"Well, that step cost you a hundred and twelve dollars. And I will point out that if you'd been at home instead of downtown inciting a riot, you wouldn't have stepped in anything."

"You know good and well it wasn't me who started the riot."

"Maybe not. But what I know for certain is that you broke

the toilet."

"Maybe if it wasn't a million years old, it could have stood up to me dipping my foot in it."

"Probably true, which is why I was sorely tempted to leave that ancient, leaky, moldy pile of bricks and move into the old firehouse building when it came up for sale. But the old firehouse doesn't back up to the bayou, and I didn't want to drive somewhere to access the sheriff's boat."

"Maybe you should give up the boat altogether and just walk on water with all your perfection."

He sighed. "Look, I know you want to help your friends, and I find that admirable even though it usually causes me grief, but how many times do you have to have a brush with death before you realize you're supposed to leave law enforcement work to law enforcement?"

It was an argument I couldn't win. Not unless Carter knew the truth about me. Sandy-Sue Morrow, librarian extraordinaire, had absolutely no business insinuating herself into a crime spree. And even though I thought billing me for the toilet was sort of a low blow, I understood where he was coming from. Carter thought he was protecting the defenseless of Sinful, and as far as he knew, I was just one more added to his list.

"I don't want any more brushes with death than I've had already," I assured him. I held up my hand. "Scout's honor."

That much was true, anyway.

"That's not Scout fingers," he said. "You look like you're swearing in for a trial."

"Fine then, grab a Bible and I'll swear to stay out of police business." I just wouldn't tell him I was crossing my fingers under the table.

Before he could say anything else, Ally bounded back into the kitchen, dressed in shorts and a T-shirt and looking perkier than anyone should before noon.

She stopped next to the counter and stared at me. "Is he making you ask permission to speak? Because it's kinda your house."

I dropped my hand. "No, I was considering slapping him, but it seemed sort of girlie."

She looked back and forth from Carter to me, then shook her head. "I don't think I want to know."

Carter leaned back in his seat and took a bite of muffin. "These are great."

"Of course they are," Ally said as she slid into the chair next to me with a fresh cup of coffee. "Did you just stop by for muffins or did you get anything on the creeper?"

"Nothing on the creeper, but I'm asking around." He swallowed the last of his muffin and downed some coffee. "I spoke with the arson investigator this morning."

"Oh." Ally sat up straight. "How long does he think it will take to figure out what started the fire? I mean, I guess they have to test stuff and all…"

"Actually, he was able to identify the source fairly quickly, and I'm sorry to say, it was deliberate."

Ally's hand flew up to cover her mouth. "No!"

"He found traces of gasoline on your back porch flooring and walls."

Ally's hand shook slightly as she lowered it back to the table. "Why would someone set my house on fire?"

"I don't know," Carter said. "I hoped that was something you could help me with."

Ally's eyes widened. "Me? I don't see how."

"Have you had an argument with anyone lately? Even something small—even at work—anything that someone could have built up into a grudge?"

Ally slowly shook her head. "I can't think of anything. I mean, Aunt Celia's given me some grief over being friends with Fortune, but I hardly think she'd come burn my house down over it."

"No," Carter agreed. "That's a stretch, even for Celia."

His attempt at lightening the mood generated a small, forced smile from Ally. "I haven't had problems with anyone," she said. "I swear. Not even a disagreement at the café. Ever since Ted's murder, things have been really quiet, almost painfully civil."

Carter nodded. "I don't want you to worry about this. I'm going to figure it out, but in the meantime, it might be a good idea if you stayed here while the repairs are being made to your house."

"I thought you said I'd be able to move back in after the initial cleanup and when the house could be secured."

"You can…I'm just not recommending it."

"Oh," Ally said quietly.

Carter rose from the table. "Try not to worry about this, and if you think of anything, call me anytime."

He looked at me as if he expected I'd escort him to the door, but I was too irritated over the toilet bill to be bothered with manners. "Thanks for dropping by," I said, then went back to eating my muffin.

Without another word, he turned around and left. I took a big gulp of coffee and watched him as he disappeared down the hall.

"Well," Ally said, "that wasn't the least bit uncomfortable. What exactly did I interrupt when I came back downstairs?"

"The usual—Carter telling me to stay out of his investigation. Me promising to stay out. Him not believing me."

"Surely he doesn't think you get involved in things on a

whim? None of the things that have happened to you since you came to Sinful were your fault. The only thing you're guilty of is trying to help your friends."

"Yes, and he'd prefer that I did not continue that tradition."

"I see. And you promised not to."

"Yeah, but I had my fingers crossed under the table."

Ally stared at me for a couple of seconds, then laughed. "Oh my God. You're serious, aren't you?"

"Of course. Did you really think I was going to take a backseat when someone is out to get you? Even if you didn't bake the best muffins in the world, you're my friend. And I'll be darned if someone is going to hurt one of my friends on my watch."

Ally smiled. "I love that you feel that way, but what can you do about it? I know you've gotten to the bottom of some things recently, but you're a librarian. You could have been hurt or worse. I don't want that on my conscience."

"I have no intention of putting myself in danger," I said, and that wasn't a lie. It usually wasn't my intent that got me in a pickle—it was Ida Belle and Gertie's.

"But you already have," Ally pointed out. "You invited me to stay here. If someone is out to get me, that means you're in danger simply by doing a good deed."

She sucked in a breath and her eyes widened. "Oh my God! What if the creeper was the guy who tried to burn down my house? That has to be it, right? He could have killed you last night."

"The way he screamed when I rounded the corner and darn near ran into him, I doubt killing someone was on his mind. I think I scared him more than he scared me."

"That's only because he didn't expect anyone to be out there. The point still is, I've already put you in danger."

"I don't think so. He took off running. What kind of killer runs away from his prey?"

"But why was he here in the first place? You didn't have any trouble before last night. So it has to be because of me."

"Okay, let's just say that's true. What are your options? Staying with Celia would put her in danger, and regardless of my profession, I think I'm better equipped to handle a potential threat than her. There's no hotel in town. Your job is here. Your house is uninhabitable."

"It's not inhabitable right now." Ally rose from the table. "I'm going to call my insurance adjuster and see if they can put a rush on things. As soon as the house is livable, I'm moving back in."

"No way—"

She held up her hand. "Tell me you wouldn't do the same thing if the situation were reversed."

I let out a huff. The truth was, I would have stayed in the house, breathing smoke and ash, and with a sniper rifle trained on the backyard, just waiting for the guy to come back and finish the job.

"That's what I thought," she said and headed out of the kitchen.

I slumped back in my chair. That had not gone as planned. If Ally went back to her house, I couldn't protect her the way I could if we were under the same roof. And I couldn't exactly tell her that I was an assassin and not a librarian, although that would instantly fix all my problems—with this situation anyway. It would open Pandora's box for others.

I didn't doubt for a moment that Carter would do everything within his power to find out who was responsible. He was an honorable man and it was clear to me that he cared about the people he protected. What Carter wouldn't do is things *not* within his power, and I'd already decided that the legal system was quite restrictive when it came to tracking down the guilty.

Which left only one option—Swamp Team Three.

Chapter Five

Gertie plopped down on my couch, clutching a pair of tennis shoes, and looked over at me. "You're sure Ally won't be back for a while?"

I nodded. "I called you guys as soon as Celia hauled her out of here. She's taking Ally to the Catholic church for some sort of prayer vigil and lunch thing."

"Good," Ida Belle said. "Someone should make a note. This might be the first time Celia has done anything useful."

"For us, maybe," I said. "Ally might have a differing opinion."

"No doubt she does," Gertie said, as she bent over to remove her loafers and pull on tennis shoes. "So explain to me again why we're going to sneak over to Ally's house?"

"To find clues," Ida Belle said. "Someone tried to burn down Ally's house. Then was creeping around Fortune's. We need to find out who it is. Have you been paying attention at all?"

Gertie gave Ida Belle a dirty look. "I'm not senile. I'm just wondering why we're going to go slipping around the back side of the neighborhood, then tromping through the swamp, when all the information we need is at the sheriff's department."

Ida Belle threw her hands in the air. "What are we thinking? We should have Gertie walk down there and get Carter to make us a copy."

"Sarcasm is not a good look for you," Gertie said.

"Now she tells me." Ida Belle grunted as she tied her shoe.

"I'm not suggesting," Gertie said, "that we stroll down to the sheriff's department and ask Carter to hand over his files. I was merely pointing out that we have managed to get confidential information out of the building."

"Oh no," I said. "I'm not breaking into the sheriff's department again. Heck, I'm not even going to walk past it on the sidewalk."

Ida Belle stared. "What's eating you?"

I grabbed the toilet invoice from my coffee table and passed it to Ida Belle. She scanned the document, then started laughing.

"He asked you on a date," Ida Belle said, "but he's billing you for breaking the toilet? He needs some serious work on his romancing skills."

Gertie snatched the invoice from Ida Belle. "Well, this doesn't make any sense at all. Why in the world would he bring this up now?"

"To dissuade me from any thoughts of getting involved in his investigation of Ally's house fire," I said. "And given that I had a creeper and he got a cat thrown on him, he's going to be watching me closer than ever. I want to protect Ally as much as you guys, but I can't keep taking the kind of risks I have been."

"She's right," Ida Belle said. "And since Carter's interested in Fortune on a personal level, he's going to pay even closer attention to everything she does."

Gertie stared at us, a confused expression on her face. "But we're about to sneak into Ally's backyard, which has been roped off as a crime scene. Isn't that a risk?"

"Yes," I said, "but it doesn't count unless we get caught."

Ida Belle nodded. "Breaking into the sheriff's department is a far bigger risk, especially since Carter's convinced we've done it before."

"We *have* done it before," Gertie said.

"Of course we've done it before." Ida Belle's exasperation started to show. "But we're not going to *admit* to it! And Fortune's right—all the happenings here lately have put her under a spotlight. We need to do everything we can to get that light off of her."

"Who said she had to go?" Gertie asked.

I looked over at Ida Belle, who frowned. "Well, hmmm, no one, I guess."

The possibilities of what could happen if Ida Belle and Gertie set out to break into the sheriff's department by themselves flashed through my mind like a *Three Stooges* episode on fast-forward.

"Can we go with this option first?" I asked. "Bail for trespassing is going to be a lot lower than bail for breaking and entering."

"Good point," Ida Belle said and rose from her chair. "Hurry up, Gertie. You're always lagging."

Gertie grunted as she bent over to tie her last tennis shoe. "You never let up—'you should exercise more,' 'get new glasses'—now I guess you're going to try to push that newfangled yoga crap on me just because I don't think touching my head to my knees represents a skill set I need or a good time."

I shook my head. "You disarmed that killer in your house with an incredible kick. Totally Bruce Lee stuff, and that was only a few weeks ago. How can you be in such bad shape now?"

Gertie rose from the chair. "I limped for two days after that kick, and had to use ice and a heating pad for a week. My body hasn't forgotten my martial arts training, and can pull off a move or two in a pinch, but I always pay for it later."

Ida Belle frowned. "Then I'm surprised you're not in traction from all the falling off fences and out of trees that you've done lately."

"I didn't fall," Gertie argued. "I miscalculated the distance in the dark."

"It wasn't dark when you fell out of the tree at the funeral," I pointed out.

Gertie glared at both of us for a second, then stalked out the front door.

Ida Belle stared after her, shaking her head. "You know—"

"If she got new glasses it would solve everything," I finished. "Her depth perception is off because of her vision. She squints a lot and lately, her head is usually cocked slightly to the right. Likely, she's got eye strain from trying to focus and it's giving her a headache and potentially an earache, which in turn is affecting her balance."

"Nice." Ida Belle gave me an approving nod. "You don't miss much, do you?"

"In my line of work, the smallest flaw can create a big advantage. I've gotten lax since I've been in Sinful. I'm trying to get back to basics."

I hopped up from my chair and Ida Belle and I joined Gertie on the sidewalk outside.

"We should head to the park," Ida Belle said. "Ally's house is a short hop through the swamp, just behind the picnic area."

I nodded. "I hope no one is picnicking. The fewer witnesses, the better."

Gertie wiped sweat from her brow. "It was ninety-two degrees when I left my house, and a hundred percent humidity given that a storm is brewing. No one in their right mind would be picnicking right now."

Sure, I thought, but how many Sinful residents were in their right mind?

I fell in step next to Ida Belle, who set off at a brisk pace for the park. Gertie huffed behind us, and I wondered if she'd make it to the park, much less through the swamp. But then I had no room to talk. I'd finally jumped on a scale this morning and had almost screamed at the horror.

Five pounds!

I'd gained five pounds since I'd arrived in Sinful. If this is what happened when one converted to civilian life, I may have to skip retirement. If I didn't do something soon, I wouldn't pass the physical for a mission, and I'd have to shop for new clothes. It was the shopping for new clothes part that scared me the most.

As I felt my hamstrings tighten, I made a deal with myself—from now on, only one bad food item a day, and I had to run at least five miles every morning to counteract the bad food. Marge had some free weights in her bedroom closet. I probably needed to haul those out as well.

"We can cut across here," Ida Belle said and stepped off the sidewalk and into the park.

We cut diagonally across the park and through the picnic area, which was empty, as predicted.

"Hold up for a second," Gertie said as we stepped into the edge of the swamp. "I've been thinking about things."

Ida Belle raised an eyebrow. "What things?"

"Things like the fire not being set by a professional."

"Well, we already knew that before Carter said anything," Ida Belle said.

"Really?" I asked. "How?"

Ida Belle shrugged. "Because it was only dusk. A professional would have waited until dark to avoid being seen."

I nodded. "And that's a logical thought except for one

thing."

"What?"

"Assuming the arsonist is a Sinful resident, no one would think anything of seeing them walking or driving down the street, or walking through the swamp."

Gertie's eyes widened. "She's right. We keep going into these things with some shadowy image of the bad guy, but we keep forgetting that it's probably someone we already know."

"Okay, I'll give you that," Ida Belle said, "but people *would* notice a man walking down the sidewalk with a gas can. Anyone who saw him would assume he ran out of gas and stop to offer a ride."

I shrugged. "So he went through the swamp, hid the can beforehand, and then returned later to set the fire."

"Before dark." Ida Belle shook her head. "One indicates clever. The other plain stupid."

"Creeping around my house wearing a makeshift mask is plain stupid, too," I said, "but somebody did it. Who else has a reason to besides our arsonist?"

"Okay," Ida Belle said. "I'll play along. Let's say the arsonist took the same path that we are to Ally's house to avoid being seen by any residents who were out and about. Why hide the can? If he's ballsy or stupid enough to torch the house before dark, then why come back later? Why not just do it while he was there?"

"Because Ally was cooking," I said, "and the kitchen is on the back of the house."

Gertie nodded. "He couldn't have entered the backyard without Ally seeing him."

"So either he got there and waited until she went upstairs or he left the can and came back later. Either way, he might have left a clue—footprints, a cigarette—and that's what we're going to look for. I can't see that this needs any more thinking."

"What if he lived next door?" Gertie asked.

Ida Belle and I both stared.

"What?" Gertie asked. "You said it was probably someone we already knew. He has to live somewhere, doesn't he?"

I frowned. "That sounds too easy."

"But it would be clever," Ida Belle said, "or plain stupid."

"Who lives next door to Ally?"

"Floyd Guidry," Ida Belle said and frowned. "Gertie may be onto something."

"I take it this Floyd is a problem?" I asked.

Gertie nodded. "You best believe it. The first time Floyd was arrested he was still in kindergarten."

I stared. "Then shouldn't he be rotting in prison by now?"

Ida Belle frowned. "He got smarter. Skirts on just this side of the law, based on what you can see. But who knows what else he's got going on."

"He's mean as a snake, too," Gertie said. "It wouldn't surprise me if Ally had problems with him."

"But Carter asked her," I said, "and she couldn't think of anyone."

"Maybe he didn't come to mind because it's the norm," Gertie suggested.

"Well, no use speculating about it," I said. "Let's get going on this and we'll ask Ally about him when we get back to my house."

We cut through the swamp toward the back of Ally's house. About fifteen minutes in, I caught a flicker of color through the trees and figured we were getting close. Then I heard the sound of water.

"Is that the bayou?" I asked.

"Yes," Ida Belle said. "It runs right behind Ally's house."

Gertie came to a dead stop and put her hands on her hips. "You're right. What the heck are we doing tromping through the swamp when we could have taken a boat?"

Ida Belle lifted one eyebrow. "Really? What boat, exactly, do you suggest we take—mine, which is still in the shop having the hull repaired, or yours, which was pulled from the bottom of the bayou two days ago and may never run again?"

Since both situations lay primarily at Gertie's feet, I figured I'd keep my mouth shut on this one. Gertie frowned, then huffed, and I thought she was going to argue, but she must have thought better of it.

"Whatever," she said and waved a hand in dismissal as she stomped off toward Ally's house.

We fell in step behind her. The closer we came to the neighborhood, the more building detail I could see, which didn't make much sense at the height I was looking. What I expected to see was a fence. When we got about twenty feet away, I realized what the problem was.

"Ally has a wrought iron fence," I said. "The only place to hide is behind her shed, and he'd have to get there first without being seen."

Ida Belle frowned. "It used to be wood."

"How long ago was that?" I asked.

"Until yesterday, it's probably been a year or more since I've been inside the house. Ally's mother isn't exactly a likable person, so no one really wanted to see her when she was well. When she got sick, she refused to let anyone inside the house except Ally."

"Who she treated like a slave," Gertie threw in.

Ida Belle nodded. "I have no idea when she made the change to the fence, but we know for sure it was before the arson. So we take this into account and move forward."

"Why are there only two houses here in this stretch?" I

asked. "I thought Ally's house was part of the neighborhood." It had been almost dark when I'd arrived at Ally's house the night before with Carter. The streetlights had provided most of the visibility, and that wasn't stellar. I'd seen tall hedges and the tree line nearby, but had been too distracted to realize there weren't more houses in this row besides Ally's and Floyd's.

"She's in the neighborhood," Ida Belle said, "but the way the bayou snakes around, you couldn't put houses on either side of Ally and Floyd's places. The ground was too unstable. A builder tried once, but the foundation cracked to pieces within a week."

I peered into the swamp in both directions but couldn't see anything but green and brown. "How far away are their next-door neighbors?"

"About fifty yards in either direction," Ida Belle said.

"So Ally and Floyd are isolated."

Ida Belle nodded. "On the sides, they are, but there are houses across the street."

Right. I remembered that the neighbor who'd reported the fire lived across the street. I studied the property line of the two homes. "I suppose the arsonist could have hidden behind Floyd's fence, but with the placement of that tree, his view of the kitchen window wouldn't be very clear."

"We've already decided he was either clever or stupid," Gertie said. "If we're going to assume it's a Sinful resident, I say we move forward with the stupid idea and look for clues behind Floyd's fence and Ally's shed."

I nodded. "Then let's spread out along Floyd's fence line and look for bare areas on the ground where we may be able to spot a footprint."

We separated, and with a distance of roughly thirty feet between us, moved toward Floyd's fence, canvassing the ground as we progressed. When we reached the back of the fence, I looked over to my left at Ida Belle and Gertie, and they both shook their heads.

They headed over and Ida Belle shook her head.

"Not even a smudge in the mud," she said, "much less a cigarette or matchbook or any of the things you see on television."

"Yeah," I said. "I don't know why I hoped something might be easy."

"No matter," Ida Belle said. "This is still what police look at first, so if we want to conduct a real investigation, we have to do the things they will do."

Gertie nodded and leaned back against Floyd's dilapidated fence. I saw the fence panel wobble, but before I could say a word, the entire section went crashing down into Floyd's yard, carrying Gertie with it.

Ida Belle and I rushed over to help Gertie up. As we reached down to lift her from the mangled mess, I heard a banging noise at Floyd's house. I looked up to see a beefy man with a bald head, wearing sweats and a white muscle shirt, stomp out the back door.

"What the hell are you doing on my property?" he yelled.

He reached back inside the house and pulled out a shotgun. I yanked Gertie up from the ground. "Time to jet."

We dashed around the back of the fence, out of Floyd's line of sight, and kept running along the length of it, hoping we'd lose him in the swamp.

"I'm sick of you lurking around my property. And you're going pay for that fence!" Floyd yelled. "Get 'em, Shorty!"

Crap! I had no idea what a "Shorty" was but I already knew I wasn't going to like it. Visions of my past run-in with Carter's rottweiler, Tiny, flashed through my head. This was so not good.

We had zero chances of outrunning a dog.

And in an instant, our odds got even lower.

A roar, not associated with any dog I am familiar with, echoed through the swamp. I looked up just as a large gold animal launched off the fence directly at me.

"A lion!" Gertie screamed and took off into the swamp faster than I'd ever seen her move before.

The flying cat hit me directly in the shoulder and I stumbled backward. It wasn't a lion—it was way too small—but I had a feeling the claws sticking out of the paw raised in front of me were about to make Merlin's seem like a gentle back rub. He growled again and swiped at me, but I jumped back in time to avoid his onboard razors, my T-shirt catching the worst of the damage.

Ida Belle yelled at the cat and swung at him with a big stick. The cat backed up and growled again, and for a moment, I thought he would pounce on Ida Belle, but in one fluid movement he whirled around and leaped back over the fence into Floyd's yard.

"Let's go!" Ida Belle said and we hauled butt in the direction Gertie had fled.

Minutes later, we burst out of the swamp and into a vacant lot. A rusty green sedan slid to a stop at the curb, and I saw Gertie frantically gesturing from the driver's seat.

"Hurry up! I bet anything Floyd called the police," she yelled as we ran for the car and jumped inside.

Ida Belle jumped into the passenger's seat and I dove for the back, not even getting the door shut before Gertie took off from the corner like a NASCAR driver. I grabbed the front seat and pulled myself up, so many questions running through my mind, I wasn't sure where to start.

"Did you steal this car?" I asked, deciding to go with the

worst illegal thing we might have just done.

"Of course not," Gertie said. "This is Maisey Jackson's car. She always leaves the keys under the floor mat."

"So that people will take her car?"

"Well, not exactly. Mostly it's so that she can always find them. Maisey's mind isn't what it used to be."

I lowered my head, out of view of pedestrians. "You stole the car."

Chapter Six

Gertie yanked the wheel to the right and I lost my grip and fell across the backseat.

"She's in the hospital," Gertie said. "She'll never know."

I pulled myself up again just in time for Gertie to slam on the brakes. I hit the back of the seat and my breath rushed out of me in a whoosh.

"You should wear a seat belt," Ida Belle said as she opened her door and jumped out. "Get a move on, will you?"

I climbed out of the car as Gertie ran around from the driver's side and they both took off running across lawns. A glance told me we were a couple houses down from mine, so I set out after them. We barely got the front door closed before Carter's truck pulled down the street and stopped at the curb in front of my house.

"Uh-oh," Gertie said as she peeked out the front window. "He looks pissed."

"He can't prove anything," Ida Belle said.

"Look at my shirt," I said. "It's sorta a giveaway." The bottom half of my T-shirt hung in ribbons.

"He's coming up the walkway," Gertie said, her voice going up an octave.

Ida Belle reached over and yanked Gertie's necklace from around her neck, then dumped the beads off the string and into a glass bowl.

"Hey!" Gertie whirled around but Ida Belle stopped her with a single hand in the air, then plopped down on the couch and waved at me.

"Stand in front of me," Ida Belle said. "Gertie, get the door."

Gertie looked as confused as I felt, but I hurried over to stand in front of Ida Belle, wondering how she was going to pull this one out of her butt. As Carter started banging on the front door, Ida Belle grabbed a piece of my torn T-shirt and began winding it around into a tight strand.

Gertie looked back at us, clearly unsure this was a good route.

"Answer it," Ida Belle hissed as she reached for a bead.

Gertie opened the door and Carter stepped inside. Even a blind person couldn't have mistaken his anger. You could practically feel it. Gertie slipped around him and hurried over to the couch to sit next to Ida Belle.

He pointed a finger at me. "I told you to stay out of my investigation, and you didn't even wait an hour before trying to access a crime scene."

"I have no idea what you're talking about," Ida Belle said. "We've been here with Fortune for the past hour or so."

Carter snorted. "Oh, I'm sure you were with Fortune, but I don't believe for a moment you were in this house the entire time."

"Why would you think we were anywhere else?" Ida Belle asked.

"Because Floyd Guidry called and reported trespassers at his house who he described as a young one and two old crows."

"That's rather a rude description," Gertie said. "You should talk to Floyd about manners."

"Lack of manners isn't against the law," Carter said.

"Tearing down a man's fence and trespassing on his property is."

"You know darn good and well," Ida Belle said, "that if we'd been on Floyd's property, he would have shot us." She threaded a bead through the twisted strand of my T-shirt and pushed it up.

"According to Floyd, he didn't have to. He sent his pet bobcat out to defend his property line."

I frowned. A bobcat sounded much less intimidating than what had attacked my shirt. "Bobcat?" I said. "What's a bobcat?"

Gertie perked up. "It's when a tiger and a house cat mate."

"Is that even possible?" I asked.

"Of course not," Ida Belle said.

"It is too," Gertie argued. "A housecat couldn't carry cubs that large, but as long as the mating is a female tiger and a male house cat, it would work."

"Doesn't seem all that satisfying for the tigress," Ida Belle said.

"Enough!" Carter yelled. "Bobcats are their own wild species and not a result of some porno interspecies mating, especially not with domesticated animals."

"Is it even legal to own one?" I asked.

"That's not the point," Carter said, his face starting to redden.

"It might be," I said. "You were ready to arrest me last night when you thought I'd thrown a house cat on you. Seems to me that siccing a wild animal on people ought to carry a stiffer penalty."

Gertie nodded. "If I'd been attacked by a vicious animal, I'd sue the owner."

"Me too," I said, completely agreeing with the sentiment if not the actual process.

Carter's eyes widened and his jaw dropped. "Are you

kidding me? You're standing there with your T-shirt in shreds and you want me to believe that some other group comprised of one young woman and two older ones just happened to be snooping around Ally's house?"

"For your information," Ida Belle said, "I tore up Fortune's T-shirt. We're beading the bottom of it, see?" She pointed to the row of beads she'd attached to one of the strands. "I think it's tacky as hell, but the kids seem to like the look. I think the choir should sell them at our next benefit, but I needed a sample."

"And Fortune has to wear the T-shirt while you work?"

Gertie frowned. "I suppose it would be easier on Fortune to let her try it on afterward."

Ida Belle nodded. "We should have thought of that."

"Unbelievable." Carter shook his head. "I'm going to say this one more time and that's it—stay out of my investigation, or I swear, I will have every one of you sitting in my jail the rest of the summer."

Ida Belle rolled her eyes. "So dramatic. Can you just get on with your job and leave us alone to do ours?"

Carter gave us one last disbelieving glare before whirling around and stalking out of my house. As soon as the door slammed shut behind him, I plopped down in a chair.

"He didn't buy that for a minute," I said.

"Of course he didn't," Ida Belle said, "but if Floyd wanted to press charges, he'd have to go down to the sheriff's department and identify us, then fill out a bunch of paperwork, something Carter would have informed him of as soon as he complained."

Gertie nodded. "The sheriff's department could be full of free beer and hookers, and Floyd still wouldn't set foot in the place."

I held up my shirt. "He doesn't exactly need the police

when he's got an attack cat. What the hell?"

Ida Belle perked up. "Yes, that was most interesting."

"You think my almost being mauled by that wild animal is interesting?"

Ida Belle waved a hand in dismissal. "Don't be dramatic. A bobcat can't kill you. You would only have sustained some scratches. It's interesting because I don't know anyone who's ever had a pet bobcat."

"I wonder if Ally knows about it." Gertie said.

"We'll ask her about it when she gets here," I said. "I want to know more about this Floyd. He sounds like just the sort of guy who'd have no qualms about setting fire to someone's house."

"Without a doubt," Ida Belle agreed. "But we need a motive."

"And opportunity," I said. "Did either of you see him at Ally's last night?"

They both shook their heads.

"That's strange, right?" I said. "I mean, he lives right next door, but the neighbor across the street reported the fire. If he didn't see it, you'd think he would have come outside when the fire department showed up."

Ida Belle nodded. "Even if only to make sure his own house wasn't in danger."

"If there's any chance Floyd could be our guy, we need to find out where he was last night. Surely someone in town knows."

Ida Belle and Gertie exchanged glances.

"What?" I asked.

"His usual hangout is the Swamp Bar," Gertie said.

I groaned. The Swamp Bar was second only to Number Two Island on the list of places that I had no desire to ever visit again. My first trip hadn't been overly pleasant, and the resulting law enforcement detainment when we were fleeing the scene was one of the most humiliating moments of my life.

And since I'd arrived in Sinful, that was saying a lot.

"I think there's an even bigger issue at work here," Gertie said.

"What's that?" I asked.

"You and Carter. I'm afraid that if you don't move toward a romantic entanglement soon, the opportunity might pass, especially given your choice of ignoring his requests to sit still like a lady."

My mind flashed back to how uncomfortable I was searching for a topic of conversation the night before in Carter's truck. "That's probably for the best. The closer he is to me, the more opportunity he has to discover the truth. Last night was a bad idea from the get-go. We all knew it."

Ida Belle and Gertie exchanged glances, then changed the conversation to the best way to get information out of the crew at the Swamp Bar. I was only partially listening.

Everything I'd said about Carter and me was true. Forming a relationship, especially the romantic kind, with the local law enforcement was the worst idea I'd had since arriving in Sinful. And that was a tall heap to top.

What surprised me was the disappointment I felt at acknowledging this.

I forced my mind away from thoughts of lost potential with Carter and tried to focus on the matter at hand. When Ally was safe again, I'd have all the time in the world to dwell on my failings as a normal woman.

I had a feeling it would be a very long dwelling.

Ally returned from her candle-lighting prayer vigil about an hour after Carter's visit. We were in the kitchen having roast beef sandwiches and what was left of the blueberry muffins from that morning. Ally went straight to the refrigerator, grabbed a beer, and flopped into the remaining kitchen chair.

"That good, huh?" I asked.

She took a breath and huffed and I readied myself. I'd seen her do that once before after a visit with Celia and shortly after the huff, a good five minutes of complaining had poured out. Not that I blamed her. Ten minutes praying with her Aunt Celia would have me bitching for the next thirty years. Spending an entire afternoon with her would require a solid year of international broadcasting.

"I cannot believe that woman," Ally began. "I know she's my family and she just lost her daughter and had nasty business all around, but Jesus H. Christ, does she have to be such a smug bitch?"

Ida Belle, Gertie, and I glanced at one another and all wisely remained quiet. The answer, after all, was implied.

"She actually said that all of this was my dad's fault for not building the house correctly in the first place." She threw her hands in the air. "Like my dead father popped out of the ground, threw gasoline on my house, and threw a match at it. I tried to tell her that Carter said it was arson, and you know what she told me—she said that was ridiculous because no one in Sinful would burn down another person's house. We've had a rash of murders lately, but arson is apparently a worse sin to Aunt Celia."

Ally chugged back a good quarter of the beer and slammed it down on the table. "Then she shifted gears and started blaming me. If I'd stop having 'ideas' about being a career woman and settle down with a good man, he would have kept the house in better repair and this wouldn't have happened. When I suggested that there wasn't a man in this town worth marrying, she told me that Carter would have been if I'd bothered to make my move before he locked his sights on 'that visiting Yankee.'"

"And just when I thought we were becoming friends," I mumbled. My short history with Celia had been full of ups and downs. Apparently, we were on a down trend.

"Oh, coming from Aunt Celia, that was complimentary, trust me."

Gertie cleared her throat. "Was there any actual, uh...*praying* at this prayer vigil?"

Ally nodded. "Celia finally had to come up for air, and one of her friends with a piece of backbone left suggested we move to the prayer part of the gathering. That was pleasant, I suppose, but given my short sleeping stint last night, I almost nodded off. The final chorus of 'amens' startled me back into consciousness."

Ida Belle shook her head. "At that point, you'd have had to use jumper cables on me."

"You mean a defibrillator?" Gertie asked.

"No, I meant jumper cables."

"But then things got hairy again," Ally said. "Carter showed up at the church and had the nerve to question where I'd been the last two hours. An entire room of women told him I'd been right in front of them the entire time, except for the one potty break, but he still seemed suspicious. Mumbling about trespassing and bobcats and beaded shirts. I swear, he sounds like he's losing it."

Gertie, Ida Belle, and I exchanged looks and Gertie started to laugh. Ida Belle held out for a bit then laughed as well.

Ally sighed. "I should have known. What were you guys up to while I was gone?"

I gave her a rundown of our activities. Her expression

shifted from amused, to horrified, to disbelief, to laughing so hard she had to put down her beer.

"I can't believe you tried to pass the whole thing off as beading a shirt," Ally said. "And are you sure it was a bobcat?"

I stood up and showed her what was left of my tee. "Something far larger than Merlin did this, and it was definitely in the cat family."

"It was a bobcat," Ida Belle said. "There's plenty of them in the swamps, but this is the only one I know of living in the suburbs. You didn't know Floyd had a bobcat?"

Ally frowned. "I try to avoid anything and everything to do with Floyd."

"Has he given you trouble?" I asked.

"Floyd is nothing but trouble." She shook her head. "He and Mama had a running feud over property lines at the back. Floyd swears that the fence between our lots is thirty feet over into his property. They went to court about it a couple years before Mama got sick. He still contends that the courts only sided with Mama because he was a criminal."

"And did they?" I asked.

"No. Anyone who's seen the original surveys and plats can tell straight off that the fence is fine."

"Thirty feet is an awful lot to claim as a mistake," I said.

Ally nodded. "There was a method to his madness. Both properties are narrower up front but branch out as you move toward the rear."

"Like a trapezoid?" I asked.

"Exactly. But Mama's trapezoid runs right into an inlet of Sinful Bayou. Floyd wanted that inlet in his property line so he could build a boat shed and dock his boat there. To irk him even further, Mama put up a ten-foot board fence across the back of the property. It didn't even have a gate on the back end."

"So as far as Floyd was concerned, she was wasting the space."

Ally nodded.

"But there's an iron fence there now."

"Yeah, the wooden one took a beating in Hurricane Katrina. Some of the men from church managed to keep it propped up while Mama was sick, but after she moved to the facility in New Orleans, I used some of the insurance money to replace it. The whole thing was one good gust of wind away from being in the bayou, and I would have been responsible for cleanup. I figured a fence with a view increased property value."

"Have you had any problems with Floyd?" I asked.

Ally frowned. "He called the cops once when he thought I was playing my music too loud in the backyard. I was gardening. Carter told me to turn it down a bit, and I've worn earbuds ever since."

"So no score to settle?"

Ally's eyes widened. "By burning down my house? I can't imagine—I mean, if he was still mad over the property line, wouldn't he have done that before Mama left?"

"It does seem a bit of a stretch," Gertie said.

"It may if he were a normal person," I said, "but this is a guy who lives with an attack bobcat." I'd known my share of psychos. Logical thinking didn't enter into their decisions if they had an emotional investment in whatever act of terror they decided to engage in.

"She's got a point," Ida Belle said. "Even though we can't come up with a clear motive, we should still see if he had opportunity." She looked at Ally. "I don't suppose you know whether or not he was home when the fire started?"

Ally shook her head. "The firemen said they knocked but he never answered. That doesn't mean he wasn't home, though. It would be just like him to be inside ignoring the entire scene."

"So we're back to the Swamp Bar," I said. "Oh, goody."

"What are you bitching about?" Gertie asked. "The last time I was there, I got shot at."

"You stole a boat," I said. "The last time I was there, I almost drowned, and Carter caught me wearing a garbage bag and little else."

Ally's eyes widened. "Holy crap, you never told me that. Why have you been holding out on the good stuff?"

"Because vast humiliation is not something I relish sharing."

"You should if it's funny," Ally said. "If we can't laugh at ourselves, who can we laugh at?"

I stared at her. "Other people?"

"Got that right," Ida Belle said.

"Absolutely," Gertie agreed.

Ally laughed. "Tonight, we are going to open up a bottle of wine, and you're going to share the trash bag story with me."

"What do I get out of the deal?"

"Chocolate cake?"

I felt myself weakening. "Maybe."

"And I might tell you about the time I went skinny-dipping with Bobby Hanson and his little brother stole our clothes."

I waved a hand in dismissal. "I bet everyone around here has one of those stories from their childhood."

"It happened last year."

I smiled. "Chocolate cake and ultimate humiliation it is."

Chapter Seven

I managed to convince Gertie and Ida Belle that we should delay our Swamp Bar trip until the next day, and they headed out to return Maisey's car. Ally decided that hours of prayer and insults from Celia rated a long, hot shower, and hurried upstairs to indulge. I took advantage of being alone to make a trip to the General Store to talk to Walter, the owner.

The reason I'd given Ida Belle and Gertie for wanting to delay the Swamp Bar trip was because I wanted to keep a close eye on Ally since we'd had a creeper the night before. And that wasn't completely a lie. Except for the part where I wanted to keep a close eye on Ally. What I really wanted to do was set my sights on the creeper. And assuming he was stupid enough to return, I wanted a way to make him pay without involving myself in a law enforcement incident. But I wanted to keep my plan on the down low.

It was much easier to cover your tracks if no one else was stepping in them with you.

Walter, unlike Ida Belle and Gertie, was happy to give advice without wanting to have any part in the actual activity, especially if the activity bordered on the illegal kind. The really cool thing about Walter was that despite being Carter's uncle, he didn't seem to have any desire to inform his nephew of other people's business. Basically, conversations with Walter were in a locked vault, which probably made him the most valuable person in Sinful.

Despite my new goal to exercise more, I drove my Jeep to the store. If things went the way I expected, I would be returning with goods—the kind of goods I didn't want people to see me walking down the sidewalk with.

The store was empty when I walked in. Walter looked up from his newspaper and gave me a smile and a wave. "About time someone came in here and took me away from boredom," he said.

I slid onto a stool across the checkout counter from him. "I thought you were reading the newspaper."

He folded the paper closed and tossed it on the counter behind him. "It's all political nonsense and sports statistics. No one has anything interesting to say anymore. How are things going with the cat?"

"Considering I can't keep cactus alive, I guess it's going well."

"Tomcats have survival skills that match the best of military special forces. He'll be fine."

"He's definitely interesting. I've never been around cats before and the things he does are fascinating. The other day I was cleaning one of Marge's guns and activated the laser sight. He bolted off the couch and chased that pointer until he was too tired to move. I've never laughed so hard in my life."

"Hunting instinct. It's still strong with him because he was fending for himself for so long. And most cats can't ignore a moving light."

"Hunting instinct…that makes sense."

He nodded and his expression shifted from cheery to serious. "I hear Ally's staying at your house. Why don't you bring me up to speed?"

"When Carter suspected the fire was deliberate, he asked

me to keep an eye on her, so as far as I'm concerned, she can have the guest room until Carter is certain it's safe for her to go back home."

Walter shook his head. "I can't imagine any reason that someone would want to hurt Ally. That girl has got to be the nicest person in this town."

"That might be reason enough."

"Ha. You got a point there. But still, I can't think of anything to be gained. I don't know her mother's financial situation but I don't think she has much to speak of besides that house."

I nodded. "That's my understanding as well. And if someone were looking to kill Ally to inherit, the last thing they'd do was burn down the only asset she had."

"Exactly. But what other reason could there be?"

"I have no idea. Ida Belle, Gertie, and I ran through every possibility we could think of this afternoon but Ally can't come up with a single reason someone would be out to get her. We've decided to go with the 'completely insane attacker' idea for the time being."

"Given the lack of facts, it seems the only possibility, but then that doesn't really narrow down your suspects—not if you're assuming it's a Sinful resident."

"We thought we'd start with Floyd Guidry."

Walter raised his eyebrows. "He's certainly got the backbone for it, and the anger issues."

"That's what I hear. We're going to try to establish opportunity tomorrow—"

Walter held up a hand. "The less I know, the better. Carter was in here earlier stomping around and muttering about the three of you and a bobcat. I didn't even ask."

"Floyd has a pet bobcat, and I'm not going to share how I

know that."

"That's probably best."

"Anyway, Floyd wasn't the reason I stopped by. I have a personal project that I want to work on tonight, and I'd like you to keep it between the two of us."

"I'm intrigued. What's the project?"

I glanced behind me to make sure the store was still empty, then leaned across the counter. "Did you hear about the creeper at my house last night?"

Walter nodded. "Carter mentioned that as well. Said you threw a cat on him."

I rolled my eyes. "The creeper threw my cat on him. Anyway, I don't know what the guy was up to—maybe it's related to the fire, maybe not—but I have this feeling that he'll come back."

"And you want to catch him?"

"Not necessarily.

Walter's eyes widened. "You don't want to kill him, do you?"

"No! At least, not until I know what he's up to. Then I reserve the right to change my mind."

"That seems reasonable."

I grinned. Even though every minute of my existence in Sinful, I felt like a fish out of water, I had formed a huge appreciation for Southern practicality. "I was looking more to mark him."

"Paint gun?"

"I was thinking something that lasts a bit longer and can't be washed off. What can you tell me about shooting someone with rock salt?"

Walter gave me an approving nod. "You're thinking the salt will scare him off from whatever nefarious thing he has planned and give him some marks you may be able to see the next day or so."

"That was my thinking, but I've never shot rock salt. Would it work?"

"If you're within thirty feet of him or so, it should leave some good red marks, maybe break the skin a place or two."

"Sounds perfect."

He reached beneath the counter and pulled out a box of shotgun shells. "It so happens, I keep a few in stock. For my better customers, of course."

I pulled one of the shells out and studied it. It didn't look any different from a regular shotgun shell. "You do good work. This looks factory."

Walter blushed at my praise, the red tips of his ears almost glowing against his silver hair. "Oh, everyone around here knows how to load shells."

"I bet they don't like this. If you were thirty years younger, I'd marry you."

His blush deepened. "It so happens there's a version of me in town who is a bit younger. I'm not admitting to thirty years."

"I think the bobcat incident might have killed things on that front," I said.

Walter shook his head. "If a couple of scratches and a little trespassing scares the boy off, he wasn't worth your time in the first place."

I smiled. "How come you're so reasonable and he's so…not?"

"Well, I don't have anything to prove professionally, don't need to defend my manhood, and I'm not trying to impress a young lady."

"Then maybe he should take a job here with you and stop trying to impress ladies. I'm not touching the manhood thing.

That's just asking for trouble."

Walter started chuckling, then slapped his knees and laughed so hard tears formed in his eyes. "By God, you are just what that boy needs," he said when he'd finally regained control.

"Somehow, I doubt that. So how much for the ammo?"

He grabbed a handful out of the box and set them on the counter. "On the house…with the condition that you come back tomorrow and tell me what happened."

"Deal. If anything happens." I hopped off my stool. "And Walter, not a word to Ida Belle."

He shook his head. "I may be in love with the woman, but I'm not blinded by it. My lips are sealed."

"Then here's hoping I see you tomorrow."

I slipped the shells in my purse and headed out of the store, where I ran right into Carter.

"Oh crap," I said.

"Do you always exit buildings without looking?"

"Sorry. I was looking in my purse."

"Uh-huh. I just spoke to one of Ally's neighbors. She said she saw three women speeding down the block in Maisey Jackson's car."

I stared at him for a couple of seconds. "Sooooooo, you should ticket Ms. Jackson for speeding?"

His jaw flexed. "Mrs. Jackson's been in the hospital for a week now."

"Someone stole her car? Wow. Is that a problem here too?"

"You know good and well who stole her car."

"Look," I said, starting to get bored with the whole cat-and-mouse thing. "I have a Jeep, so I have no reason to steal someone else's car. If you want to help people, then I suggest you contact this Mrs. Jackson and assist her with the insurance claim."

He frowned.

"What?"

"The car was returned," he said, and I could tell how much those words irritated him.

"So it wasn't stolen."

"Of course it was stolen."

I threw my hands in the air. "What kind of thief returns what they stole? Look, with the arson, creepers, bobcat owners, and car thieves, it sounds like you have a lot to do. I'm going to head home and check off the only thing on my list, which is keeping Ally safe and secure inside my house."

I whirled around and headed to my Jeep. When I turned around to climb in the driver's seat, the sidewalk was empty. I felt momentary regret that I'd intentionally provoked Carter to anger. It wasn't nice, and normally, I didn't do that sort of thing to people I liked.

Unfortunately, I liked Carter too much.

And that was something I needed to correct before things got messy. And the easiest way I knew how to do that was to make him stop liking me.

Around 11:00 p.m., I poured Ally into bed and pretended to turn in myself. Instead, I pulled on black sweats, a long-sleeved T-shirt, and black shoes, secured a 12-gauge with a strap from Marge's secret weapons stash behind a hidden panel in her closet, then headed downstairs and unlocked one of the windows in the living room to give myself a backup plan in case the doors weren't an option when I returned.

The creeper wasn't likely to try the front of the house, where he could be seen by neighbors across the street. If he was smart, he'd head to the back of the house as he had before, but tonight I had the benefit of moonlight to help illuminate the backyard. I figured the creeper had probably been trying the windows on the back of the house when I startled him. This time, I planned on giving him an even bigger surprise—one he'd never see coming.

I slipped out the back door and locked it behind me, slipping the key into my pocket, then skirted the side of the house and crawled through an enormous hedge and into my neighbor's side yard. Ronald J. Franklin Jr. was an odd-looking man with a long beak nose and frantically moving limbs. Gertie said he looked like Ichabod Crane, but I had no idea who that was.

His oddities didn't end with his looks. From an upstairs window, I once watched him dancing around his backyard in full ballerina dress—female, not male—while waving a stick with a long streamer. I decided he was on something really good and much stronger than Sinful Ladies Cough Syrup, which was basically cherry flavoring and homemade Everclear. At least, I hoped he was high on something because...well, damn.

He was also the neighbor who lived with one finger on speed dial for 911. I had no doubt that every call the sheriff's department had received on me, about occurrences at my house, had been made by Ronald. But his roof was the best line of sight I had, and by God, I was using it.

I looped the 12-gauge strap over my shoulder and positioned the gun diagonally across my back, then grabbed one of the lower limbs of a giant oak and pulled myself up into the tree. I scaled the tree quickly until I reached the same height as his roofline. I stood on one wide branch that reached almost to his roof and crept out on it like a tightrope walker until I stepped onto his roof.

I immediately dropped down on my knees and inched down

the back side of the roof until I had a clear view of my backyard. I gauged the distance between my position and the back corner of my house at about twenty-five feet, allowing for the height. If he approached the house from the opposite side, I'd have to wait until he got two-thirds of the way in before taking a shot; otherwise, I ran the risk of only scaring him but not leaving anything for him to remember me by.

Satisfied with my position, I loaded a shell and got into a prone position, the 12-gauge at my side. Now the waiting was all that was left. And the waiting was always the worst, but at least I had a time limit on this one. I was giving the creeper two hours to show up before calling it a night.

To keep from dozing off, I launched into my usual routine of mentally reciting every weapon in my private collection back in DC. If I got to the end of the weapons list and the creeper still hadn't shown, I'd move on to the disassembly-reassembly process for each of the rifles and pistols.

It was close to midnight when I saw movement below me at side of my house. I reached into my pants pocket for the sight I'd removed from one of Marge's rifles and took a peek. It was the creeper all right, makeshift ski mask in place. How many beanie hats did the guy own?

I pulled the shotgun from my side and into a shooting position, but as I placed my finger on the trigger, a dark cloud rolled in front of the moon and the light disappeared, leaving me in the pitch black. It was only for a couple of seconds, but each one of them ticked by as if it were an hour. When the dim glow finally encompassed the yard again, I could just make out the back of the creeper as he inched around the corner and headed for the bushes that ran across the back of the house.

Perfect!

I sighted his rear and moved my finger to the trigger.

Now or never.

I squeezed the trigger and the *boom* from the shotgun shattered the utter silence of the night. A split second later, I heard yelling and knew my shot had been a good one.

I lifted the scope again, expecting to see the creeper running the opposite way, but instead he whirled around and headed straight for me. And that's when I realized he wasn't wearing a mask. And he wasn't the creeper.

I'd just shot Carter.

Chapter Eight

I jumped up and ran across the roof in the opposite direction of my house. With any luck, the echo from the shot wouldn't alert Carter that the shot came from above...at least not right away. If I could get to the other side of the house and find a way down, I could double back and sneak into my own house and pretend I knew nothing about all of this.

I was almost to the opposite edge of the roof when the lights on Ronald's back porch flicked on and I heard a gunshot.

"Damn it!" Carter yelled. "It's Deputy LeBlanc. Put that gun down."

I took a second to gauge the distance between the roofline and a branch of an oak tree, then jumped, praying the branch was sturdy enough to hold me. I overjumped and crashed into the trunk, but managed to get my hands up before my face collided with the thick bark. I could still hear Carter and Ronald arguing, so I wasted no time scrambling down the tree. The lowest branch was still a good fifteen feet off the ground, so I readied myself and jumped, prepared to roll when I hit the ground.

Unfortunately, the strap from the shotgun caught on a limb behind me and instead of hurtling to the ground, I ended up hanging in the tree like a wind chime. I reached back, frantically trying to release the strap from the gun, but my weight had the strap and buckle pulled so tight I couldn't.

I heard running feet and my heart sank. Carter was finished with Ronald and back to pursuit. I kicked my legs out, thinking a swinging motion might dislodge the strap from the branch. As I swung out a second time, the strap came loose and I flew into a set of bushes.

It took far less time for me to get up than it did to fall. I leaped out of the bushes as if they were on fire, grabbing the shotgun as I whirled around. Then I sprinted across Ronald's front lawn and to my house, where I threw open the window I'd left unlocked earlier. I tossed the shotgun through the window, then dived in after it. I cleanly completed my somersault but as I started to rise, something hit me on the back of the head.

Pain exploded on my skull and in my eyes, and I heard the sound of ceramic shattering.

"It's me," I hissed.

"Fortune!" Ally's voice was a mixture of frightened and bewildered. "I thought you were the creeper. Why did you come in the window?"

I ran to the wall to push the window down and lock it, relieved that Ally hadn't turned on any lights when she'd come downstairs to clock me. Dim light from the kitchen was the only light in the room. I'd no sooner clicked the window latch in place when I heard running in front of the house. "No time to explain. Answer the door and make up a lie about the vase. You never saw me."

I grabbed the shotgun and dashed upstairs, leaving Ally staring wide-eyed behind me. I pulled off my clothes as I ran, and by the time I got to my bedroom, I was down to sports bra, underwear, and socks. I yanked off the socks, pulled on yoga pants and T-shirt, and grabbed my headphones. I paused long enough to check myself in the dresser mirror and was glad I had. Several leaves and some small branches stuck out of my hair. I plucked them out, redid my ponytail, and prepared for the showdown that was about to come.

I could hear Ally talking to Carter as I started for the stairwell.

"I don't know anything at all," Ally said. "I was asleep and heard a gunshot. I could hear a commotion outside, but couldn't see anything. I'd left my pistol and my cell phone downstairs, so I hurried down here to grab both, intending to call the sheriff's department."

"So what happened to the vase?"

"I didn't want to turn on the lights and make it easier for someone to see inside. I thought I could make it to the kitchen in the dark, but I guess I don't know the house as well as I'd hoped. I jammed my leg into that decorator table and wasn't able to catch the vase before it hit the floor. Then you started knocking and here we are."

I pulled my headphones around my neck and skipped down the stairs. "What's all the racket?"

Carter looked up at me, his expression a mixture of incredulity and suspicion. "You're telling me you've been upstairs sleeping this whole time?"

"It's after midnight. What am I supposed to be doing?"

Carter narrowed his eyes at me. "You didn't hear anything that just happened outside?"

I pointed at the headphones. "Remember my problem with the frogs? I can only handle a few days of bad sleep before I resort to these. They're pretty good. I heard some noise downstairs, but it was faint. At first I thought I was dreaming, but then I figured it was Merlin messing with something so I came down to check."

Carter looked back and forth between the two of us. I could tell he was caught in a struggle between wanting to believe us and thinking there was no way in hell that he could.

"What's going on?" I asked, figuring that's the exact question an innocent person would have.

Ally looked over at me. "Carter saw the creeper outside of the house, and there was a gunshot."

I widened my eyes, feigning a look of surprise. "He came back? Seriously? I didn't think he'd be that stupid."

Carter blew out a breath. "Apparently, he didn't get your memo on what constitutes intelligent behavior."

"So you shot him?" I asked. "Who is he?"

"No. I didn't shoot anybody. Someone else fired a shotgun, which is why I'm here."

"Wasn't me this time," I said, crossing my fingers behind my back. "Hey, maybe it was the creeper?"

Carter looked aggrieved. "At this point, it could have been John Gotti."

Ally frowned. "Isn't he dead?"

"Who's John Gotti?" I asked. Gertie wasn't the only one who could play the ignorance card.

Carter sighed. "You swear neither of you saw or heard anything?"

"Nothing beyond what I've already told you," Ally said.

I shook my head. "Not until I came downstairs and heard the two of you talking."

"Then I'll let you get back to sleep. Make sure all the windows and doors are locked."

He looked so defeated, and I couldn't stop the wave of guilt that coursed through me. When he turned around to leave and I saw the white marks on the back of his jeans, my guilt ticked up a hundred more notches.

Ally closed the door behind him and locked it, then watched out the window for several seconds. Finally, she turned around and stared at me, hands on her hips. "What the hell is going on here? What did you do that I just lied about to cover up?"

"I…uh, might have shot Carter."

***

After swearing Ally to silence, I headed upstairs to take a shower and hit the bed. Convincing Ally to stay quiet about the entire fiasco had been easier than I'd thought it would be, but then technically, she'd just lied to cover up a felony. I supposed that might factor in.

With all the running, shooting, hanging around trees, and getting hit with vases that was going on, I hadn't had time to process the facts of the night. But under the hot stream of the shower, my mind finally slowed down and I started at the beginning, focusing on when I first saw the creeper.

Initially, I considered that I might have been wrong and had confused Carter for the creeper from the get-go, but that couldn't be right. The creeper had been wearing a beanie mask, just like the night before. And obviously, Carter had seen him too or he wouldn't have been tracking him around the back of my house.

Crap!

That also meant that Carter had been watching my house again. Stupid. I should have known he'd be nearby. One, because he wanted to nab the creeper before he could finish whatever nefarious thing he had planned, and two, before I shot the beanie-wearing freak myself. The interesting thing is that I hadn't seen Carter at all when I'd left the house, and the moonlight had the yard lit up pretty good all the way across the bayou.

I'd checked the street when unlocking the living room window and hadn't seen his truck, so either he had it tucked away somewhere else, or he'd walked over from his house and had been hiding across the street. None of this boded well for any future creeper hunting. I'd already expensed more lives than Merlin had. At some point, I would run out, and the last place I wanted that to happen was in front of Carter.

I shut off the shower and dried off. Settling for underwear and T-shirt, I dressed and headed into the bedroom and slid in between the cool sheets with no intention of leaving for a good eight hours or more. Ally had to be at work early and would be up and gone with the chickens, but hopefully, I'd be able to sleep through it.

First thing tomorrow, I'd check in with Gertie and Ida Belle and formulate a plan to go to the Swamp Bar. At some point, I had to check in with Walter, who would be expecting an update. He wasn't going to be thrilled with the one I provided, but that was his own fault for making me promise. Then I wanted to sit down with Ally and have another talk about who could be out to get her.

The timing of the arsonist and the creeper couldn't be a coincidence.

Someone in Sinful had an agenda. And I was going to find out what it was.

Given that it had taken me two hours to slow my mind down enough to fall asleep, I surprised myself when I popped out of bed at 8:00 a.m., completely rested and ready to go. Ally had prepped the coffeepot for me and left a note that said to press Brew. Unfortunately, we'd polished off the blueberry muffins the day before so I stood looking inside the refrigerator for a while, deliberating between a bagel and a protein shake. Finally, I closed the door and poured a cup of coffee, having decided I'd finish off the pot, then head into town for breakfast at Francine's.

I inhaled two cups of coffee like a true addict then, in keeping with my vow to exercise every day, pulled on my tennis shoes and set out at a good jog to the café. It took me about a block for my breathing to relax into rhythm, and my thighs complained a bit, but finally my body settled into its normal pace and it wasn't very long before I hit Main Street. I slowed to a walk, wanting to get my heart rate and breathing slower before I consumed breakfast.

That run had consumed a good bit of calories. Maybe enough calories for me to splurge at breakfast.

The usual crowd of locals were already seated in the café and digging into their breakfast. I snagged my usual two-top table in the corner at the back of the café, and Ally cruised by a minute later and pushed a cup of coffee in front of me.

"I bet you're starving," she said. "Special today is chicken-fried steak and eggs."

My stomach rumbled and my mouth was well on its way to blurting out "Hell, yeah" when I remembered my new fitness plan. "Not today. I'll have an egg-white omelet with spinach and mozzarella."

Ally raised one eyebrow. "Really?"

"Yeah, I have this whole fitness thing. When yoga pants start to get tight in the waist, you've got a real problem."

She laughed. "I get it. Ever since I've started all this testing to open my own bakery, nothing in my closet fits right. I guess you've consumed some of everything as well."

"Maybe a bit more than 'some' in most cases."

"I'll put this in," she said and headed toward the kitchen.

The bells above the café door jangled and I looked over in time to see a middle-aged man I didn't recognize step inside.

Midforties, decent to okay shape, nearsighted, left leg slightly shorter than right. I'd beat him in a footrace hands down.

His looks were normal—brown hair, brown eyes, common face—but his clothes were a little off. He wore a polo shirt and slacks, with the shirt tucked in, and loafers. I wouldn't have even noticed him in DC but in Sinful, he was dressed a little too fancy to blend, especially as it wasn't Sunday.

When Ally stopped by a minute later to refill my coffee, I inclined my head in his direction. "Who's that?"

Ally glanced over, her brow scrunched in concentration for a couple of seconds, then her expression cleared back to normal. "I couldn't remember at first. He's a real estate agent from New Orleans. Wanted to buy Mama's house after she went to the facility in New Orleans. Given the way things have turned out, I should have sold it."

I frowned. "So he just showed up from New Orleans, somehow knowing you might have a house for sale. That sounds a little odd."

"He said his client had family that used to live here and he was interested in retiring somewhere quiet but not too far away from New Orleans. I guess someone suggested me, thinking I'd want to sell and go back to New Orleans with Mama."

"Were there any other houses for sale at the time?"

"I think so. The Pauleys had just moved to Natchez, and I'm pretty sure Mrs. Verna's grandson had her house up for sale after moving her to an assisted living center."

"And did anyone from New Orleans buy either of those houses and move here?"

"No. Both were bought by oilfield guys who'd been working in the area and commuting." Ally glanced over at him again and frowned. "You don't think he was up to something, do you? He made that offer six months ago."

I shrugged. "He may be completely on the up-and-up, but it sounds a little strange is all."

"I hate this," Ally said. "It forces me to look at everyone differently. I don't want to even think about someone I know being involved in something so cruel."

"Yeah, that's pretty crappy." And it was. Until now, I hadn't really thought about it in relation to my own situation, but I supposed when it boiled right down to it, our situations were similar. In my case, I was hidden away in the Louisiana swamps, pretending to be someone else, because my boss was certain that a leak at the CIA was what had put me in harm's way. It sucked to think that another agent was the reason one of the most dangerous men in the world had put a price on my head. What kind of scumbag did you have to be to betray one of your own?

And the more I thought about it, the angrier I got. When Director Morrow found out who the leak was, I swear I was going to take a piece out of them.

"Don't worry," I said, returning to my here and now. "Carter will figure it all out."

"Let's hope he doesn't figure *all* of it out." She gave me a small smile and headed to the next table with her coffeepot.

I sighed at the reminder of my mission failure. The absolute last thing I'd wanted to do was draw attention to myself with Carter, especially when he was 100 percent in cop mode. Instead of sitting inside with locked doors and windows, minding my own business, I'd tried to play sniper vigilante and had ended up shooting the one person I was trying to avoid.

The number of miscalculations I'd made since I'd been in Sinful had to be some sort of all-time record, at least for nonresidents. Gertie probably held the local record for foul-ups. That woman could probably figure out a way to make watching television dangerous.

The door bells sounded off again and I looked over to see Carter walk in. I felt my back and neck tighten. I had hoped he'd be too busy working this morning to stop for breakfast, but I supposed work didn't preclude needing to eat. Not seeing any other choice, I lifted my hand to wave him over.

He headed over and slowly lowered himself into the chair across from me. Dark circles were beginning to form under his eyes and he looked exhausted.

Ally made her way over, looking a little apprehensive, but plastered on her usual smile as she stepped up to the table. "Morning. Do you want your usual?"

"No time to sit and enjoy it today," he said. "Can you just get me a sausage biscuit and a coffee to go?"

"Coming right up," Ally said, then headed off for the kitchen again.

"What's wrong with you?" I asked. "You're moving all stiff." Carter had never mentioned being shot last night, so I needed to act like someone who knew nothing.

"I got shot last night at your house."

I sat up straight and forced my eyes as wide as I could get them. "What?"

"That gunshot last night was a load of rock salt, and it got me right across the back."

"You don't sit on your back," I pointed out.

"Fine. I got shot in the ass. Does that clear things up?"

"Completely." I frowned. "Actually, I'm lying. I have no idea what any of that means. What is rock salt and how do you shoot it? Ally said it was a shotgun blast. And where were you when you got shot? Why was someone shooting in the first place?"

Carter held a hand up to stop my barrage. "Rock salt is just what it sounds like—lumps of salt formed into tiny rocks. You can load shotgun shells with it. Some people use it to scare away animals they don't want near livestock. Others use it to scare away trespassers."

"Is that legal?"

He gave me an aggrieved look. "I shouldn't even be saying this to you, but technically, if they're trying to enter your home, vehicle, or business, and you have reason to believe they will harm you, then you can shoot trespassers with *real* bullets."

"See, this is where the legal system gets stupid. If an intruder, like the creeper, for instance, clearly knows I'm home, then why would I have a reason to believe he's *not* going to harm me? If he simply wanted to steal something, he'd wait until I was gone."

He nodded. "And that is the way most juries see it. But in this case, he wasn't inside your house."

"Not yet."

"We don't know what he was planning to do."

"Well, we know he wasn't planning to drop by at a decent hour with a fruit basket and ring the doorbell. Doesn't creating a ski mask count for premeditated something-not-good?"

"Maybe. Or he could just be a Peeping Tom."

I stared. "Seriously. With all the people toting firearms in this town, is someone really stupid enough to try to peep in windows? I discovered quite recently, and much to my horror I might add, that you can see all kinds of naked and perverted on cable TV. Why leave the safety of your house?"

"Television can't replace the real item."

I raised one eyebrow. "So you're telling me someone is risking getting shot just to catch a glimpse of me in some form of nakedness? It can't possibly be worth it."

"Well, I'm not sure if it's worth it...yet." He gave me that lazy, sexy smile of his that turned my legs to jelly. And despite my private decree that a relationship with Carter was completely and totally out of the question, I felt my resolve slipping away.

My face flushed hot and I cursed myself for such a typical girl reaction. I may be a girl, but I was anything but typical. Carter's grin widened at my obvious discomfort.

"So do you think the creeper is the one who shot you?" I asked, trying to get the conversation back around to safe ground.

The smile disappeared. "I didn't think so last night. I was watching your house from across the street and saw him slip down the hedges to your backyard. I made it to the corner of your house as quickly as possible without making a ton of noise. I didn't think he had time to circle around the house and come up behind me."

"Maybe he never went down the back of the house. Maybe he saw you or heard you and hid in the bushes on the side until you went by."

"I suppose that's possible," he said, but I could tell he didn't want to admit the creeper might have gotten the best of him.

"More possible than yet another guy lurking around my house shooting people."

He sighed. "Probably so."

Ally stepped up to the table and placed a to-go cup of coffee and a small bag in front of Carter. "It's on me this morning," she said. "For looking out for me and Fortune."

She hurried off before he could argue. He rose from the table and picked up his coffee and biscuit. "I better get back to it," he said.

"You'll let me know if you find out anything, right?" I asked, although I don't know why I bothered. If Carter figured out that I was the one who shot him, I'd know by virtue of the handcuffs I'd be wearing.

"Of course," he said and left the café.

Not ten seconds later, David, the fireman who'd helped Ally at her house, walked in, looking as though he'd just been summoned into a brothel rather than a café. The tips of his ears were pink and he glanced nervously around.

My curiosity piqued, I gestured him over. At first, he looked confused, but when he stepped up to the table, his expression cleared. "You're the lady I saw at Ally's house."

I extended my hand. "Sandy-Sue Morrow. But everyone calls me Fortune."

He shook my hand. "David Leger."

I waved at the empty chair. "Have a seat."

He glanced back at the kitchen again and I held in a smile as what he was up to finally hit me. He was here to see Ally, and he didn't want her to think he was hitting on me.

"Please," I said, now more interested in talking to him than before. "People sit with me all the time when the café's full. That chair is a regular revolving door."

"Thanks," he said and sat down, looking a little less nervous. "So you're a friend of Ally's?"

I nodded.

"You guys been friends a long time?" he asked, not quite meeting my gaze.

"Not even a month. I'm not from here. My aunt passed away and I'm here for the summer to settle her affairs."

"Oh, I'm sorry about your aunt."

"Thanks," I said. He seemed like a nice guy. Maybe he could end Ally's bad streak with Sinful men. "So I'm basically new here, like you, although I suppose you spent time here when you were a kid."

He nodded. "I usually spent a couple weeks every summer with my grandparents when I was young. Then Grandpa died and when Grandma got ill, Mama put her in an assisted living center in Houston. I always remembered the town, though, and liked it. Lake Charles, where I'm from, is no big city, but it a sight bigger than Sinful. It doesn't have that tranquil feel, you know?"

I nodded. If he only knew just how far from tranquil Sinful really was.

"And the fishing is great," he said.

"If you like to fish."

"You don't?"

"Nope. If possible, I only get into boats to drink beer and sleep."

He hesitated just a second before laughing, probably assuming I was joking. I glanced over at the kitchen as Ally came out with my food. She did a double take and almost stopped short when she saw David sitting there. Quickly recovering, she put on her smile and sat the plate in front of me.

I pointed to David. "Look who I found waiting for a table."

David looked up at Ally with a shy smile. "Are you doing okay? I mean…since the fire?"

"I'm doing fine. The insurance adjuster is supposed to be out today. Hopefully, it won't take long to get things fixed."

"The damage didn't look too terribly bad," he said. "But you'll probably get a new kitchen out of it."

Ally perked up. "You think so? That would be fabulous!"

"Ally is going to open her own bakery," I said. "Her pastries are worth killing over."

Ally blushed a little. "Fortune exaggerates, but I do like to bake."

"True," I agreed. "I do exaggerate, but not this time. Why do you think I invited her to stay with me while her house is being repaired?"

David nodded. "I'm living in a one-bedroom apartment over the preacher's garage right now, but I'd gladly take the couch if I could find a roommate who cooked. I can't even heat up microwave dinners without making a mess."

"Well, there you go," I said to Ally. "If you get tired of me, you have another offer on the table."

A blush ran up David's face and Ally looked slightly horrified.

"Oh, that's not what I meant," David said, clearly flustered. "I mean, I would never make a presumption like that about a lady."

"I'm just kidding," I said. "Besides, do you really think I'd give her up that easily?"

"Good Lord," Ally mumbled. "Can I get you anything to eat, David?"

David glanced at his watch and his eyes widened. "It's later than I thought. Can I get a sausage biscuit and a coffee to go?"

"Of course." Ally gave me a dirty look, then spun around and headed for the kitchen.

I leaned across the table, locking my gaze on David. "She's single," I said, my voice low. "In case that's what you came in for."

His jaw dropped for a moment and he stared at me in dismay. "I, uh…well, thanks."

After an uncomfortable thirty seconds of silence, Ally appeared with his coffee and biscuit. He handed her a twenty, thanked her, and hurried out of the café.

"Jeez," I said as the café door swung shut. "I'm running them off in record numbers this morning."

"I cannot believe you!" Ally glared down at me, hands on her hips. "Suggesting I move in with that guy."

"I didn't suggest you move in with him. I was only pointing

out that you had another option besides me and Celia."

"If I didn't know any better, I'd swear you were playing matchmaker. You, the woman who finds every excuse in the world to avoid the hottest guy in town."

I glanced around, then whispered. "That whole shooting thing isn't an excuse. It's more of an explanation."

"What else did you say to him?"

"To Carter? Nothing that would incriminate me."

Ally threw her hands in the air. "Not Carter. David."

Some of the patrons looked over at her and she smiled at them. "Sorry."

"I didn't say much—just how I was fairly new in town myself and didn't like fishing."

She narrowed her eyes at me. "That's it?"

"I might have told him you were single."

Her hand flew up and covered her mouth. "You didn't."

"Was I supposed to lie? Because I could tell the next guy you're married or took a vow of celibacy or something."

"You're not supposed to give him any information at all."

"Wouldn't that be considered rude? I mean, up north, no one would think much of it, but seems like not participating in casual conversation over coffee would get you a reputation in a place like Sinful."

She closed her eyes and shook her head. I was fairly certain she was praying—whether it was for strength or a vial of untraceable poison, I wasn't certain.

"He looked interested," I said.

She opened one eye. "Really?"

"Definitely."

She opened the other eye. "Then maybe I'll let you off the hook."

I grinned. "So you *do* like him."

She blushed. "I don't know him, but yeah, he seems nice."

"And he's not hard on the eyes—all that fireman muscle and stuff."

Ally waved a hand at my plate. "Eat your breakfast before you get both of us into trouble." She gave me a grin before heading back to the kitchen.

I choked down my omelet—eggs without the yolk are gross—then tossed some money on the table and headed across the street to the General Store. It was ten minutes past opening time, and with any luck, I'd get to explain my slight mishap from the night before to Walter before word got to him another way.

Then I saw the look of dismay on his face when I walked inside the store.

Darn it! Someone had beaten me to the punch.

Chapter Nine

I trudged across the store and plopped onto the stool. "I take it you heard?"

Walter shook his head. "Hard not to. I had Carter here when I opened the door, asking me if I'd sold any rock salt bullets lately."

Crap!

"What did you tell him?"

"The truth. I didn't sell you the bullets, remember?"

I stared at Walter for a moment, the light slowly dawning. "You didn't charge me on purpose. You thought something would go wrong and you'd have an out."

"If one considers your track record, it was a fairly safe assumption."

"Then why didn't you try to talk me out of it?"

"What would have been the fun in that? I mean, granted, I didn't think you were going to shoot my nephew, but it makes one helluva story."

"How do you even know it was me?"

He stared.

"Okay, fine, it was me. But I'm not sure the story is all that interesting."

"Uh-huh. Why don't you let me be the judge of that?" He poured me a cup of coffee and pushed it across the counter. "Get to talking."

I took a sip of the coffee, then launched into my story, which was heavily edited to eliminate scaling trees and running rooflines and instead incorporated hiding in Ronald's bushes. I had to pause a few times for Walter to finish laughing, but finally, the entire sordid mess was laid bare on the counter at the Sinful General Store. A version of it, anyway.

Walter reached for a tissue and wiped his eyes. "Oh my God. I don't think I've laughed that hard since...well, since the last time you had a run-in with my nephew. You're like his own personal Pandora's box."

"That doesn't sound so nice."

Walter waved a hand in dismissal. "He deserves it. That boy's been strutting around this town, ignoring all of the good advice I give him, thinking he knows what's best. See, the real problem is that he wasn't challenged. Not by his job and certainly not by any of the local single women trying to get his attention."

"And then I showed up and the entire town went to hell in a handbasket."

"Ah, don't be thinking you're to blame for things going on in this town. You showing up the same time as this town melting down is just a coincidence. But it's all the perfect storm for Carter. He's needed some shaking up for a while."

I crossed my arms across my chest. "I'm not trying to shake anything up."

Walter nodded. "And that's the beauty of it. Things in this town were collecting behind a dam that just burst, but you're riding on top of that first wave." He leaned forward. "Don't you see? Your being here is a good thing. If you weren't, I don't know that things would have gotten sorted out on some of those crimes as quickly as they did. And if they hadn't been sorted out quickly, then more people might have gotten hurt."

"I'm sure Carter would have figured everything out without

my help."

"I'm sure he would have, too, but at what cost? Seems to me that as much grousing as that boy does about you, Ida Belle, and Gertie nosing into his business, you're helping protect the people in this town." He pointed his finger at me. "But if you repeat that to Ida Belle and Gertie, I'll swear you're a bald-faced liar."

"Your secret is safe with me." I sighed. "You really think I'm helping and not hurting?"

Walter nodded. "It's a lot harder to look at people you've known your entire life and imagine them as criminals. You don't have the same bias as Carter because you're not from here. Without emotional attachments, it's easier to see everyone as a suspect."

I nodded, but I wondered how much longer Walter's assessment would apply. Despite my lifelong ability to avoid emotional entanglements, I'd acquired friends and people I cared about in Sinful in a matter of weeks. I still wasn't sure what was more disturbing—that I'd made friends so easily here or that I'd gone three decades without doing so in DC.

"Thanks for everything," I said as I hopped off my stool, "but I'm afraid this time Sinful crime has me stumped. I have no idea what the arsonist and the creeper are up to, or if they're even different people."

"You'll figure it out."

Walter delivered that sentence in a tone that implied he was completely convinced of the truth in it. I wished I had as much confidence in my abilities as he did.

As I exited the store, I saw the real estate guy from the café crossing the street. I adjusted my stride to quite literally bump into him as he stepped onto the sidewalk in front of me.

"Oh, sorry," I said. "I was too busy looking at the display

and not watching where I was going."

His expression remained completely bland. "Not a problem."

I frowned. "You're not from here."

"Excuse me?"

"Your accent. It's not thick but definitely not Southern. New York?"

His left cheek twitched. "Originally, but not for a while now."

I put on my biggest smile. "What a relief to finally find another Yankee in this town." I extended my hand. "I'm Sandy-Sue, but everyone calls me Fortune. I'm from back East myself."

His expression said he couldn't care less, but he managed a reply. "Do you live here now?"

My interest ticked up a notch when he didn't volunteer his name. "No. I'm just here for the summer, settling up my aunt's estate. She's got a big house full of lots of stuff, and it's all on me to get organized. I'm a school librarian, so I have three months to tackle it all."

"I'm sorry about your aunt."

"Thanks. Hey, someone at the café told me you were in the real estate business. I'm going to be selling my aunt's house. Would you be interested in taking a look at it?"

His eyes flickered with a tiny bit of interest. "My client has a very specific set of desires in a home. Where is your aunt's house located?"

I gave him the address.

"Is that along the bayou?"

I nodded. "It's got a huge backyard. The bayou runs horizontally across it. It's very serene."

I glanced up, hoping storm clouds weren't brewing for fear of a lightning strike. Calling that property serene was one of the bigger lies I'd told since arriving in Sinful. Since I'd been in residence, the location had seemed to attract nothing but trouble.

"Is the property located in a residential area?"

"Yes, but the lots are huge and everyone keeps things so nicely. It's really amazing the foliage you can grow with all the rain." I hoped to God that sounded reasonable, as my knowledge of landscaping was mostly limited to the trees and bushes I've tumbled into and out of since I'd been in Sinful.

He frowned. "I'm sure it's lovely, but I don't think it will work. My client is looking for something with fewer neighbors."

"Oh well, if you want remote, there's plenty of that around here. Just pick a direction and wander into the swamp."

"He's looking for something a little more civilized with city services. It's been nice talking to you…er, Fortune, but I've got an appointment to make."

"Sure. It was nice meeting you, uh…I'm sorry, I didn't get your name."

He barely managed to disguise his displeasure. "Robert. Have a good day."

He strode off down the sidewalk at a speedy clip and got into a shiny new Lexus. I watched as he backed up and drove down Main Street in the direction of the highway.

All of my senses were on high alert. I'd used a real estate agent to find my place in DC. I'd thought hiring a man would mean less talking and business only, but I couldn't have been more wrong. My agent and the real estate agents representing every property we looked at could win Olympic events in talking about absolutely nothing. If the moment ever came that they ran out of things to say, I was convinced they would recite the alphabet simply to hear their own voices.

Either this guy wasn't a real estate agent, or he was lying about what he was in Sinful for. Why offer on Ally's house and not mine? What was he trying to buy? And for whom?

"I look like a hooker," I said.

"Good," Gertie replied. "That means we've gotten it right."

I looked at myself in the mirror and wondered how in the world I'd let Gertie talk me into this outfit. The jeans were a size too small and I'd had to lie down on the bed to zip them. The bottom half of the white lacy top was missing, and the part that surrounded my boobs had padded wire underneath, pushing my already decent-size chest up so high I could probably perch a plate of food on it. At least the boob-covering part was double-lined. With its thin straps, a bra was out of the question.

But the shoes were the worst part—six-inch spike heels with straps of studded leather wrapped around my feet. I'd need ski poles if I intended to walk very far. And my ankles may never be the same again. I found myself wondering why ballerinas intentionally adopted this position. It was excruciating.

Gertie was busy doing something to my hair she'd called "ratting." The side she'd finished stuck out into a different zip code and I had no doubt when I went to comb it later on, the "ratting" part of the equation would be readily apparent.

She finished up the second side of my now-enormous hair and stepped back to give it a critical look. "If you had a heavier bang, it would be sexier. Maybe we could just cut a little."

"No! Remember, this is not my own hair. I can't exactly grow more of it. I'm already worried those knots you just put in it will never come out and I'll be stuck this way forever. Who in the world finds this attractive?"

I turned around to face Gertie just as Ally stepped into my bedroom. She took one look at me and raised an eyebrow. "Since you look like a hooker," she said, "my guess is most men who aren't dead will find it attractive."

I sighed. Men really needed to get higher standards.

Ally gave me an apprehensive look. "Please tell me you're not going on a date with Carter. He may be one of the few men in this town who won't go for that look."

I waved a hand in dismissal. "I've put that whole dinner thing way on the back burner. Maybe even off the stove."

"I'm almost afraid to ask, then," Ally said.

I glanced at Gertie, who barely shook her head. Crap. Ally had an appointment with her insurance adjuster this evening, and I'd hoped I'd be gone before she got back. She was already worried about my safety and I knew if she found out about our plan, she'd try to talk me out of it. If I'd known about the outfit and the hair ratting, I might have let her.

I knew Gertie wanted me to lie so that Ally wouldn't worry, and normally, I'd have no problem with that. But for the first time in my life, I couldn't think of a single plausible explanation for this horror.

"I'm thinking of auditioning for *American Idol?*" I said.

Ally stared. "Try again."

"I thought jogging in the heels would pump up my calves?"

"The truth. What are you up to?"

I sighed. "I'm going to the Swamp Bar to see if I can get the lowdown on your friendly neighbor."

Ally's eyes widened. "You can't go to the Swamp Bar looking like that. You'll cause a riot."

Gertie perked up. "But if men are hot for her, they might talk."

Ally shook her head. "The only sounds that will come from them is the cussing they'll be doing while fighting. The Swamp Bar crowd is not an overly civilized bunch."

Gertie frowned. "Maybe we should try a bigger pair of

jeans…in case you need to run or something. You can't really bend well in those."

"If I have to run, I'd need to strip naked first. These shoes are a broken ankle waiting to happen. And if I ran with my boobs pushed up like this, they'd probably give me black eyes, not to mention that the straps wouldn't hold very long."

Ally gave me a critical up-and-down. "Where did you even get those clothes? I know you didn't pick them out."

"They were in the donation boxes at church for a charity drive we're doing," Gertie said. "We didn't have time for a trek to New Orleans, and Walter doesn't carry anything suitable, so I picked through some new arrivals."

Ally nodded. "I thought I recognized those shoes and that top. They used to belong to Pansy, back in junior high. Aunt Celia must be cleaning out some of her old stuff. She probably didn't want anyone at the Catholic church to see them, so she donated them at the Baptist church."

No wonder. I glanced back at the mirror and cringed. Ally's late cousin could have charitably been referred to as "easy." Her run on married men had caused herself and others a ton of trouble, ultimately ending in her death.

"Maybe this is too much," I said. It didn't really bother me to wear a dead woman's old clothes, but the limits on my physical ability did. "The last time we went to the Swamp Bar, we had to leave in a hurry. I'm at a serious disadvantage dressed like this. There's not even a place to carry my pistol."

Ally cocked her head to one side. "Well, there's *one* place."

"I'm not carrying my pistol in between my boobs."

She shrugged. "Then there's no other place. Look, I don't want you to go at all, but I know you're too stubborn to be talked out of it. If you insist on going and want to carry a weapon, which I'm all in favor of, then maybe you should switch to a skirt. It probably wouldn't be comfortable, but at least you could strap it to the inside of your thigh."

"Hmmm." I looked at Gertie. "Did you happen to find a skirt when you were confiscating charitable donations?"

Gertie reached for the trash bag she'd hauled upstairs and dumped the entire thing onto my bed. "I think I grabbed a black one with that stretchy fabric. It might work." She pawed through the pile of sleazy-wear and finally pulled something small and black out of it.

"Here it is," Gertie said, looking triumphant.

I stared at the object in dismay. "That's a headband."

"Stop exaggerating," Gertie said. "It's a perfectly good skirt. Go put it on."

I took one wobbly step in the heels and plopped down on the bed. The tight jeans sent me careening backward and two attempts to bend into a sitting position were met with failure. "I'm going to need some help here."

Ally and Gertie each unbuckled a shoe and pulled them off. I unfastened the jeans and pushed at the waistband. After a minute or two, I'd gotten it worked down around my hips. I looked up at Ally and Gertie, who looked rather amused at my discomfort.

"Either start pulling or cut these off of me," I said.

They both grabbed a pants leg and tugged, moving the jeans down maybe an inch.

"You're going to have to work harder than that," I said.

They both got a grip and pulled again, this time so hard they almost pulled me off the bed.

"Hold up," I said. "This isn't working." I inched back onto the center of the bed and rolled over. "I'll hold on to the other side of the bed so that I don't move when you pull."

"I think the scissors would be easier," Gertie said.

"Or dynamite," Ally agreed.

I reached over the side of the mattress and clutched the bed rails. "Just pull."

I felt them grab the jeans again and this time they counted.

One. Two. Three.

It was a really good yank.

The jeans ripped down my legs like a magician performing a big reveal. A second later, I heard a crash, followed by a thud and a yell, then tumbling and another crash.

I jumped up from the bed and turned to see Ally staring out the bedroom door, one hand over her mouth. Gertie was in a heap in the hallway, the blue jeans completely covering her head. At the bottom of my stairs, Ida Belle used a newel post to pull herself upright.

I rushed out into the hallway and snatched the jeans from Gertie's face, then scanned her for injuries.

"Is she all right?" Ally asked, leaning over beside me.

"I think she knocked herself out," I said and started tapping her face with my fingers.

I heard stomping on the stairwell and a couple seconds later, a somewhat disheveled Ida Belle appeared on the landing. "What the hell is going on?"

"Gertie knocked herself out," Ally explained.

Ida Belle, who was dressed in all black and wearing combat boots, stepped up beside me and peered down at Gertie. "Well, that's what happens when you run around with blue jeans on your head."

"She wasn't doing it on purpose," Ally said. "We were trying to get the jeans off of Fortune and we might have pulled a little too hard."

Ida Belle shook her head. "Well, next time, check behind you first. Being knocked down a flight of stairs is never on my list of things to do." She stalked off into the bathroom and came back with a cup of water that she promptly tossed into Gertie's face.

Gertie bolted upright, sputtering and sending water droplets spraying. "What happened?"

Ida Belle stared down at her, hands on hips. "You knocked me down the stairs, you old coot."

Gertie noticed the cup in Ida Belle's hand and glared. "Afraid you're going to break a hip, Methuselah?"

"No. But I might have torn a perfectly good shirt."

I held up a hand. "We do not have time for a senior citizen insult fight."

Ida Belle looked me up and down. "Do you plan on putting on pants before we go to the Swamp Bar?"

I realized I was standing there in a hooker top and my underwear. "I'm wearing a skirt, actually."

"Whatever," Ida Belle said. "Just put on something or you'll stand out even more than you already do. Underwear Night is Friday."

I blanched and headed back into my bedroom to grab the skirt. The words "Underwear Night" and "Swamp Bar" did not belong in the same sentence together. I found myself hoping the underwear part was for the ladies only. Otherwise, good God, the horror.

I pulled on the skirt and took a look in the mirror. It wasn't quite as small as a headband, but if I bent over, someone would see my weapon. The pistol, that is. I contemplated digging through the clothes pile for something else, but if the clothes had been part of Pansy's junior high wardrobe, the chances of my locating better coverage were slim to none. At least I could run in the skirt.

Ida Belle and Ally had gotten Gertie into a standing

position, and I sat down on the edge of the bed to buckle myself back into the death shoes.

"You're late," Gertie said. "Don't tell me you've been waxing that car again."

Ida Belle's Corvette was a source of contention between Ida Belle and most everyone who'd ever gotten in the way of what she considered her best relationship. After my disastrous trash bag ride, I would be the first to admit that the thought of the Vette did not inspire good feelings. But we had already decided that speed might be a necessity if things went south, which put Gertie's ancient Cadillac and my Jeep out of the running and left Ida Belle's Corvette as my ride for the evening.

"I sold the Corvette."

"What?" "No way!" "Seriously?"

We all spoke at once, and I bolted up from the bed, grabbing on to Ally as my feet threatened to fall out of my shoes. "When did this happen?" I asked.

"Yesterday," Ida Belle said. She scanned our faces. "What? I've been saying I was going to sell the car. I thought you'd all be happy?"

Gertie shot me an apprehensive look. "I guess I never figured you'd really do it."

Ida Belle shrugged. "It was a great car, but I didn't find it exciting any more. It was time to try something new."

An uneasy feeling ran through me. Ida Belle was dangerous enough in the Corvette. The thought of her navigating a new vehicle on the narrow, curvy road to the Swamp Bar, especially if high speeds were required, didn't leave me with a good visual.

"So what did you replace it with?" I asked, already sure I wasn't going to like the answer.

Ida Belle grinned. "A motorcycle."

Chapter Ten

Gertie's jaw dropped and Ally's hand flew up to cover her mouth.

"You're joking," I said.

Ida Belle gave me a dirty look. "No, I'm not joking. What? You think I can't handle a motorcycle? I'll have you know I was a pretty good off-road rider in my day."

I immediately saw two problems with her last statement. One, we were supposed to be *on* the road. And two, "in my day" was not something that yielded confidence when the woman making the statement was as old as the dirt she used to ride on.

"You're supposed to be giving me a lift to the Swamp Bar, remember?"

"Of course I remember. I'm not senile. Are you telling me you're scared of motorcycles?"

I shook my head. "It's not the motorcycle that concerns me."

"You need a way in and out of the Swamp Bar. If things go south, a motorcycle is the best bet for speed and maneuverability."

It wasn't that I disagreed with her, exactly. But the number of things I could see going wrong with this situation was so large that I couldn't even wrap my mind around it.

"Bottom line," Ida Belle said. "It's either my motorcycle,

Gertie's Cadillac, or your Jeep."

"You could use my car," Ally said.

"You're a nice girl to even offer," Ida Belle said, "but I don't want a Ford Escort to be the thing I'm depending on to get me to safety."

"What about my boat?" Ally suggested.

I perked up. The Swamp Bar sat right on the bayou. A boat would be a much better option than playing Evel Knievel with Ida Belle.

Gertie shook her head. "As much as I hate to say it, a boat won't work. Walter said the dock at the Swamp Bar is being rebuilt, and you'd never make it up the bank walking."

"Especially in those shoes," Ally agreed. "Those heels would sink down into the mud and it would harden around them like concrete. They'd probably have to rebuild the dock right on top of you."

"Fine," I said. "We'll take the motorcycle."

I grabbed my nine-millimeter and a thigh strap from my nightstand and waved them out of my room. "Let's get this over with."

If I didn't need therapy before I got on the motorcycle, I was pretty sure I needed it now. I don't know what I'd expected—maybe a Harley—but what sat in my driveway was a dual-sport bike. One of those that could be ridden on or off road. Given that the road was the only solid piece of ground running to and from the Swamp Bar, I found the off-road option a little more than disconcerting.

Then the real fun began.

Ida Belle handed me a helmet that I think I'd seen in a black-and-white movie the week before. "No visor?" I asked.

"You're sitting behind me," Ida Belle said. "That will be fine."

I wasn't convinced, but I grabbed the straps and placed the helmet on top of my hair. It took me pulling and Gertie and Ally pushing to get the helmet down far enough to buckle, but no way was I riding without one. This one may have come over on Noah's Ark, but it was still better than nothing. I shuddered to think what my hair would look like when we got to the bar. Probably like one of those Albert Einstein posters. Once the helmet was in place, I used Gertie and Ally as balancing posts and swung a high-heeled leg over the seat, then they arranged the toes of my shoes on the foot pegs.

Despite my earlier objection, I decided my boobs were the best carrying option for my pistol, at least until we got to the bar, so I wrapped the holster around my biceps and shoved the gun into the middle of my cleavage. Ally's lips quivered but no one was foolish enough to laugh at an irritated woman packing a pistol in her boobs.

"You talked to Myrtle?" I asked Gertie.

"Yes," she said. "She's working dispatch until midnight. If any calls come in about the Swamp Bar, she'll call me and I'll figure out a rescue option."

"Great," I said, with a lot more enthusiasm than I felt. This entire plan was so full of holes it wouldn't hold water.

Ida Belle had already donned her helmet and a black leather jacket, complete with a Sons of Anarchy patch. "Ready?" she asked.

"As ready as I'm getting."

She dropped the visor on her helmet. "Good enough for me."

She fired up the motorcycle and revved the engine. It was so loud I was certain it rattled the windows on every house on the block. I wrapped my arms around her thin frame, she put the bike in gear, and off we went.

I'll be the first to admit that I rode the first block with my eyes closed. If I was going to die, I didn't see any point in seeing it coming. It was one of those areas where I felt ignorance was bliss. When a bit of time passed and we didn't hit the skids, I opened one eye and saw we'd made it safely down the block. Considering it was better than I'd expected, I decided to give both eyes open a whirl and took in a wide-angle view just as we pulled onto Main Street.

The sound of the engine alone had everyone on the sidewalk turning to look, although with our helmets and completely odd clothes, I doubt anyone recognized us. If anything, they probably all thought some skinny dude had picked up a hooker.

Ida Belle surprised me by maintaining a reasonable speed and executing good control over the motorcycle. In fact, the highway riding was almost pleasant. And then we turned off the paved road.

The road to the Swamp Bar was basically a narrow path of dirt and rocks that wound though the bayou. In some places, it wasn't even wide enough for two cars to pass each other, explaining the partially submerged automobiles that littered each side of the road. The road was also covered with potholes—some only big enough to provide a jolt up my spine, others big enough to disappear in. Ida Belle wove in and out of the big ones, seeming to hit every single small one on the road. I was fairly certain she shook loose a filling or two.

It was dusk when we pulled into the Swamp Bar parking lot, which was essentially one big patch of dirt that was either dry or muddy, depending on the weather. Ida Belle parked at the far end of the space, near the bayou and on the other side of a van.

The light from the bar didn't extend to where we were, so no one inside would be able to see us. The van blocked us from the view of people pulling into the lot.

I did a quick check of the van to make sure it was empty and not a roving meth lab or something equally as dangerous, and grimaced when I saw two child seats in the second-row bench. I hoped they, at least, had one responsible parent at home. People who showed up at the Swamp Bar weren't usually part of Sinful's most reputable. Showing up before dark added a whole level of unsuitable to the mix.

"Do you see Floyd's truck anywhere?" I asked.

Ida Belle shook her head. "No, but it's a bit early."

There were twenty or so vehicles in the parking lot. I knew from my last visit that there would be three times that once the place was hopping. "Should I wait for more people to show up?"

It was a catch-22. If I went in while it was quiet, I'd draw more attention, but not the kind I was looking for. If the place was busy and everyone had belted back a few, they wouldn't care as much when a stranger walked in. If it was quiet and people were still sharp, they might take a closer look and realize they'd seen me before. Things would go further downhill if they recognized me as a friend of Carter's.

"I think it will be easier to blend if there's more people inside," Ida Belle said.

"Okay, but I'm taking off this helmet."

Ida Belle nodded. "You can certainly try."

I unhooked the helmet strap and pulled the helmet up. It didn't budge. I yanked harder and only succeeded in wrenching my neck. "A little help, please?"

Ida Belle motioned for me to bend over and she grabbed the helmet. With her pulling and me pushing, it finally popped off my head. Ida Belle took one look at me and started laughing.

I reached up with one hand and met with hair a good two feet from my head.

I bent over to take a look at my hair in the mirror on the motorcycle handlebars, but the mirror was too small to see much. I rose up and twisted the side mirror on the van and gasped. My hair stood straight out as though I'd stuck a fork into a 220-volt plug.

I pressed my hand on the top of the hair, trying to push it flat. "I've got to get this down."

"It would take a downpour and weights to accomplish that," Ida Belle said.

"I don't have weights and I'm not standing here until a downpour passes by."

Ida Belle shrugged. "There's always the bayou."

"You want me to stick my head in the bayou?"

"Jesus, do I have to think of everything?" She bent over and grabbed an empty soda bottle from the ground, then stomped over to the bayou and filled it with dirty, icky swamp water. When she walked back over to me, bottle in hand, I shook my head.

"No way," I said. "You're not putting that stinky water on my hair."

"It's either this or you go in looking like a porcupine hooker."

Crap.

"Okay, but just pour a little in my hands and I'll try to pat it down."

She gave me a skeptical look, but dumped some of the dirty water into my hands. I tried not to think about what was in it as I flopped my hands on the top of my head and rubbed the hair down. "Is that better?" I asked.

"Better than what?"

"Than before."

"I suppose it will have to do."

I leaned over and looked in the van mirror again. My hair was still poofier than it had been after Gertie finished with it, but I had cut it down in volume by at least a third.

"Here comes the crowd," Ida Belle said and pointed over the hood of the van.

I peered around and saw a line of headlights coming toward the bar. "It looks like a funeral procession."

"That's probably the regulars, so same difference, really."

I watched as the vehicles pulled into the parking area, switching off in different directions to park. Burly middle-aged men and the occasional sleazily dressed woman climbed out of cars and trucks and headed straight for the bar.

"I didn't see Floyd in the mix," I said.

"Me either. Now that more people showed up, it's probably a good idea for you to get in there before Floyd arrives. People aren't likely to talk about him if he's sitting in there with them."

"Maybe I can get the skinny on Floyd from the others, and if he shows up, I might be able to find out more."

Ida Belle pointed her finger at me. "If he shows up, you get the hell out of there before he realizes you're one of the people who tore his fence down."

The mental image of the giant leaping cat and my torn T-shirt flashed through my mind. "You're probably right." I unwrapped the holster from my arm and secured it around my thigh, then pulled my pistol out of my cleavage and tucked it into the holster.

"Am I good?" I asked.

"Not if you bend over, or maybe even sneeze."

"I'll be sure not to do either."

"I wouldn't breathe too deeply, either," Ida Belle said.

"You've got your phone, right?"

I grabbed the tiny purse at the end of the gold cross-body chain hanging over me and pulled out my phone. "It's all that would fit in this completely useless purse. One bar for service. That's not exactly encouraging."

"Typical this far out in the swamp. Don't worry about it. I'm going to move the motorcycle to that small spot of grass over near the front door. I brought a ball cap and a pack of cigarettes. I'll stand around the edge of the porch and keep watch. If anything goes down, make a break for the door. I'll be ready to go."

"You took up smoking?"

"No. I took up blending with this crowd. Standing outside for a smoke doesn't attract attention."

"Good plan." I tucked my phone back in the purse, pulled down my skirt, and pushed up my boobs, then carefully picked my way across the parking lot in those god-awful heels.

I'd made it halfway to the bar when Ida Belle called out, "The bar closes at two a.m. In case you want to pick up the pace."

"Smart-ass," I grumbled as I forced myself into a faster wobble.

Fortunately, the owners of the Swamp Bar were not only disreputable but cheap, and the flooring on the entire front porch and inside was sheets of plywood. That gave me long stretches of flat board to balance on and I managed a more natural-looking walk as I strolled to the front door.

I paused a couple of seconds at the threshold and took a deep breath before shoving the door open and stepping inside. A second later, a tidal wave of cold water hit me in the face, completely drenching me. I heard a cheer inside the bar as I sputtered and wiped at my eyes with my fingers.

"You idiot," the bartender yelled. "Throw the water on the chest, not the face, or they'll get all upset over your ruining their makeup."

Directly in front of me stood a man holding an empty bucket—I assumed the source of my current soaking-wet status. He stared at my chest and yelled back at the bartender. "They's so big, they're up next to her face. Can't aim that narrow with a bucket."

"Why are you throwing water in the first place?" I asked,

The bartender pointed to a wall behind him with a list of events. Next to Wednesday, in barely legible handwriting, were the words "Wet T-Shirt Contest."

Oh hell no.

From the weathered age of the board and the flaking paint spots on the lettering, I knew that list had been in place for a while. Which meant Gertie and Ida Belle already knew about wet T-shirt night. And when I got out of here and into fighting clothes, they would both pay. Dearly.

"Ma'am," the bartender yelled. "Contestants drink free. I have a nice white wine."

I shook the water off of my arms and gave Bucket Man my go-to-hell stare as I did my best to stalk by. It was a bit wobbly, but I figured I still pulled off pissed. The bartender handed me a stack of napkins.

"Sorry about ole Billy," the bartender said as I wiped off with the napkins. "He means well but he's a bit of a half-wit."

"Then maybe you should let someone with a higher IQ toss the water." Of course, I had no reason to suspect that anyone who frequented the Swamp Bar even possessed a higher IQ, but it didn't hurt to throw the suggestion out there.

A man slid onto the stool next to me. "That's what happens when you let Buckshot Billy handle moving objects."

Midforties. Six foot tall. A hundred sixty pounds. Wearing dark sunglasses at night in a bar. 1970s sweeping disco hairdo.

I could definitely take him, but he had such a weird vibe that I wasn't sure I wanted to touch him. If I'd been drinking a beer, I could have gone for a good clock in the face with a beer mug, but I wouldn't even make a dent with the cheap wineglass I held.

"Buckshot Billy?" I asked.

Weird man nodded. "The locals gave him the nickname because he couldn't hit the broad side of a barn with a football. The only time he could hit something hunting was using buckshot—it scatters a good bit."

I looked at the bartender. "You're letting a guy nicknamed 'Buckshot' control the water bucket?"

The bartender looked a little sheepish. "Billy's sorta a sad case. I was trying to be nice."

"Then give him free beer. Take away the bucket and be nice to every other woman who walks through that door."

He rubbed his chin, as if the idea required deep thought. "You may be right."

It was all I could do to keep from rolling my eyes.

Weird guy's cell phone rang and he looked at the display and frowned. "Excuse me," he said, as if I cared where he was going. Then he walked across the bar and outside. The bartender stepped back behind the bar with the bucket, poured a beer, and shoved it across the counter to Billy, who gazed longingly at the bucket.

"I haven't seen you in here before," the bartender said. "You new in town?"

"Just visiting. Thought I'd look up an old friend. Someone told me he hangs out here."

"What's his name?"

"Floyd Guidry."

The bartender narrowed his eyes at me. "Best I know, Floyd ain't got no friends, and it don't take women long before they know to steer clear of them. He's got no qualms about backhanding one."

I frowned. "Is that so? He wasn't really my friend. Just someone my brother met doing a job down here. My brother thought I might look him up and say hello if I had the time. He seemed pleasant enough the one time I met him, but I guess I was wrong."

The bartender still didn't look convinced. "He's in the phone book. Coulda called him."

I smiled. "But then I wouldn't have gotten a bucket of water thrown on me."

He studied me for a second more. Based on my outfit and my flippant attitude, he must have decided I looked like the party type because he finally nodded. "That's true enough. And I'm happy to have some new blood for the contest. Floyd's been in here this week, but he usually shows up a bit later."

"I'm in no hurry. I stopped by Monday night, but I only stayed long enough to see he wasn't here, then left. Figured I'd catch him a different night."

"He didn't come in two nights ago," Billy interjected, "on account that he was in jail in New Orleans."

My heart dropped. If Floyd was in jail, then he couldn't be the arsonist.

"That sounds about right," the bartender said.

"Sounds like Floyd walks on the edge a little too much for my taste," I said. "Maybe I should take your advice and just give him a call."

The bartender nodded. "Probably a lot safer bet to have Southwest Bell between the two of you instead of just a barstool."

"Great, then I guess I'll be going."

"Wait," the bartender said. "You can't leave yet. We're about to start the wet T-shirt contest."

"Oh, I think I'll have to pass. I've had all the excitement, and water, I can take for one night."

The bartender's face fell. "You were a shoo-in for the win. The usual crew of women in here look a little rough." Someone yelled at the other end of the bar and the bartender headed off to serve them. I hopped off the stool and pulled down my skirt.

Billy, who'd been staring intently at the wall behind the bar, came out of his stupor. "That's funny. You and that other guy both looking for Floyd tonight."

"What other guy?"

Billy's eyes widened. "I shouldn't have said nothing."

"No, it's okay. You can tell me. I won't say anything."

Billy looked at me, glanced at the door, then the makeshift stage at the front of the bar, then bit his lower lip. His expression went from worried to calculated—as calculated as an idiot could look, anyway. Then he grinned. "I'll tell you if you do the wet T-shirt contest."

My first inclination was to simply say "hell, no" and leave. After all, what did it really matter that someone else was looking for Floyd? If he liked to hit women and spent regular time in jail, then the list of people looking for Floyd might be as long as the Mississippi River. But something about it bothered me, even though I couldn't put my finger on it. Maybe it was the timing of someone else looking for Floyd the same night I was, or maybe it was the fact that the other man could have called Floyd or even gone directly to his house, as the bartender suggested I do.

Or maybe it was just because in Sinful, things were never quite surface level.

But a wet T-shirt contest? Was satisfying my curiosity really worth the humiliation just to get an answer that probably didn't matter anyway?

I glanced around the room, checking out the women who might be competing. "I don't have to do anything special, do I?"

Billy frowned. "You have to have boobs and stand there."

"Yeah, I got that part. I mean, do I have to walk around, dance, sing the national anthem?"

"No. You all just line up and then someone throws water on you—used to be me but I traded the job for free beer—then the bartender holds his hand above each of you and the one with the loudest cheers wins."

I looked at the makeshift stage. It sounded simple enough, and I was already wet, so nothing lost on that end. Maybe the other man didn't mean anything. Maybe getting the name was a total waste of my time.

But what if it wasn't?

I sighed. "Fine, I'll do it. But as soon as I get off that stage, you'll be standing at the door ready to give me that name on my way out. No other requirements. Deal?"

Billy nodded. "Deal."

He stuck out his hand and we shook on it. I had a feeling I was going to regret it.

"Attention please!" the bartender yelled into a microphone that screeched.

Everyone covered their ears with their hands.

"Sorry," the bartender said in his regular voice. "It's time for the contest you've all been waiting for. If you beautiful ladies would make your way onto the stage."

Three other women stood up, adjusted their chests, and pranced up to the stage. Not to be outdone, I gave my chest a shake and attempted a slow, smooth glide. Hip-shaking was completely out of the question if I had any intention of remaining upright, but I finally managed to navigate the crowd and stand at the end of the row of contestants.

The bartender stepped off the stage and grabbed a water hose from one of the patrons. "And now for the fun part."

He turned the water hose on full blast and shot a chest-high line straight across the stage. The other women squealed and jumped as the water hit them. I thought I was prepared, but I swear, he must have pumped the water in from a cooler. It was so cold it took my breath away.

"No fair," one of the contestants yelled. "She doesn't have on a bra." She pointed at me.

"That's what I'm talking about!" one of the patrons yelled and a cheer went up around the bar.

"Is one required?" I asked.

"Only during hurricane season," the bartender replied. "Safety issues."

"Can we get on with this?" I said. "I need to go stand in front of a heater."

The bartender grinned and held his hand over the first woman. "Let's hear it for Sheena."

A small cheer went up and Sheena frowned.

"Damn it, Lester," Sheena yelled into the crowd. "You better open your mouth and yell for me, or you'll be cooking your own dinner for the rest of the year."

A man sitting up front rose from his chair, a bit wobbly as he went, and started yelling. "Let's hear it for my wife's hooters."

Sheena grinned. "That's my old man. You tell 'em, baby!"

Good. God.

The next two women either didn't have an "old man" in the bar or didn't want any help marketing their wares, so the bartender moved quickly in my direction. Before he even put his hand above my head, the patrons started going wild.

The other three women shot me dirty looks, then piled off the stage.

"We have a winner!" the bartender yelled. A couple seconds later, I felt something drop onto my shoulder and glanced down in horror at the satin banner draped across my chest proclaiming me "Best Boobs." Before I could rip the sash off, lights flashed and a bevy of smartphones took my picture.

I looked over the crowd to the door and saw Billy standing there, giving me a thumbs-up. But just as I started to step off the stage, Floyd walked in the door and his gaze locked directly on me.

I should have taken advantage of the fact that his stare started with my chest. Maybe if I'd have reacted quicker, he wouldn't have had a chance to move up to my face, but the absurdity of the entire mess combined with my surprise at him walking in the bar at the worst moment possible caused me to hesitate. And that hesitation was my undoing.

His eyes widened and he pointed his finger at me, his face contorted in anger. "You're the bitch that ruined my fence."

Chapter Eleven

I jumped off the stage, ready to run, but one of my feet landed on a rotten piece of plywood and the heel went straight through the wood and lodged there. I pulled as hard as I could, but it didn't budge an inch.

"You're not getting away this time," I heard Floyd yelling in the crowd, but even more disturbing was it didn't sound as if he was very far away.

I gave the shoe one last tug, but it was no use, and I had neither the time nor the flexibility to undo the straps myself—not without flashing the entire bar my weapon, anyway. I reached up and grabbed a bottle of beer out of a man's hand, broke the bottle on the table, and swiped at the straps with the broken glass. I held in a string of cursing as I felt the burn of a glass cut on my ankle, but with my foot free, I stumbled forward, like a drunken, peg-legged pirate, hunched over so Floyd couldn't see me.

I made it to the back door and pulled Billy outside. "Who was the man?"

"That was great," Billy said. "I knew you'd win. You got a great set of hooters."

"The man who was looking for Floyd. Who was he?"

"Oh, right." Billy scratched his head. "He was that dude you talked to at the bar. Marco something. Said Floyd was in big trouble…or little trouble. I can't remember exactly."

"Marco's last name?"

Billy shrugged. "I didn't catch it."

"You bitch!" Floyd appeared in the doorway, clutching a beer bottle and wearing an expression that said he had every intention of using it. As I took off down the steps, he shoved Billy off the porch. "Move out of the way, you moron."

I heard the motorcycle engine fire up and took off down the steps. Ida Belle roared toward me and slid the bike around in a one-eighty right in front of me, showering me with dust and rocks. I might have screamed just a little before she skidded to a stop, but I'll never admit it.

I leaped onto the back of the bike and barely grabbed on to Ida Belle before she took off, handing me my helmet over her shoulder as she went. I felt Floyd's fingers run down my shoulders as he just missed pulling me off the back of the bike. I turned around and saw him running for his truck. A couple seconds later, the engine fired and he roared backward out of the parking space, scattering dirt and rocks in every direction.

"He's coming after us!" I shouted as I tugged on my helmet with one hand and held on for my life with the other.

Ida Belle rolled the throttle back as far as she could manage and keep us upright, but I knew the motorcycle was no match for Floyd's V-8 engine. Ida Belle took a sharp corner too fast, and the back end of the motorcycle broke loose and started to slide. My mouth was clenched so tight my jaw started to ache, and I was afraid that with the death grip I had on Ida Belle, I might bruise one of her ribs.

The back tire gained a hold on the dirt road again and the bike jerked upright. Ida Belle didn't even hesitate before rolling the throttle again. I glanced back and saw that Floyd was gaining on us at an alarming rate.

"He's going to run us over," I shouted.

"We've got to get off this road," Ida Belle said.

"What? The only thing off this road is swamp."

"Closer to the highway, there's a stretch of mostly solid land."

Mostly?

No one placed a bet on "mostly."

The glare of headlights beamed over my shoulders. I held one hand over my forehead and glanced back. "We're not going to make it."

The truck's engine revved and it leaped forward, coming so close that I could count the squares in the grille. It took nerves of steel and the limbs of a contortionist, but I let go of my stranglehold on Ida Belle with one hand and worked my pistol from the holster between my thighs. I swung my arm around, trying to get an aim on a tire, and fired.

Missed.

Between the shoddy road, the glare of the headlights, and the small amount of tire showing beneath the massive bumper, my chances of making the shot were low, even given my abilities. I took aim again, this time at a headlight, figuring that if he couldn't see where he was going, it would slow him down.

Direct hit.

Plastic and glass exploded from the driver's side headlight and the glare I stared into was instantly cut in half. I shifted the pistol to my right hand and twisted around to take aim at the remaining light.

Aim. Fire.

Right as I squeezed the trigger, the motorcycle dropped into a huge pothole and the shot went low, pinging off the bumper. The truck swerved and fell back ten yards or so, then the engine revved up again and it launched forward. I aimed again and fired.

Bingo!

The remaining headlight shattered and the truck immediately dropped back as we shot off down the road, putting good distance between us. I turned around to try to gauge how close we were to the highway, but before I could make out any of the markers I'd taken note of on the way to the bar, bright lights encapsulated us and I twisted backward, trying to see where they came from.

Not good.

Floyd's truck was gaining on us again, a row of four spotlights in full force on top of the cab. Crap. That was an option I never had to consider back in DC. Of course, back in DC I wasn't usually balanced on the back of a motorcycle trying to avoid being run over by an angry redneck who thought bobcats made great pets. In fact, now that I'd processed the entire scene, it just might be the most ridiculous thing that had happened to me since I'd arrived in Sinful.

Might be.

In the meantime, I needed to figure out a way to live to tell about it. Otherwise, it was going to be a very sad ending to a short career in unintended private investigation. Even worse, I would die dressed like a hooker. It was the sort of thing nightmares were made of.

I only had one bullet left and four spotlights. No matter how you arranged the numbers, they didn't add up in my favor. I could always fire through the windshield. I had a really good chance of hitting Floyd, but that meant I had a really good chance of killing him, too. Floyd may be trying to kill me, and he was definitely an asshole, but taking him out went against everything I believed. He may be a bad guy by Sinful standards, but in my world, he was just another civilian. Before I could change my mind, I took aim at the tire again and fired.

Miss.

My pulse shot up as I realized how quickly the truck was closing the gap between us. I peered over Ida Belle's shoulder, hoping to see lights from the highway, but we'd just entered a stretch on the road with rows of tall cattails surrounding us and I couldn't see anything at all through the thick reeds. I whipped back around and my heart fell when I saw only a couple of feet between me and the truck.

Inch by inch it crept toward me, until I felt the heat coming off the engine. I could make out a dim outline of Floyd in the driver's seat and for whatever reason, I was certain he was smiling. Just when I thought it was all over, Ida Belle swung the bike around a corner and the truck dropped back as it negotiated the corner. The breath I didn't know I'd been holding rushed out of me so quickly my chest hurt, and I prayed the road had enough turns to keep us ahead of the truck until we reached the "mostly" solid land.

Two more stretches passed with the truck just about to overtake us as we reached the corner. Two more times we narrowly avoided being roadkill. But the next stretch seemed to be longer than the others. My head was a swivel, looking back to see how close the truck was, then forward, praying I'd see a turn coming up.

Just when I thought we were toast, Ida Belle yelled, "Hold on!"

And she drove straight off the road and into the swamp.

The initial drop from the road into the marsh was enough to vault my stomach up in my throat. Then the bike slammed down onto the ground and jarred my spinal cord so hard I would probably come out of this a half inch shorter. The truck skidded to a stop at the edge of the road and I heard Floyd yelling. Then he backed up and continued down the road. If Ida Belle's shortcut turned out to be a bust, Floyd would be waiting at the edge of town, ready to mow us down.

The bike bounced along at a much faster clip than I'd imagined Ida Belle would be able to manage, and I found myself grudgingly giving her credit for her driving ability. I'd worked with professionals who wouldn't have been able to negotiate a motorcycle in this terrain, and definitely not at the speed she was managing.

I looked over Ida Belle's shoulder, trying to gauge how close to the highway we were, but I was sorry I did. Nothing but inky blackness stretched in front of us, and the motorcycle's headlight didn't illuminate more than five feet in front of us. Panic coursed through me. No way did she have the terrain memorized, and unless she had infrared vision, she couldn't see any farther than I could, so that meant she was completely winging it. It was a wonder she'd made it this far.

My mind raced for alternatives to the death trip we were currently on, but with no place to hide, no other means of transportation, no bullets, and likely no cell phone service, I couldn't think of a single viable option. Just when I was about to give up all hope, the motorcycle launched upward and into the air, slamming into pavement when it dropped.

The highway!

In the distance, I could make out lights from downtown Sinful. If we could get into town, we would be safe. I whipped around to check behind us and saw the truck turning onto the highway about fifty yards behind us. It was a good distance, but was it enough? Ida Belle had the throttle pegged but every time I glanced back, the truck had closed in by ten yards or more. With Sinful still fifty yards in the distance, we weren't going to make it.

With thirty yards to go, and the truck bearing down on us, my hopes of a narrow escape started slipping away. Then without warning, Ida Belle made a sharp right turn and drove off the highway and down a slope into a rice field. I remembered a farm that sat just on the edge of town and hoped it wasn't owned by the kind of farmer who shot first and asked questions later. As we raced along a row in the rice field, I saw the truck fading into the distance and my spirits shot up.

Then an ear-shattering boom of thunder shook the earth and rain plummeted from the sky as though it was the end of days. The drops were huge and at the speed we traveled, pelted my skin like rocks. With her visor and leather jacket, Ida Belle was in much better shape than I was. With the way I was dressed, I may as well be riding naked through a hailstorm. I held one hand over my eyes and squinted over Ida Belle's shoulder, happy to see we were drawing near lights, probably from the farmhouse. That meant we were west of downtown and headed toward my neighborhood.

And that's when the first shot rang out.

It whizzed right past my head, so close that I could hear the rush of air breaking, even wearing a helmet in the downpour. "Someone's shooting at us!" I yelled.

As Ida Belle made a hard right, a second shot shattered the headlight on the motorcycle, pitching us into complete darkness. But that didn't slow Ida Belle down any. I only had two options left: let go and face the gun-slinging farmer, or pray. Given my outfit and the fact that I was deep in the Bible Belt, I figured God would come a lot closer to understanding my situation than the farmer.

Before I could even get out the first word of prayer, the motorcycle broke through a thin plywood wall and the air exploded with chickens. Feathers and hay swirled around us, and I covered my face with one arm as the squawking, frantic birds flapped their tiny wings in a desperate attempt to get out of the way. Seconds later, we broke through the opposite side of the coop, Ida Belle never slowing.

I heard a yell and looked over to see a woman run out the front door of the farmhouse, shaking her fist at us. Ida Belle made a hard right up a slope and we launched up and onto a side street in my neighborhood.

I said a quick prayer that Floyd had no idea who I was and where I lived, and counted every second of the dash to my house. The farmer would be certain to call the police, and Swamp Team Three was Carter's first choice to check out when odd things happened in Sinful. I had no doubt that he'd be banging on my door tonight, and it would be a miracle if we could pull off a cover story in time.

We were soaking wet, covered in feathers, and beneath the domestic fowl look, I was still dressed like a streetwalker. Ida Belle, at least, could shed her clothes and helmet and would be able to pass for normal…as normal as things got, anyway. But short of being sandblasted, I wasn't sure there was any hope for me.

As we rounded the corner to my house, I saw the garage door open and Gertie standing in my driveway, frantically gesturing us inside. Ida Belle flew into the garage and slid to a stop next to my Jeep. Gertie yanked the garage door down and before I even stepped off the bike, Ally fired up a Shop-Vac and started sucking the feathers off my arms and shoulders.

Ida Belle jumped off the bike and started pulling off her clothes and replacing them with her sweat suit that Gertie had placed on the toolbox. Steam rose from the motorcycle, and slightly charred chicken feathers were stuck to at least half of the engine. The odor they put off had me choking. Gertie grabbed a tarp from a shelf and tossed it over the steaming mess of metal.

"I guess the farmer called the sheriff's department?" I asked as I tugged off my helmet.

Gertie nodded. "Myrtle said a call came in that a giant chicken rode a motorcycle through the coop and off down the street. She called me before she called it in to Carter."

I stared, wondering which was more unnerving—that the farmer thought a giant chicken was riding a motorcycle, or that Gertie had apparently known what had happened and was prepared to handle it. "And so you ran out into the garage to ready a tarp, a change of clothes, and a Shop-Vac?"

"Of course," Gertie said.

"But how did you know that's what you needed to do?"

"Oh, well, there was this one time in junior high school when Ida Belle and I stole Sammy Crawford's minibike...took us hours to pick the feathers off by hand. I always keep a Shop-Vac handy now. Just in case."

"Just in case you decide to drive a motorcycle through a chicken coop during a rainstorm?"

"Yes," Gertie said.

I opened my mouth, but I was completely out of words. Ally stopped vacuuming for a couple of seconds and shoved a glass of Sinful Ladies Society cough syrup into my hand. "It's not worth trying to understand," she said.

I chugged back the shot of whiskey in one gulp.

"You need to get out of those clothes," Gertie said. "Cutting the shoe strap will probably be easiest."

"It was for the other one," I said. "As far as I'm concerned, you can cut off the entire mess." I pointed my finger at Gertie. "You and I need to talk. You sent me to that bar dressed like a hooker on wet T-shirt contest night. And don't you dare try to pretend you didn't know."

Ally sucked in a breath and stared at Gertie, her eyes wide. "You didn't?"

"Well, of course I knew," Gertie said. "How'd you do?"

Ida Belle yanked what was left of my sash out of the back of my top and waved it in the air.

"I knew it!" Gertie said and gave Ida Belle a high five.

I glared at Ida Belle. "I wondered why you had nothing to say about my outfit. You were in on this the entire time."

Ida Belle shrugged. "We needed you to get enough attention to loosen lips, and if we'd told you ahead of time, you would never have gone in."

"Damn right I wouldn't have. I single-handedly set women back fifty years tonight."

Gertie waved a hand in dismissal. "You're trying to catch a criminal, not make a political statement. Besides, the people in that bar formed their opinions on women years ago. Your boobs aren't going to make a difference one way or another in regards to women's rights."

"What about my rights? What about my humiliation?"

"That's just a bonus," Gertie said.

Before I could respond, she bent over to cut off my shoe. I stumbled to the side as my foot slipped out of the heel and grabbed on to Ida Belle to steady myself.

Ally popped up from the floor. "That's as good as I can get, but you should be able to rub the rest off with a towel."

Ida Belle nodded. "And make it quick. Carter won't spend five minutes listening to Farmer Frank's wife and her insane story. He'll head straight here when he's done."

"I'm more worried about Floyd showing up here," I said. "He was trying to kill us."

Gertie's eyes widened and Ally stiffened. Ida Belle gave me a shove. "We'll talk as soon as you're wearing something suitable. Right now, you look like a worker at the Chicken Ranch, on more levels than one."

Since Gertie had insisted on watching *The Best Little*

Whorehouse in Texas the week before, Ida Belle's comment wasn't lost on me. "Fine," I said, "but when I get back downstairs, the two of you are going to answer for a lot. And somebody light a candle or something. It smells like we're burning down a KFC."

I dashed upstairs, taking the stairs two at a time now. Amazing what one's feet could accomplish when they weren't strapped to stilts. I raced into the bathroom and slid to a stop in front of the vanity, where I caught a look of myself in the mirror and for a split second, thought someone else was in my bathroom.

My hair was still damp from the wet T-shirt event and I had to pull some feathers from the ends of the strands that hadn't been covered by the helmet. Despite the helmet, most of the hair still stood out a good two inches from my head. My eyes looked like I'd been the loser in a bar fight. Black smudges of makeup circled both of them, with the remnants dripping down my cheeks like a scene from a bad horror movie.

I turned on the shower and removed my holster and pistol before jumping into the stream of hot water with a bar of soap and a hunting knife. While I closed my eyes and let the soap lather go to work on my face, I carefully cut the clothes off of me with the knife, letting them drop into the tub as I went. When I was free from the last garment, I rubbed my face until my eyelashes were no longer sticking together.

I jumped out of the shower and dried off as I hurried into my room to grab shorts and a T-shirt. I threw on the clothes, forced my wet hair into a ragged ponytail, then hurried downstairs. I flopped down on the couch and leaned back to catch my breath. My pulse was still racing from all the rushing around.

Ally immediately leaned over and did some sort of swirly thing with my hair, wrapping it into a knot on the top of my head. "That looks neater. I baked chocolate chip cookies while you were at the bar," Ally said. "I know you're cutting back, but do you want some?"

"Given that I've just gotten in an hour's worth of aerobics," I said, "I think I deserve it."

Ally grinned and headed off to the kitchen, returning a couple minutes later with a plate of cookies and a beer. I shoved an entire cookie in my mouth and sighed from the awesomeness. "Where are the trouble twins?" I mumbled while still chewing.

"The candles weren't making a dent in the burned chicken smell, so they opened the garage to air it out, and they're hiding the motorcycle in your back hedges."

"Not the ones right along the back of the house?"

Ally shook her head. "I told them not to. Our luck, Carter would decide he wanted to investigate the creeper while he's here, and find the motorcycle. Then the whole gig would be up."

"The whole gig is up, anyway. He'll know it was us. Two of us, anyway."

Ally grinned. "Or one of you wearing a snowsuit covered in feathers."

I laughed. "By the time Farmer Frank's wife saw us, we probably looked like the Stay Puft Marshmallow Man with wings. When I think about how she saw it and then what she said to Myrtle, it's funny. But don't you dare tell Ida Belle and Gertie I said so."

"No way. We can have a chuckle about it now, but the bottom line is that you both could have been killed."

"Yeah. That Floyd is a real hothead. I can't believe he made such a big deal over that rickety fence of his. A good wind would have taken it out."

"A good wind already has. He keeps propping it back up."

"Then what's his major malfunction?"

"I don't think he likes women much."

"The bartender at Swamp Bar said he likes to slap them around."

"Really?" Ally asked. "That doesn't sound like the kind of information a bartender would volunteer about one of his regulars."

"I told him I was looking for Floyd, but I don't think I fit the profile for Floyd's usual woman. I passed it off as looking up an old acquaintance of my brother's while I was in town. I guess since I played it as not really knowing him well, the bartender felt obligated to give me a warning."

Ally frowned. "Maybe I've been lucky, living right next to him and nothing happening."

I nodded. "It kinda sounds like it, but if it makes a difference, he probably isn't the arsonist."

Ida Belle and Gertie walked into the living room from the kitchen. "Why do you say that?" Ida Belle asked.

"Some idiot at the bar—" I started.

"There she goes," Gertie said, "calling the good people of Sinful idiots again."

I could tell she was being facetious, so I ignored her. "Called Buckshot Billy," I continued.

"Definitely an idiot," Gertie said.

"He told me Floyd wasn't at the bar the night of the fire because he was in lockup in New Orleans."

Ida Belle and Gertie looked at each other, then back at me.

"Certainly a possibility," Ida Belle said. "I'll have Myrtle call New Orleans and verify."

"She can do that?" I asked.

Ida Belle nodded. "She gives them some ID number and they'll assume she's checking because of an investigation. I'll give her a call."

Ida Belle pulled out her cell phone, but before she could dial, someone pounded on my front door. She shoved the phone back in her sweatpants and hurried off to the kitchen. Gertie dashed across the room and pressed Play on my DVD player.

Ida Belle returned a couple seconds later and put chips and dip on the coffee table. "We've been watching a movie." She flopped down in the recliner and motioned for me to get the door.

Chapter Twelve

It wasn't the most creative cover in the world, but at least it was one that couldn't be disproven. I jumped off the couch and swung open the front door. Carter stood on the front porch, his I-know-you've-been-up-to-something scowl already in place.

"Hi," I said, forcing a smile. "What's up?"

He glanced inside and frowned.

"Make it rain!" Gertie stood in the middle of the living room floor, clutching a fistful of dollar bills. Every couple of seconds, she'd pull some bills from the stack and toss them at the television. Ida Belle stared at her as if she'd lost her mind. Ally was doubled over on the couch, tears streaming down her face.

"What the hell is going on here?" Carter asked.

"Movie night?" I answered, not nearly as confident of that fact as I had been thirty seconds before.

I stepped back around the entry wall into the living room, Carter right behind me, and took a look at the television. Half-naked men danced on a stage, crazed women screaming at them and clutching their chests.

Gertie cheered like the women in the movie and tossed more bills at the television set. "I told you this *Magic Mike* movie was the best thing ever."

Carter's scowl disappeared and his expression shifted to slightly horrified. Probably because straight men weren't overly excited to see another man dancing around with his stuff in a G-string, even if it was on television.

"We agreed to indulge her," I said. "Did you need to talk to Ally? I think I can revive her." Ally now hung half off the couch, laughing so hard her entire body shook.

"You've been here all evening?"

"I have, but it's my house. Ally met with the insurance people for a while, and Ida Belle and Gertie showed up about an hour ago with snacks and Gertie's version of girls' night porn. Why?"

"Dispatch got a call from Farmer Frank's wife. Someone ran a motorcycle through her chicken coop."

"I don't own a motorcycle."

"Lack of legal possession hasn't been a deterrent for you in the past."

I felt my back stiffen, somewhat insulted by his accusation and his tone. "I see. So if something weird happens in this town, and it involves anything remotely illegal, then it must have been me. Remind me why you asked me on a date again? Clearly your opinion of me doesn't match the standards of the badge you carry."

He had the decency to look embarrassed. "It's not about you, necessarily. It's about the company you keep."

Because he had a point, I decided to let his comment slide. "Well, I'll admit that I wouldn't mind if you arrested Gertie for both her behavior and her awful choice in movies, but that's the only thing even remotely inappropriate that has gone on here tonight."

Which was technically true, because dressing like a hooker was stupid but not necessarily inappropriate and everything questionable or illegal had taken place somewhere else. Well, technically, hiding the motorcycle in my bushes might count as questionable, but I wasn't about to admit it.

He glanced at the television again and flinched, then shuffled, clearly uncomfortable. "I guess I'll be going then."

I followed him to the front door and watched as he stepped outside, then turned around. "Oh, I forgot to tell you, your garage door is open."

"Thanks. I must have forgotten it."

He started down the steps, then paused and sniffed the air. "Smells like someone's burning trash again." He shook his head and headed across the lawn to his truck. I waited until he'd driven off, then ran outside to close the garage door. It was a good thing he hadn't gotten any closer to it or he would have realized it was the source of the smell—sort of a cross between burned chicken, vanilla, and Febreze.

I hurried back inside, closing and locking the door behind me, then headed into the living room and flopped back down on the couch. My living room floor was still littered with dollar bills, but the television was off and Gertie had taken a seat and was plowing through the chips and dip.

"That went well," I said.

The others looked at me for a couple of seconds, then glanced at each other.

"What?" I finally asked when no one replied.

Ally gave me a sheepish look. "I'm sorry he was so rude to you. That must have hurt your feelings."

I scanned their faces. "Is that what this is about? Good Lord, do you people know me at all? He pissed me off all right, but I assure you, not a single feeling was injured in the exchange."

But even as I said the words, I knew they weren't entirely true. Sure, I'd been mad, but there was more to it than that. I had felt a pinch when I'd thought his opinion of me had diminished.

Granted, I should have been happy if it had. The bigger the risk Carter thought I presented to his reputation and his job stability, the less likely he'd be to ask me out again. Then I wouldn't have to tell him "no" when I really meant "yes."

"If you say so," Ally said, "but I still think he was harsh."

"He's a man," Gertie said. "And a young one at that. He'll put his foot in his mouth a lot more times before he departs this earth."

Ida Belle nodded. "Seems almost a requirement, really. With everything that's happened the past couple of weeks and now the arson situation, he's stressed. Everyone knows Sheriff Lee is decades past when he should have retired, and they're all watching every move Carter makes so when the vote comes up, they know where they stand."

I sighed. "And we're not making it any easier on him, are we?"

"No," Ally said. "You're not and that's why this has to stop. Given the way you returned tonight, I knew something had happened." She looked at Ida Belle. "Fortune told me Floyd tried to kill you. Is that true?"

"He was chasing us," Ida Belle said. "I can't swear he was trying to kill us."

Ally shook her head. "So he was chasing a motorcycle in a huge, fast pickup truck, on a narrow road. And just how close did he get to you?"

"I was too busy driving to look," Ida Belle said.

I shook my head. "Your rearview mirrors were so full of headlights that you couldn't see in them. I'm not going to lie about Floyd's clear intentions when Ally lives next door to him. Even if he's not our arsonist, he's clearly unhinged, and Ally needs to know by just how much."

Ida Belle sighed. "You're right. I just don't want her

worrying about us, but she needs to know that Floyd is more of a loose cannon than we originally thought, even if he's not the arsonist. Let me give Myrtle a call and see if he was in the tank in New Orleans the night of the fire. That will answer one question, at least."

She pulled out her cell phone and made the call. "Myrtle's checking now."

I nodded and lifted a slat on the blinds behind my couch to peer out into the darkness. If Floyd wasn't the arsonist, then that meant someone else in Sinful had an ulterior motive or was an unhinged as Floyd was. And where did the creeper fit into all of this? Floyd had seemed such a simple answer for everything, but I had a feeling things were much more complicated than I wanted them to be.

Ida Belle's cell phone rang and she answered, taking only a couple of seconds before disconnecting. "It's confirmed. Floyd was in the clink in New Orleans until eight the next morning. He's not our arsonist."

Ally rose from the couch. "Look, I appreciate everything you guys have done, but you have to stop. None of you are qualified to tangle with criminals. All Fortune did was invite me to stay in her house a few days, and she's already got a creeper lurking around. Tonight, the two of you could have been run down by Floyd or shot by Farmer Frank."

"But we weren't," Ida Belle said.

Ally threw her arms in the air. "You're a librarian and two long-retired average citizens. When are you going to realize that the only reason you're still sitting here is because you've been really lucky? Do you think I want your deaths on my conscience? I'm asking you as friends to please stop and let Carter do his job."

I glanced at Ida Belle and Gertie, who shuffled

uncomfortably in their chairs.

"Fortune?" Ally prompted.

"Fine. I promise not to put myself at risk again, but I'm still going to watch everyone closely and listen."

Ida Belle shook her head. "Gertie and I will do our best to stay out of trouble, but I can't promise you that it will happen. We were poking our nose into Sinful business long before Fortune arrived—actually, before you were even born. It's like asking us not to breathe."

Ally sighed. "If that's the best I can get, then it will have to do." She looked at me. "The insurance adjuster said they're sending a crew to secure the kitchen wall tomorrow morning. He thinks I should be able to move back into the house by tomorrow evening."

"I think you should stay here," I said, "at least until Carter knows more."

"If I stay here, it keeps you in the middle of this mess and on the outs with Carter. I don't want that on my conscience either." She yawned. "It's been a long day and I haven't been sleeping very well. I'm going to go to bed. Try not to cause any trouble while I'm sleeping."

I watched as Ally trudged upstairs, then motioned to Ida Belle and Gertie. "Recon in the kitchen," I whispered. "Voices in the living room carry upstairs."

We headed into the kitchen and took up our usual seats at the table. "So what do you guys think?" I asked.

"Did you find out anything else at the bar?" Ida Belle asked.

"Nothing that seems to matter. There was some weird dude in the bar who Billy said was also looking for Floyd, but that could be anything or nothing." I gave them a description of the guy, but it didn't ring any bells with them.

"Did you get the guy's name?" Ida Belle asked.

I shrugged. "All Billy knew was Marco, but I'm not sure Billy is the most reliable source."

"Probably not," Gertie said. "His mother dropped him on his head when he was a baby."

"I thought baby's heads were pretty tough."

"She was on top of the water tower."

I grimaced. "Okay. Anyway, we're back to square one."

That wasn't technically true, but I didn't want to tell them about the sketchy real estate agent until I'd talked to Ally and gotten some more information. If the guy turned out to be on the up-and-up, putting Ida Belle and Gertie on his scent would be like unleashing the hounds of hell on the guy.

"What are we going to do about Ally moving back home?" Gertie asked. "It's not safe for her there."

"I know," I said, "but she thinks she's putting me at risk by staying here. If I were really Sandy-Sue, librarian and regular girl, she'd be right."

Ida Belle nodded. "We can't exactly blame her for her stance. She cares about all of us and would feel responsible if something happened while we were helping her. Without any knowledge of our real qualifications, she's going to assume that we're at a complete disadvantage."

"Maybe this time, she's right."

I tossed and turned most of the night—the time I didn't spend pacing, anyway—upsetting Merlin with every flop I made in another direction. He seemed to think I was intentionally ruining his sleep. From all appearances, he slept a good twenty-two hours out of the day, so I didn't feel even remotely sorry for disturbing him. It wasn't as if he had a big workday ahead of him or anything. In fact, given that he used to reside outside, living inside with me was pretty much a permanent vacation.

All night, I kept one eye and ear open, in a state of semi-slumber, wondering if the creeper would return. I hoped that my shooting Carter the night before was enough to warn him away, and maybe I'd been right. But what about when Ally went home? She assumed the creeper was after her because he'd started up when she came to stay with me, but that wasn't necessarily the case.

Since I'd been in Sinful, I'd made a few enemies—family and friends of those I'd helped send to prison and a few who might have died in the process of criminal activity. It was quite possible that one of those disgruntled few might try to take action against me.

Or it could be Ahmad.

I bolted straight up in bed, startling Merlin out of a dead sleep. He bolted out of the room and I was left alone with my heart pounding so hard that it felt as if my chest would burst open. I sucked in a huge breath, then slowly released it, concentrating on slowing my pulse.

Where the hell had that come from?

With all the things that had gone down these past few weeks in Sinful, it had never once crossed my mind that Ahmad was behind any of it. Why did he pop into my mind now? There was no way Ahmad or any of his men were the creeper. If any of Ahmad's crew came to Sinful, I'd be dead within minutes and they'd be gone without a trace. They wouldn't lower themselves to lurking outside of windows. They would simply make quick work of the lock, slip silently inside, and smother me in my sleep.

I glanced at the alarm clock. Five a.m. Even if I thought I could manage it, there was no use going back to sleep. In fact, until things got back to normal—whatever the hell that was—it was probably in my best interest to sleep during the day so that I could be on alert at night. Especially if Ally moved back home. No way was I letting her sit inside that house without protection. She may be able to refuse me entry, but she would never see me keeping watch from the swamp behind her house.

I threw back the covers and climbed out of bed, my muscles protesting a bit at the speed at which I elected to stand. I rubbed my thighs and biceps for a bit, mortified that my physical conditioning had been put to the test by high heels and a senior citizen on a motorcycle.

I threw on shorts, headed to the kitchen, and flipped the switch on the coffeepot. I always prepped it the night before so I could get that first cup as quickly and with as little effort as possible. After I'd completed the heavy lifting of pushing the button, I flopped down at the kitchen table and opened my laptop, accessing the secret email I used to communicate with my CIA partner, Ben Harrison, and typed a message.

To: hotdudeinNE@gmail.com
From: farmgirl433@gmail.com
How are things in NE? Everything is business as usual here on the farm. It's a warm summer, but I'm doing my best to stay cool. How is the heat in NE? I know it was hot before, but I'm hoping you get a break in the weather soon.

I'm looking forward to seeing you this fall.

Email or call when you get a chance.

I hit Send and closed the laptop. Even though the only people who knew about the email accounts were Harrison and me, and he only accessed the account on a spare laptop that bounced his proxy around so that it couldn't be traced back to him, we still talked in code. The weather was the easiest way to convey how the Ahmad situation was going. Hot meant things were still too bad for me to return home. What I hoped to see was an email telling me it was cooling off.

It would probably be a while before Harrison replied, so I opened the back door and strolled outside. Bits and pieces of my azalea bushes were scattered across the backyard, casualties of the motorcycle hiding and unhiding. I wondered briefly if Ida Belle would ditch the bike now that Carter was looking for it, but she was so cagey about most things that I bet she would keep it and deny the chicken coop incident until death.

I stepped down onto the lawn and walked the hedges down the side of the house, looking for any sign of passage. I'd raked the dirt in front of and behind the bushes the day before. If anyone had stepped on the loose dirt, the prints would show, but the dirt was undisturbed. I felt a bit of the tension leave my shoulder and neck. Maybe the rock salt fiasco had scared the creeper away, at least from my house. Now my concern would be protecting Ally in her own house.

I headed back inside, itching for that cup of coffee, and was surprised to find Ally in the kitchen, getting coffee cups out of the cabinet. "I thought you worked the lunch shift today," I said.

"I do." She poured the coffee and handed me a cup before sitting at the table. "I couldn't sleep any longer."

Dark circles had settled under her eyes, and even her movement screamed how exhausted she was. I felt guilty about adding to her strain. "I'm really sorry we upset you last night. I had no idea things would get that out of control."

Ally gave me a small smile. "With Ida Belle and Gertie involved, you can almost always bet that things won't go quietly into that good night."

"After Gertie's choice of movies, I'm not about to disagree with you. But still, I thought the worst thing that could happen was Ida Belle wrecking the motorcycle and my having to live down that outfit with the emergency room staff."

"If Ida Belle had crashed that bike," Ally said, "I don't think there would have been much left of that outfit."

"Especially since it was only half of one to begin with."

"If that."

"Hooker clothes aside, we didn't mean to cause you more worry."

Ally reached over and squeezed my hand. "I know you guys were trying to help, and I love you for it. And yes, when Gertie got that call from Myrtle, I did panic a little. Then when you told me about Floyd, I almost had a heart attack right there in your living room, but the reality is, last night was only one small piece of my worries and that part was over by the time I went to bed."

"Then what else is bothering you? I mean, besides the obvious?"

"Staying here. Moving back to my house. Living in a construction zone. Living next to Floyd. The creeper. The arsonist. Do I need to go on?"

"No. That's a pretty good list."

"I also have a date tonight."

I nodded automatically, my mind still locked on her list, and it took me a couple of seconds to realize what she'd just said. "What?" I sat up straight, sloshing my coffee onto the table.

She grinned and handed me a napkin. "That got your attention."

"Who is your date with? The cute fireman?"

"Yes," she said, a light blush creeping over her face. "I ran into him yesterday at the General Store after I finished with the insurance adjuster. He asked me if I was doing all right and if there was anything he could help with at my house. We got to talking for a bit and one thing led to another."

"And?"

She laughed. "And he asked me out. What did you think—we had wild monkey sex in the General Store and Walter videotaped it?"

"No! I would never… I'm just not that good at the whole male-female interaction thing. You kinda have to spell it out for me."

Ally shook her head. "You really weren't kidding about that, were you? What the heck did you do with all your free time before?"

I frowned, not certain how to answer. I was supposed to be a librarian, but I wasn't a big reader except for books on weaponry and historical battle stories. I almost never watched television until coming to Sinful, so I could hardly claim an addiction to that. I didn't knit or paint or anything else that women might do with their time.

"Well, I worked out every day."

Ally rolled her eyes. "Your life must have consisted of more than going to the gym."

I nodded. That much was true, as the majority of my exercise hadn't been the controlled-environment kind. "I did other things."

"You make it sound so secretive."

My mind flashed back to a documentary I'd watched the week before. "I…I guess I don't like to talk about it. I work with some organizations. Usually I spend my summers overseas doing, uh, humanitarian work."

That wasn't a lie. Killing bad guys benefited humanity.

Ally smiled. "I think that's great. I promise never to rib you about not having a life. It sounds like you have one filled with purpose."

I nodded, but I felt like a hypocrite. My job was filled with purpose, if one considered a mission objective to be the same thing, but my life was sort of a void—the blank time I spent waiting for the next assignment.

"I'd appreciate it if you didn't tell anyone," I said. "The work is very personal to me. When people find out, they tend to ask a lot of questions, and I get uncomfortable answering them."

"I understand. Your secret is safe with me."

Relief and guilt washed over me. Before I'd arrived in Sinful, I could lie as easily as I told the truth, but once you knew people on a personal level, and liked them, it changed everything. Mostly, it made everything more complicated. My personal life was a lot simpler when I didn't care about anyone and no one was counting on me for anything outside of my job. Now I actually called people friends and liked it, but it came with costs.

Because of the risks they took, I worried about Ida Belle and Gertie, but my relationship with them was easier because they knew the real me. With them, there was no obfuscation. My relationship with Ally was a finer line to balance, always hovering between a truth and a lie. My…whatever…with Carter was even more confusing. The only progress I'd managed to make was admitting to myself that I was attracted to him, and I knew he was attracted to me.

Except it wasn't really me.

And that's the thing that got me every time. I may lack experience in the male-female arena, but I knew that no relationship worked if it was founded on a lie. Carter was attracted to a woman who didn't really exist, and I had no doubt that if he found out about my duplicity, his interest would disappear completely. To experience that firsthand would suck, which is why I had no intention of Carter finding out who I really was until I was long gone from Sinful.

Which brought up the question of the ethics of getting involved with him now.

Part of me argued that he knew I was only here for the summer, so he couldn't possibly be thinking long-term either, but now that I'd made real friends, I realized relationships didn't work that way. When I returned to DC, my feelings for Ida Belle, Gertie, and Ally wouldn't just disappear because I'd changed zip codes. And those relationships weren't even the romantic sort. The feelings I had for Carter were already different from any I'd felt before. Allowing them to develop even more would just make things harder when my life could return to normal.

"Fortune?" Ally's voice broke into my thoughts.

I blinked and looked at her.

"You were doing some heavy thinking," she said. "Care to share?"

If someone had asked me that question the month before, I would have told them they were nuts, but oddly enough, I felt compelled to talk. Unfortunately, my situation prevented it. "I was just thinking about how much I'm going to miss you guys when I go back home."

Ally stared at me several seconds. "Is that the reason you're dragging your feet with Carter?"

It was such a direct hit, I was momentarily taken aback. "Maybe. I guess. Hell, I don't know."

She nodded. "I guess I can see that. You're worried that you'll really like him and then where does that leave you? Granted, I still have this thread of hope that the end of summer will come and you won't be able to leave, but I know that's not likely."

I shook my head. "I like it here—might even grow to love it—but my entire life is somewhere else. The important parts of it can't be relocated, especially to Sinful. It's too late for me to reinvent myself. The person I am back East is the only person I know how to successfully be."

"It's never too late to reinvent yourself. God help us all if that weren't true." Ally took a breath and blew it out. "Look, I went to New Orleans for schooling that I had no interest in because that was what my mother pushed me to do. I quit and came back here to take care of my mother when she got sick—at least that's what I told myself. But when I think back and am honest with myself, I was just looking for a reason to make a change. Then Mother had to be moved to the facility in New Orleans. And instead of going there with her, where there is a ton more opportunity, I stayed here, not making a move to do anything about my life until you showed up and told me to go for it."

I smiled. "Easiest advice I've ever given. You were born to own a bakery."

"I agree, but it took a stranger saying it before I thought seriously about it. Oh, it was always the pipe dream that I think about while taking a bubble bath or right before I doze off while pretending to fish, but I never took steps to make it a reality. I don't think I even believed it could be."

"But now you do."

She nodded. "And you can do the same thing. You're not that much older than me, so don't give me the 'old dog, new tricks' argument. It won't wash. Besides, Ida Belle and Gertie are ancient and those two are up to new tricks every day."

I smiled. "Ida Belle and Gertie are in a class by themselves."

"True, but that doesn't mean you can't change direction."

"I know I can. I don't know that I want to."

"And that's fine too. But promise me you'll give yourself permission to at least consider your alternatives."

"I promise." The words were easy enough to say, and I could even entertain thoughts of what my life might be like if I quit the CIA and became a regular civilian. But the likelihood that anything would change in the end was still so slim it might as well be vapor.

"I'm going to run take a shower," Ally said. "If you can hold out, I'll make French toast when I come back down."

"I can definitely hold out."

She downed the rest of her coffee and rose from her chair.

"Hey," I said. "That real estate agent that wanted to buy your mom's house—do you remember his name?"

She frowned, probably thinking I was asking because I wanted to sell Marge's house. "It's been so long. Mark, John…it was something common. Robert! That was it. Robert Patterson. I can't believe I remember that."

"Thanks," I said as she hurried out of the kitchen.

I pulled my laptop over in front of me and did a quick search for Robert Patterson and real estate agent. A website popped up on the first page of search results and I clicked on the link. Robert's profile picture was right there on the top left corner of the website. I clicked on the Services link and saw that he specialized in commercial properties and most of his clients were shipping and distributing companies.

So why did he offer to buy a residential property?

I shook my head. Maybe the buyer was a friend or family of a coworker. There was no telling, really. The bottom line was that Robert Patterson looked legit, even if he wasn't all that forthcoming with information.

I opened a new tab and accessed email on the off chance that Harrison had replied. My pulse ticked up a notch when I saw the email in my in-box.

To: farmgirl433@gmail.com
From: hotdudeinNE@gmail.com
I'm glad to hear things are going well on the farm. I know

you're looking forward to harvest season. Unfortunately, it's hotter than ever here in NE. I thought we were going to catch a break a couple of days ago, but the expected cooling disappeared and we were left wondering where it went. I'm still hoping we find some soon.

My dad was asking about you yesterday, and was happy to hear things are good. He's hoping you'll have time for a visit after harvest.

Take care!

My back tightened and I reread the email, making sure I'd interpreted it correctly. It sounded as if Harrison thought they were going to have a breakthrough on the case, but it hadn't happened. But what I didn't understand was the "disappeared" comment. Did he mean that Ahmad had disappeared? If so, that was really, really bad. I opened a new tab and pulled up harvesting schedules for the Midwest. Corn was what we'd agreed on.

October.

Crap. October wasn't summer at all. It was dangerously approaching Thanksgiving.

I leaned back in my chair and blew out a breath. If this mess wasn't settled by the end of August, what was I supposed to do? The real Sandy-Sue had to settle the estate, and I doubted she was interested in moving to Sinful. That meant she'd sell the house and contents. Even worse, it meant she'd come to Sinful to handle it all. The gig was definitely up then.

I'd hoped the news would be better. That the situation with Ahmad was close to solved and I'd be able to return to DC before things got more complicated here. But not only was the situation not solved, things had clearly gotten worse. Now I had to worry about not only finishing the summer out in Sinful, but where I would go afterward.

Far too many sobering thoughts for not quite 6:00 a.m.

Chapter Thirteen

I stuffed myself so full of breakfast that I was certain I'd start speaking French. What I should have done was gotten up from the table and run from Sinful to Peru, but I didn't feel like moving that fast or that far. Instead, Ally and I grabbed books and headed outside. I climbed into the hammock and she dragged a lounge chair under the tree close by and flopped down on it.

Between my lack of good sleep, the huge breakfast, and the cool breeze, it wasn't long before I nodded off. I had no idea how long I'd been sleeping when I felt someone shaking my arm.

"Fortune," Ally said. "Wake up. Carter is here and said he needs to talk to both of us."

My eyes flew open. "What happened?"

"I don't know, but he looks really unhappy."

"Crap. He must have found out about the motorcycle."

She glanced back at the house, an uncertain expression on her face. "I don't know. If that was the case, then he'd take it up with Ida Belle first, and she would have called to warn you. Besides, I didn't have anything to do with last night—except covering it up, of course—so why would he need to talk to me?"

I frowned and climbed out of the hammock. "So what do you think is going on?"

She shook her head. "I have no idea, but I have a feeling it's not going to be good."

I trudged beside her toward the house, feeling the same way.

Carter was pacing my kitchen when we walked in the back door, and based on his expression, I had no doubt he was in full-on cop mode. He gave me a quick nod, then gestured to the table. "You'll probably want to sit."

"That bad?" I asked. "Or is it going to take that long?"

"Maybe a bit of both," he said.

I glanced at Ally, who bit her lower lip and slipped into one of the chairs. I took the chair next to her, leaving Carter to sit across from me.

"I don't know how else to say this," he began, looking directly at Ally, "so I'm just going to come right out with it. The crew hired to work on your house found Floyd dead in your backyard this morning."

Ally gasped and I straightened in my chair.

"Oh my God," Ally whispered.

"How did it happen?" I asked, hoping Floyd had drunk himself into a stupor and impaled a lung on a random board or something. Anything but murder.

"I'll have to wait for the report, of course, but someone cracked him in the head with a two-by-four. It was lying next to him."

Damn it.

"What was he doing in my backyard?" Ally asked.

"That's a good question," Carter said, "and one I'd like an answer to. I assume you and Floyd did not have a late-night-back-door sort of relationship?"

"The only relationship I had with Floyd was the avoidance type," Ally said.

"Probably wise," Carter said. "Based on the crime scene, I have no way of knowing what he was doing there. Maybe he thought it would be an easy way to lift some things. Maybe he was just being nosy. What concerns me more is that someone was either already there or followed him there."

"I prefer option two," I said.

Carter nodded. "So do I, because it means Floyd's murder is only about Floyd. But until I know for certain option two is the correct one, I can't ignore the fact that someone might have already been at Ally's house and didn't want Floyd as a witness."

"I don't understand," Ally said, clearly distressed. "Over twenty years I've lived in this town and been almost a nonentity. Now, all of a sudden, everything bad in Sinful is happening around me. Why? I haven't changed anything. I haven't done anything."

I placed my hand on her arm. "None of this is your fault. Something strange is going on, but I don't think it's because of you."

"How can you say that?" she asked. "Someone set my house on fire. Someone has been creeping around your house ever since I came to stay here. Now someone was murdered in my backyard. I'm the only common denominator."

"I agree that things appear to be orchestrated around you," Carter said, "but we have no reason to think it's because of something you've done."

"So what? It's random victim selection month and he drew my name out of a hat? Threw darts at a local phone book?" She shook her head. "Look, I know you're trying to make me feel better, but trying to tell me this isn't about me is asking me to take leave of reality. It's not going to happen."

"I'm not trying to sugarcoat this," Carter said. "It's in your own best interest to remain suspicious and on alert. I'm just saying that although the circumstances surround you, I don't believe you have anything consciously or directly to do with what's happening."

Ally relaxed a little. "I guess I can agree with that." She glanced at her watch. "Is this going to take much longer? If so, I need to call Francine and let her know I'll be late."

Carter shook his head. "That's all I needed. The rest of my conversation is all about Fortune, and if you don't mind, I'd prefer to have it alone." His jaw hardened and he frowned.

Ally glanced over at me, one eyebrow raised, then rose from her chair. "Then I'm going upstairs to get dressed for work. Do I need to ask either of you to disarm yourselves before I leave?"

"I'm not armed," I said, "so if there's any shooting, it's all on Carter."

Ally gave me an encouraging smile before leaving the kitchen, but I knew she felt the undercurrents just as I did. Whatever Carter was about to say wasn't going to be pleasant.

I waited until Ally's footsteps faded upstairs then said, "Let me have it."

Carter moved into the chair next to mine and pulled his cell phone from his pocket. "Floyd was hit on the back of the head with a two-by-four, but that's not what killed him."

He turned his phone around and showed me a picture of Floyd's body, splayed out faceup next to the charred remains of Ally's back porch. "He was stabbed in the chest," Carter said. "Notice anything interesting about the weapon?"

I took the phone from him and enlarged the image to zero in on his chest. The object impaled in his chest was thin and black and wasn't very long. I squinted at the screen. Something about the object was familiar but I couldn't put my finger on it. I twisted the phone a bit from side to side, and tiny flecks of silver glistened on the object.

Holy crap!

It was the heel from my shoe—the one that I'd left stuck in

the plywood floor of the Swamp Bar. Instantly, the scene with Ahmad's brother and my shoe—the incident that had caused me to be hiding in Sinful in the first place—flashed across my mind. Clearly, the universe was telling me I shouldn't wear high heels.

"That is the spike from a woman's shoe," Carter said. "A woman that Floyd chased out of the Swamp Bar last night, threatening to kill. A woman who jumped on a motorcycle with another person to get away."

"Do you think it's the same motorcycle that ran through the chicken coop?" I asked, trying to keep my voice normal. Patrons of the Swamp Bar weren't the sort I ran into at the General Store or Francine's Café. Chances were any of them would pass me on the street today and never recognize me for the floozy who was in the bar last night. So until Carter had solid evidence that it was me, ignorance was still my best defense.

"I think it's definitely the motorcycle that ran through the chicken coop, and I think you already knew that."

"Me? I don't know anything about it."

"Really?" He removed his phone from my hand and scrolled to the next picture before turning the phone back around. "Are you going to deny that this is you?"

I looked at the phone and cringed. It was a picture of me standing on the stage, drenched across the chest and sporting the Best Boobs sash.

"I also have video," he said, "in case you want to argue this was Photoshopped. And the video has a clear shot of the shoes you were wearing."

Busted.

"Do I get any brownie points for winning the contest?"

"I think your title has to rank a little higher than Best Boobs to keep you from being arrested."

"Are you accusing me of killing Floyd?" I asked.

"No. When Floyd was killed, you were pacing in your bedroom."

I frowned. "You were watching me?"

He shook his head. "I was watching your house in case the creeper returned."

"Oh. How do you know what time Floyd died?"

"His watch broke when he fell."

"So I'm in the clear?"

"With me, but how do you think the evidence would look to the state prosecutor?"

I blew out a breath. "Not good."

"That's a huge understatement. The man chased you out of a bar, threatening to kill you, and was found stabbed to death with the heel from a shoe you were wearing when he took off after you. A jury wouldn't be out ten minutes on this."

"But you saw me in my house. You're a deputy. Surely that means something."

"Uh-huh. I'm also the deputy who asked you out on a date."

"Oh. Crap."

He leaned forward and looked me straight in the eyes. "So, even though it's my sworn duty, I'm asking you to give me a reason not to connect the dots for the prosecutor. I want the truth, Fortune. All of it."

I nodded. "Where do you want me to start?"

"Let's start with the weapon. Do you have any idea how the killer acquired your shoe?"

"That part is easy. Floyd walked into the Swamp Bar right when the contest ended. He saw me on stage and started yelling."

"About what?"

Double crap.

Everyone in the bar had heard Floyd. Odds were, Carter already had the answer and this was a test. I sighed. "About his fence."

Carter shook his head. "Something else you denied being part of."

"Anyway, I ran off the stage, hoping he'd lose me in the crowd and I could get out of the bar, but one of my heels got stuck in a rotten piece of plywood. He was coming at me, so I cut the straps on the shoe so I could get away."

"So you left the shoe in the bar?"

I nodded.

"Which means anyone in the bar could have taken it. Damn."

I narrowed my eyes at him. "You lied to Ally."

"What do you mean?"

"You said one possibility was that Floyd interrupted something going on at her house and whoever it was took him out. But if someone took my shoe from the Swamp Bar and used it to kill Floyd, that was premeditated."

"Unless Floyd took the shoe."

"What use would that be?"

"Maybe to identify you. Maybe to extort money out of you."

"That's thin."

He nodded. "But a better alternative than someone stealing the shoe to frame you for murder."

I slumped back in my chair. He had a point.

"So why were you at the Swamp Bar to begin with?"

"Because we were trying to find out where Floyd was when the fire started at Ally's. Ida Belle and Gertie knew he frequented the Swamp Bar, so we were trying to eliminate him as a suspect."

"And it didn't occur to you that checking Floyd's alibi was

one of the first things I would do? His bad attitude and disrespect for authority aren't exactly a secret. Floyd was the first on my list of suspects."

"So you already know he was in jail in New Orleans."

"Yes."

I sighed. "I don't know why I let those two talk me into these things. It sounded so simple—dress up sexy, go to the bar, ask a couple of questions, then leave. We just wanted Ally to be safe, and if the guy who tried to burn down her house was living right next door, that would suck."

"I get that, but can you please explain to me why you think I'm not capable of doing my job? I thought we were friends…maybe a little something more, but for the life of me, I can't figure out why my friend would consistently attempt to undermine me."

A wave of guilt washed over me and I had the sudden urge to curl up in a tiny ball and disappear. I knew my actions could potentially cause Carter trouble with his job, but I'd never stopped to consider that I might be insulting him on a personal level. I'd been so focused on my own thoughts on the matter, I'd never seen it from his viewpoint.

"I think you're very capable," I finally managed, but couldn't look him in the eyes.

"Then why do you keep interfering?"

I shrugged. "We figured the Swamp Bar crowd would be more likely to talk to a woman than a cop. I swear, your capability never entered into the equation. I mean, except for the part where you don't have boobs." I frowned. "I guess that's not much better, is it?"

"Not really. Look, I appreciate and respect your loyalty to your friends, even Ida Belle and Gertie, although they are probably the two worst influences you could have come across.

But the three of you are going to get hurt or killed with these pursuits. Do you really not see how lucky you've been?"

Although it rankled me to no end to pretend incompetence, I nodded.

"Then from this point forward, I expect you to stay out of my investigation. I won't issue any more warnings. If I catch you, Ida Belle, or Gertie doing anything that I even remotely suspect is related to my case, I'm going to throw you all in jail, for your own good."

"I understand."

He cocked his head to the side and stared at me. "Do you? Because it seems like you think I'm only trying to restrict what you do. Has it ever occurred to you that I care about what happens to you? That if something happened to you while you were nosing into my work that I'd carry the guilt of not preventing it around with me forever?"

My heart clenched and my stomach started to churn. Did he mean he cared about me more than he cared about the other citizens he protected? Attraction was one thing, but was Carter alluding to an emotional connection with me that was different? That thought made me warm and tingly and scared and panicked, all at the same time.

"Fortune?" Carter's voice broke into my thoughts.

Despite my complete discomfort, I forced myself to meet his gaze. "I'm sorry you had to worry about me. That wasn't my intention. But I do think I'm more capable than you realize."

He gave me a small smile. "I think you're capable of a lot of things, but you're still human."

"You mean I'm a civilian."

"That too." He rose from his chair. "I've got to run. I need to figure out how to document this in a way that doesn't make me a liar or incriminate you, and I'm not even sure that's possible."

I jumped up from my chair and circled to his side of the table, emotion overwhelming me. "Don't put your job on the line. Document what you know. I'm sure I'll be fine."

I knew my name going into his report would be the end of my stay in Sinful, but I couldn't allow him to risk his career for me, especially when he didn't know the truth. I put my hand on his arm. "This is my problem. Please let me handle it."

He stepped closer to me and looked me straight in the eyes for several seconds. My knees started to quiver and more than anything else in the world, I wanted him to touch me, even though I knew it would only make things worse for both of us. He leaned toward me and I knew I should back up, escape his reach, but God help me, I couldn't make myself do it.

His lips brushed against mine and all of my resolve drifted away like pollen in a hurricane. He reached up with one hand to cup the back of my head and deepened the kiss, parting my lips with his.

I swayed a bit and clutched his arm to steady myself as a wave of dizziness passed over me. Every inch of my body sprang alive—my heart raced, my breathing increased, and my skin tingled. He slipped his tongue in my mouth and began a sensual dance that had me on the verge of explosion.

It wasn't supposed to be like this. I'd already decided that personal involvement with Carter wasn't fair to him, and only complicated things for me. But damned if my body agreed with my mind.

Just when I was ready to rip off all his clothes and have my way with him right there on the kitchen floor, he broke off the kiss and looked at me. "If it's your problem, it's mine too."

Before I could formulate an argument, he leaned in for one hard, brief kiss, then spun around and left. I was still standing in the same spot when the front door clicked shut.

My problems had just gotten a thousand times worse.

"Fortune?" Ally's voice roused me out of my stupor.

She gave me a critical look. "Are you all right?" she asked.

"Yeah, fine."

"What was that about? Or can't you say?"

"I probably shouldn't decree it publicly or anything, but Carter knows about my trip to the Swamp Bar. Apparently, there were pictures and, God help me, video."

Ally's eyes widened. "Oh no. Is he mad?"

"He's mad and upset and worried. The whole bar saw Floyd tear out after me."

"That would definitely justify upset and worried."

"And I'm sure a few of them reported Floyd threatening to kill me as he left."

Ally's hand flew over her mouth. "Oh my God! Carter doesn't think...he wouldn't..."

"No. He doesn't think I did it. In fact, he's certain of it because he was watching the house last night. When Floyd was killed, I was busy pacing in my bedroom. Carter could see me from wherever he was hiding."

Ally dropped her hand and exhaled. "Thank goodness."

I nodded and left it at that. Ally didn't need to know that Floyd had been killed with the heel from my shoe, or that Carter was running a huge risk in not reporting his knowledge to the DA's office. There was nothing to be gained from both of us worrying about something that couldn't be changed.

She grabbed her car keys from the counter and I put my hand on her shoulder. "Hey, I know you planned on moving back in your house as soon as it was secure, but I hope you'll rethink that. I think you should stay here with me until Carter figures all this out."

JANA DELEON

Ally bit her lip. "All this stuff that's happening, I want to say no because my staying here puts you at risk. But I'd be lying if I didn't say that I'm scared to be there alone now."

"You don't have to be. Strength in numbers and all. Besides, apparently Carter is keeping an eye on us. We'll be alert and smart, and we'll both be safe here."

Ally threw her arms around me and gave me a hug. "Thank you for being such a good friend. I'm so glad you came to Sinful." She released me and sniffed, her eyes reddening, then she gave me a half wave and headed out of the kitchen.

I sank down in a kitchen chair, my mind whirling so fast I was afraid it would spin right out of my skull. What the hell had just happened?

My body completely sold out my mind.

That pretty much summed it up. And made it impossible for me to keep fooling myself into believing I wasn't going to get entangled with Carter. The reality was, I already was.

Chapter Fourteen

I put in an emergency call to Ida Belle and Gertie, then tried to occupy myself with busy work. By the time they arrived, I'd already put on a load of laundry, mopped the kitchen floor, and dusted the living room, and was just about to start bleaching the driveway.

Ida Belle and Gertie took one look at me, standing in the garage and holding a bottle of bleach, and immediately flew into action. Gertie yanked down the garage door and Ida Belle grabbed the tarp that had covered the motorcycle the day before.

"Where's the body?" Ida Belle asked.

"What? Jesus, there's no body!"

Gertie visibly relaxed. "Thank goodness. This is a new blouse."

"And bleach isn't really the best choice," Ida Belle threw in.

I stared, not sure whether to be impressed with their efficiency in shifting gears or horrified that they could move so easily from somewhat normal to Son of Sam. I decided to settle for impressed and slightly fearful.

"I was going to bleach the driveway," I explained and stuck the jug of bleach back on the shelf.

Gertie frowned. "Is there blood? I thought I cleaned up the bit that dripped on the floor from your ankle."

"No blood. No cleanup necessary. I was trying to occupy myself until you got here because I was afraid if I sat still, I would end up exploding."

Ida Belle glanced at Gertie, her expression worried. "Then we best get inside so you can fill us in."

As part of my domestic flurry, I'd put on a pot of coffee, but I couldn't bring myself to drink a cup. Instead, I dumped half a bottle of Sinful Ladies Society cough syrup into a tumbler and took a big gulp. Ida Belle and Gertie took seats at the kitchen table and silently stirred their coffee as I paced the kitchen.

Finally, I blurted out, "Carter knows about last night."

"How much does he know?" Ida Belle asked.

"Everything," I said. "Everything relevant, anyway."

Gertie's eyes widened. "You told him?"

I nodded.

They looked at each other, clearly surprised by my revelation.

"Don't tell me you're feeling guilty?" Ida Belle asked.

"Yes…I mean, I didn't tell him because I felt guilty, but I feel guilty now." I blew out a breath and lowered myself into the chair. "A contractor found Floyd dead in Ally's backyard this morning. He was murdered."

Gertie sucked in a breath and Ida Belle straightened in her chair.

"How was he killed?" Ida Belle asked.

"Someone cracked him over the head with a two-by-four."

Ida Belle looked a bit relieved. "Well, that could have been anyone."

"Then he stabbed Floyd with the high heel from my shoe," I finished.

"Oh." Ida Belle fell back in her chair, deflated. Gertie's jaw dropped and she remained frozen in place.

"He didn't arrest you?" Gertie managed to get out.

"No. He kissed me."

Ida Belle and Gertie both studied me, as if waiting for the punch line that would never come. If anyone had told me it was possible to feel more miserable than I did right then, I would have called him a liar.

"So," Ida Belle said finally, "I take it that means he doesn't think you did it?"

"He knows for certain I didn't do it," I said and explained about Floyd's watch and Carter's staking out my house. "But he also knows how it would sound to the prosecutor."

Ida Belle's expression cleared in understanding. "Especially if the prosecutor found out that Carter asked you out. Jesus, what a mess."

"I told him to turn all the evidence over to the DA," I said. "That it was my problem to deal with."

Gertie sucked in a breath. "And he kissed you?"

I nodded.

Gertie leaned forward. "Was it the Godfather-it-was-nice-knowing-you kind of kiss or the I'll-never-let-them-hurt-you kind of kiss?"

"The latter."

Gertie whimpered a bit and covered her chest with one hand. "That's so romantic."

"And stupid," Ida Belle said. "If there's pictures and video of Fortune at the Swamp Bar floating around, someone else can make the same connection that Carter did."

"Do you really think so?" Gertie asked. "Swamp Bar regulars aren't the sort that would associate with Fortune on a normal basis, and she was heavily made up."

"Floyd recognized her," Ida Belle pointed out.

I nodded. "Which is exactly why I told him to turn over the evidence."

"He doesn't think you'll get a fair shake," Ida Belle said,

"and he's probably right. The prosecutor assigned to this area is an incompetent, ladder-climbing idiot of monumental proportions. All he cares about is conviction rate. It doesn't matter to him whether he's actually getting crime off the streets. As long as he has a warm body in a cell, it's another notch in his belt."

"She's right," Gertie said, "and with Carter unaware of your real background and the connections you have to get you out of this, he thinks turning over that evidence would be buying you an express ticket to Angola."

"That's what I figured," I said. "I can't let him risk his future for me, especially since he doesn't know the truth."

Gertie shook her head. "I don't think you have a choice. The only way around it is to turn yourself in, and that would not only blow your cover, but get you locked up where the man gunning for you could easily have sharpshooters surrounding the place, just waiting to cap you when you leave."

"I could contact my partner," I said, "and let him know I needed extraction."

Gertie's face fell. "You mean just disappear?"

I nodded. "Then Carter could turn in his evidence and my director could deal with the fallout."

"But you'd be gone, maybe forever." Tears began to form in Gertie's eyes.

"If Carter is caught withholding this evidence," I said, "he could lose far more than his job. He could go to prison himself for conspiracy."

Ida Belle leaned forward in her chair. "Never the best option for a cop."

Gertie clasped her hands together, her distress clear. "There has to be another way."

"There is," Ida Belle said.

Both Gertie and I turned to stare at her.

"Really?" I said. "Because I haven't thought of anything."

She gave us a single nod. "We could find the killer."

I shook my head. "I promised Carter I would stay out of his investigation. He's stuck his neck out enough already. Our investigating always seems to come back in our faces, and his."

"But we've always caught the bad guy," Gertie said.

"And almost gotten killed in the process," I said.

"So we'll be more careful," Gertie said.

"There's no careful way to go after a killer," I said.

"She's right," Ida Belle agreed. "By default, any movement toward a killer comes with heavy risk, and I understand completely why Fortune doesn't want to compromise her promise to Carter." She looked directly at me. "But despite all that, I'm not ready for you to leave Sinful."

"I don't want to leave," I said, "but it's not fair for me to let Carter jeopardize his job when I'm not being honest with him."

"Then you won't be involved," Ida Belle said.

"What do you mean?" I asked.

"Gertie and I will do all the investigating. You won't have anything to do with it. Gertie and I acting like fools is commonplace. Carter won't take any flak over us."

"No. It's too risky. And besides, we have no leads."

Gertie perked up. "Billy said that weird guy you talked to in the bar was looking for Floyd, didn't he?"

"That's right," Ida Belle said. "And that guy could have taken the shoe."

"But we have no idea who he is," I argued. "We have my description and a first name from a highly unreliable source. Where would we even start? And don't you dare say we should go back to the Swamp Bar and ask."

"No," Ida Belle agreed. "I think we should steer clear of the

Swamp Bar for a while."

"If by 'a while' you mean until Christ returns, then yeah."

Ida Belle shook her head. "So back to the guy in the bar. According to Billy, the guy said Floyd was going to have big problems, right?"

"He said that Floyd was going to have big problems, or little problems."

"That doesn't make sense," Gertie said. "A problem is either big or little. It's not both."

Ida Belle jumped up from her chair. "Unless the problem *is* big and little."

Gertie sucked in a breath. "Big and Little Hebert."

"Their names are Big and Little?" I asked. "What are they— a circus act?"

"Oh, they're an act all right," Gertie said, "but not the entertainment type. They're a father and son act who work for Sonny Hebert."

"Who's Sonny Hebert?" I asked.

"He's a mob boss out of New Orleans and third cousins, or some other relation, to Big and Little," Ida Belle said. "The Feds finally busted him on something a year or so ago, but I think he only got a couple years."

"What do Big and Little do for Sonny? Hit men?"

Ida Belle waved a hand in dismissal. "Nothing like that. As far as I've heard, they don't handle any of the strong-arm stuff. Just things like loan-sharking, illegal gambling, that sort of thing."

"So Floyd could have owed them money," I said.

"Sure," Ida Belle said, "but in my experience, bookies didn't kill people who owed them money. That's a surefire way to never get paid."

I nodded. My knowledge of the U.S. Mafia was mostly limited to the movies Gertie had me watch, but what Ida Belle said made sense. Dead men couldn't pay bills, and bookies weren't the kind of business that put a lien against an estate.

"Here's a theory," I said. "What if Floyd borrowed money from Big and Little to get out of trouble with someone else?"

Ida Belle frowned. "But it wasn't enough. Or he got in trouble again and couldn't borrow more."

"And that's who killed him," Gertie said. "I bet that's it."

"It's just a theory," I said.

"Yeah," Ida Belle said, "but it's a theory that makes sense."

"So all we have to do is prove we're right," Gertie said. "Thank goodness. I thought this was going to be much harder."

I stared at her. "Just how do you intend to easily prove we're right?"

"Duh. We'll ask Big and Little."

"Have you lost your mind?" I asked.

"Probably," Ida Belle mumbled under her breath.

"You think," I continued, "that you can just stroll into their office, or whatever, and ask them if Floyd borrowed money and if so what for?"

"Sure," Gertie said. "Nothing illegal about that."

"No, but I'm sure lending money to Floyd was illegal. You think they're going to come out and admit to being loan sharks?"

Gertie frowned. "I could always ask for a loan. Then their secret would be out and they'd have no reason not to answer my questions."

I looked at Ida Belle. "Is she for real? I don't pretend to know anything about how the Mafia works in the states, but I'm not buying that they have this sort of conversation."

"Normally, I would agree," Ida Belle said, "but Big and Little have reputations for being eccentric and not too bright. That's why Sonny has them out in the swamp instead of working New Orleans. There's a possibility they'd talk to us, especially since Floyd is dead."

"They're here in Sinful?" I asked.

"No," Ida Belle said. "They have an old warehouse off the highway to New Orleans, about twenty miles from Sinful."

I leaned back in my chair and blew out a breath, my mind racing with all the things that could go wrong with their plan. But on the flip side of the thousand or more things that could go wrong was the possibility that they'd get a solid lead on who killed Floyd, which could let Carter and me both off the hook.

"You don't think they're dangerous?" I asked.

Ida Belle shrugged. "They're not harmless, but I don't think they'll shoot us for asking a question. More likely, they'll tell us they don't know anything and ask us to leave. Why bring heat down for no reason when a simple 'I don't know anything' will suffice?"

"But if you find out anything," I said, "you're going to turn it over to Carter, right?"

"Of course," Ida Belle said. "If I thought Big and Little would talk to a cop, I'd send him over there now, but I think we all know that's not likely to happen."

"No," I agreed. "It's probably not."

I was just about to launch into all the rules they'd have to follow if I were to agree with this very sketchy idea when someone pounded on my front door. I jerked my head in the direction of the living room.

"Are you expecting someone?" Gertie asked.

"No." I jumped out of my chair. "And I know that knock."

It was Carter's angry knock.

Had he bugged my kitchen? Had he changed his mind about talking to the DA and was here to arrest me? I flung the front door open, expecting to see Carter standing there holding handcuffs, but instead, a very agitated Walter had his hand lifted, about to pound on my door again. Apparently, the knocking skill was a family thing.

"Oh, there you are," he said and hurried inside my house. "Are the other two here?"

"Kitchen," I said and waved him back.

Ida Belle and Gertie stared as Walter stepped into the room, then they both looked at me. I shrugged and slid into my chair, pointing Walter to the remaining seat.

"I'm glad you're all here," he said as he took a seat.

Ida Belle cast a worried look at Gertie. "Shouldn't you be at the store?"

"Scooter's watching it for a bit. Not the best idea, I know, so I have to hurry." Walter pulled a box of chocolates out of his pocket and placed them on the table in front of me. "He said to give you these."

"You banged on my door to give me chocolates from Scooter?"

"No. When I told Scooter where I was going, he insisted, and it was easier than arguing with him."

Because I got chocolates out of the deal, it sounded like a solid explanation to me. "So what's up?" I asked as I cracked open the box. Scooter had absolutely no chance with me, but I wasn't about to let perfectly good chocolates go to waste.

"I heard about Floyd early this morning from a contractor at the café," Walter said. "I'd…uh…also been working on a radio last night when the channels got crossed and I picked up a radio call about a giant chicken riding a motorcycle."

I lowered my hand with the chocolate that I'd been about to pop into my mouth. "You old sneak. You've got a police scanner and never told us."

"Anyway," Walter continued, completely ignoring me, "I figured the three of you were behind the chicken fiasco somehow." He held up a hand. "I don't want to know the details. But I don't think any of you popped Floyd."

"I'm capable of killing Floyd," Gertie groused.

"Being capable," Walter said, "and actually doing it are two different things. We're all capable, and I'd wager that we've all wanted to at some time or another. The difference is, we have the good sense to know better. Anyway, I had a vanity cabinet that had been delivered for the sheriff's department, so I took it over, hoping to get a word with Carter."

"Was that cabinet going in the bathroom?" I asked.

Walter nodded. "Carter said to put it on your tab."

I sighed.

"I hauled the cabinet into the sheriff's department and put it in that storeroom across from Carter's office so that I could open it up. I was waiting on Carter to get off the phone but he'd no sooner hung up than two men wearing suits walked into his office and shut the door."

Gertie's eyes widened. "It's the Men in Black. Floyd must have been killed by aliens."

Walter frowned. "They weren't black suits. One was gray and the other navy."

Gertie looked disappointed. "Nothing cool ever happens here."

We all stared at her for a moment, then turned our attention back to Walter.

"Could you hear what they said?" I asked.

"Not from the storeroom," Walter said, "but I carried the vanity into the bathroom, and well, I guess I don't have to tell you that the walls are thin." He gave me a pointed look.

I threw my hands in the air. "I had gum on my shoe. How come no one believes me?"

Walter raised one eyebrow.

"Whatever," I said. "Continue."

"Anyway, I set the vanity against the wall and that's when I realized I could hear the men talking. It's not good."

"No dramatic pauses," Ida Belle said. "Give us the punch line."

"They're Feds."

Chapter Fifteen

I swallowed the half-eaten chocolate. "What kind of Feds?"

"FBI."

I relaxed a little. FBI were still mostly human. If he'd said NSA, I would have been a little worried. "Why are they here?"

"They told Carter they're taking over the investigation of Floyd's murder. He was instructed to hand over his case files and cease all action on the case." Walter scowled. "They threatened to throw him in jail if he interferes. What the hell kind of thing is that for one law enforcement officer to say to another? Carter wasn't being rude."

"He wouldn't have to be," I said. "The Feds think all local cops are territorial, so they go ahead and get that in up front."

Walter stared at me.

Crap.

"I live next door to a cop back home," I said, throwing out the first lie that came to mind. "I've heard him complain about that more than once."

"If he gets talked to like these guys did Carter, I can just imagine," Walter said. "It's bad enough to come into a man's place of work and tell him he can't do his job, but there's no cause to make threats on top of it."

He rose from the table. "Anyway, I don't know what you three have brewing, and I don't want to know, but I thought it was important that you knew this right away."

I jumped up from my seat. "Definitely. We appreciate you coming straight here to tell us."

Ida Belle and Gertie nodded, both wearing sober expressions. I followed Walter to the door and let him out, then headed back to the kitchen, still processing the latest curveball this situation had thrown us.

"So," I said as I took my seat. "What do we think?"

"Not good," Ida Belle said. "If the Feds are here about Floyd then he was into something big. Big enough to kick Carter out of his job."

I nodded. "That's my take. And it sorta supports our theory that Floyd got mixed up in something and borrowed money from Big and Little."

"Unless the Feds are after Big and Little," Gertie pointed out.

"I doubt that's it," Ida Belle said. "I mean, I don't doubt that the Feds have an eye on them, but of all Hebert's organization, my understanding is that Big and Little are small potatoes."

"True," Gertie agreed. "What do you think Carter had in the files he had to turn over?"

"Crime scene details and photos," I said. "Floyd's record and maybe information about the fire at Ally's house."

"But nothing about you or the Swamp Bar?" Gertie asked.

"He kissed her," Ida Belle said. "Do you think he's going to give her up to the first set of buttholes in suits that come along? Give the boy more credit. If anyone is going to take Fortune down, Carter would be the one to do it himself. It would be a matter of honor."

"I think she's right," I said.

Gertie looked back and forth from me to Ida Belle and grinned. "You realize what this means, right?"

Ida Belle smiled and they both looked at me.

"What did I miss?" I asked.

"Floyd's murder is no longer Carter's problem," Gertie said. "That means you wouldn't be interfering with his investigation if you got involved. You'd be interfering with the Feds."

"And who cares about that?" Ida Belle said.

A spark of excitement passed through me. "The Feds will keep a close eye on Carter. He won't be able to do much on the side without them knowing."

Ida Belle nodded. "And the FBI will be wasting their time here. No outsider is going to step into this town and solve a murder."

I grinned. "Not without an inside track, anyway."

"You're no outsider," Ida Belle said. "You've always been one of us. You just didn't know it."

"So the way I see it," Gertie said, "solving this murder would not only solve Fortune's problem, but it would also get Carter off the hook. I think it's our duty as leaders of Sinful to get this situation in hand."

"I couldn't agree more," Ida Belle said.

I looked at the two smiling faces and considered the proposal. It was risky. And borderline insane. And if anything went wrong, the best outcome was that I disappeared from Sinful forever. But if we were successful, then everything could go back to the way it was three days ago, when my biggest worry was dinner with a hot deputy.

"I'm in."

"What is that smell?" I asked and wrinkled my nose as I searched the backseat of Gertie's Cadillac for the origin of the offensive odor.

"Some perm solution spilled back there a couple days ago," Gertie said. "That's probably what you smell."

I had no idea what a perm solution was, but it smelled like death. "Is it safe to have chemicals like that in your car? Shouldn't we lower the windows or something?"

Ida Belle laughed. "A perm solution is something you put in your hair to make it hold curl. Do you think Gertie's hair grows like that naturally?"

I stared at Gertie's hair, horrified. "You put that stench on your hair...intentionally?"

Gertie shot me a dirty look in the rearview mirror. "Just because I don't want a man underfoot doesn't mean I want to look like one—like *some* people. My hair is baby-fine. If I didn't perm it to get some volume, I'd have a flat, thin layer of white cotton."

"That's what I'd go for," I said. "Flat cotton and a hat. Given that days later, this stuff is making my eyes water, maybe it seeps through the skull and fries the brain. That could explain a few things."

Ida Belle grinned.

"At least I don't dress like a hooker," Gertie said.

"With that thin, flat cotton hair, how could you?" I shot back. "If you teased 'thin cotton' it would probably file a complaint about bullying."

"Keep it up and you'll walk home."

"At the moment, I don't see a downside there. By the way, what's up with the shirt?"

Gertie, whose usual going-somewhere outfit consisted of stretchy polyester pants and a silky sort of blouse, was decked out this time in jeans and a black T-shirt with silver lettering across it that read "Ask me about the Lord." It seemed a bit eccentric, even for Gertie.

"We wore these last year when our church group went to New Orleans for the choir competition."

"Did you get many takers?" I asked.

Gertie sighed. "No, there was a *Star Wars* convention the same weekend. Everyone kept asking us which Sith we were beholden to."

I grinned. "And you thought Big and Little might go for the *Star Wars* Sith Lord fan club look?"

"No, I just thought appearing as a little old church lady might make me look less threatening. And it is the Heberts. I figured it wouldn't hurt to take God with us on the trip. Just in case."

My grin disappeared as I considered the reality of what we were doing—walking into a Mafia-run business to ask questions about one of their customers who had been murdered. When I laid it all out like that in one sentence, it didn't seem nearly as innocuous as it had felt back at my house. I'd gone for a sundress and lip gloss, thinking I'd go for the youthful, innocent look. If that didn't work, I hoped Gertie and her T-shirt were enough to sway Big and Little into the "they're probably harmless" camp.

"There's the turnoff." Ida Belle pointed to a dirt path to the left that veered off into the marsh.

"Why are these places always stuck at the end of one-lane trails through the marsh?" Gertie complained. "The options for escape are seriously limited. It's like nature claustrophobia."

Given my recent dash from the Swamp Bar, I understood exactly what she was saying. On the other hand, if we had to make a run for it, away from the Mafia, in Gertie's Cadillac, that escape was over before it started.

"Everything will be fine as long as we remain calm and cool," Ida Belle said.

Gertie nodded, but I could already see the tension in her

shoulders and neck. Calm and cool were not a normal part of Gertie's day.

"Just let Ida Belle and me do all the talking," I said. Silent was probably Gertie's best bet.

Gertie turned a corner and pulled to a stop in front of a warehouse. "Well, this is it."

I clapped her on the shoulder. "Stop worrying. Just stand there looking like the church lady and you'll be fine."

"I'll be as quiet as a church mouse," Gertie said.

I had no idea what a church mouse was or exactly how quiet they were, but I took that to mean Gertie would refrain from talking, which was a good thing. She tended to ramble when she got flustered.

"Promise?" Ida Belle asked.

"I'm taking a vow of silence," Gertie assured her. "You two can handle all the talking."

Ida Belle seemed satisfied, so we climbed out of the car and headed to the warehouse. I knocked on the door and waited, but no one answered. I tried the handle and found that the door was unlocked, so I pulled it open and peered inside.

The interior of the warehouse surprised me. I'd expected to find something that resembled regular warehouse storage, with a vaulted ceiling and rows of shelving, but in this case, the interior had been remodeled to resemble a high-end office building. Marble floors spanned a lobby area, complete with reception desk.

I looked back at Ida Belle and Gertie and shrugged before stepping inside, figuring I might find a call button on the receptionist desk. I walked over to the desk, Ida Belle and Gertie following silently behind me, and scanned the surface for a button or telephone. Nothing. Not even a sticky pad or pen.

"Hello?" I called out. I pointed to the catwalk above us that ran the length of the building. "I bet those doors lead to offices."

"We can't just go roaming around a Mafia den," Gertie whispered.

"Well, we have to find someone to help us. Standing here isn't solving anything."

"Can I help you?" A deep, booming voice sounded to our right. We whirled around and saw a beefy guy coming toward us.

Midthirties, six foot four, two hundred forty pounds of pure muscle. Deadly as hell.

He had the body of a professional wrestler and the face of a serial killer, but instead of leather, studs, or torn jeans, he dressed in a black silk suit that probably cost as much as I made in a year. He stepped in front of us and we all stared.

One glance at Gertie and I could see she was frozen in place. Even Ida Belle seemed less confident with the mountain of man standing only inches from us. If any talking was going to happen, it looked like it was up to me.

"I asked how I can help you," the man repeated.

My mind screamed at me to make up a "sorry, wrong place" excuse and get out of the building as quickly as possible, but then we'd be right back to Carter's job risk and my imminent departure from Sinful.

"We'd like to see Big and Little Hebert," I said, hoping I sounded more confident than I felt.

He snorted. "What the hell for?"

I bristled a bit at his obvious dismissal. He was a brute, but I could still take him. "Business. *Personal* business."

He didn't look remotely inclined to humor me, so I decided to try my *Godfather*, tough-guy move. The characters in those movies seemed to get whatever they wanted by pretending they were due everything. Maybe that was the only language the mob spoke.

"I don't really appreciate being questioned this way," I said. "I'm not going to provide details of my business to a guard. Are Big and Little available, or do I need to report this to my people?"

Ida Belle and Gertie stared at me as if I'd lost my mind. The Hulk stared at me for a moment, then laughed.

"Your people? Babe, you got a lot of nerve coming in here with that line of shit." He reached under his jacket and pulled out a nine-millimeter. "Do you know who I am?"

Gertie picked that moment to break her vow of silence. "Do you know Jesus Christ?"

I looked over at her and shook my head. "Not now," I whispered.

The Hulk scrunched his brow, apparently not sure what to think. I didn't blame him. The situation was probably far from his norm. I was just about to suggest we leave when a voice called out behind him.

"Yo, Mannie. You got a problem over there?"

I leaned to the side to peer around him and saw a little guy, wearing a silk pin-striped suit and alligator loafers, walking toward us.

Thirtyish, five foot three, a hundred twenty pounds soaking wet and with clothes. Less threatening than damp toilet paper.

Mannie, aka the Hulk, stuffed his gun back in his jacket. "No, boss," he said and straightened the jacket over his firearm. "These three ladies would like to see you about business, but they're not in the appointment book."

I glanced over at Ida Belle, who shrugged. Who knew the Mafia made appointments?

The small guy walked up to stand next to Mannie and gave us each the once-over. He must have decided that whatever we were up to was something he could handle, because he extended his hand toward me. "I'm Little Hebert. What can I do for you?"

This was Little Hebert? I'd taken the nickname as a junior/senior sort of thing, not an indication of stature. As I shook his hand, I tried to visualize Big using proportions of scale, but I couldn't make it work.

I realized I'd never replied to Little and said, "Well, um, it's about a loan."

He smiled. "Why didn't you say so? Let's go upstairs and talk out the details with my father." He motioned to a staircase behind the reception desk and followed behind us as we proceeded to the second floor. Mannie gave him a nod and slipped off into a room with a glass front.

One-way glass. That explained it. He'd watched before approaching us.

"Third door on the right," Little called as we stepped onto the landing. I proceeded down the catwalk, opened the door, and found myself staring at the largest human being I'd ever seen in my life.

Midfifties, six foot three, five hundred pounds—maybe in the left leg alone. Threatening only if he sat on me, but he'd have to catch me first.

Big Hebert wore the same silk pin-striped suit as his son, and no way did it come off the rack. The cost of the fabric alone probably equaled the cost of an economy car. He was seated on a park bench positioned behind a mahogany desk. Apparently a chair that could hold all of him had not yet been made. I wondered briefly if there was a freight elevator somewhere in the warehouse because clearly, Big hadn't seen a set of stairs in years.

"They're here about a loan," Little said.

Big motioned to a set of chairs in front of the desk and we all took seats, me in the middle. I was fairly certain none of us had blinked or released a breath since we'd entered the room. Little grabbed a barstool from the corner and sat next to his father. The barstool and the park bench put them at about the same height sitting down, and I had to work to suppress a grin.

Big pulled a stack of papers out of his desk and pushed them across to me. "I'll need your social security number, list of assets, last two months' pay stubs, and two forms of ID. How much do you need to borrow?"

Fascinated by all the paperwork, I picked up the stack and began to thumb through it until Ida Belle jabbed me in the ribs. "I'm sorry," I said. "I'm afraid you misunderstood."

Little's expression darkened, so I hurried to explain.

"Or I probably didn't explain things well," I said.

Little relaxed.

"I don't need a loan. I need to know if you made someone else a loan."

Big and Little looked at each other, then back at me. "You the police?" Big asked.

"Do we look like the police?"

Little scanned the three of us. "The one in the T-shirt looks like that broad on *The Golden Girls*. The stupid one."

I coughed to hold in a laugh and out of the corner of my eye, saw Ida Belle rub her mouth with her hand.

Gertie came alive. "Oh hell no. I am *not* Rose."

Little shrugged. "Didn't say you was. Said you looked like her."

"And you are?" Big asked me.

"Sandy-Sue. I'm staying in Sinful for the summer, settling up some of my late aunt's business. I'm a school librarian, not a cop."

I must have met the appearance standards for a librarian because Big nodded. "We're not in the business of providing information about our clients." He leaned back on the bench and crossed his tree-trunk arms across his massive chest. "Surely you can appreciate that, working for the school system."

"I understand and respect your policy. It's just that the person I want to know about is dead. So I figured if you gave me information about him, it wouldn't matter."

And that's when Gertie lost her cool and her vow of silence all over again.

"Unless, of course," Gertie said, "you're the one who killed him, and then I guess it would matter a lot, and it would be really stupid for us to be here asking you questions."

Chapter Sixteen

Gertie sat back in her chair and took a deep breath. I clutched my chair arms, waiting for the hammer to drop. Big and Little both studied Gertie, probably waiting to see if she keeled over from a heart attack. She already looked to be in the preliminary stages of cardiac arrest, her face ashen and her body stiff.

"I assume," Big said, turning his attention back to me, "that you're referring to the very unfortunate Floyd Guidry?"

"Yes."

"Even if this man is no longer a customer," Big continued, "why should I tell you anything?"

I stared at him, praying for a moment of clarity. What in the world would make this man talk—the jaws of life? I couldn't appeal to him on a personal level. Neither one would care if I were a suspect. They probably lived every minute of their lives as a suspect for something. I stretched my mind back to the Mafia movies I'd watched, trying to find some common thread to use as ammunition.

And then I had an idea.

"The truth is," I said, "you shouldn't tell me anything. It would be unprofessional. I'm only asking because Floyd was killed on my friend's property."

Big cocked his head to the side and started tapping his pen on the desk.

"She's a young, single woman, living alone," I continued, "and someone set fire to her house three nights ago. Her mother is dying and had to be placed in a facility in New Orleans, so she's already dealing with a lot. Now she's afraid to live in her own house. I know it's not your problem, and I'm sure Floyd didn't plan on dying, much less in her backyard. But the crux of the matter is, I feel it was disrespectful to bring my friend into all this, and I'd like to get her some answers so that she feels safe again."

The tapping stopped. Big and Little straightened in their seats and looked at each other. Little nodded and Big looked back across the desk at me.

"It's unprofessional to talk about a client, but me and Little are old-school when it comes to the importance of respect. That's especially true when it comes to women, and a young single woman already grieving her mother's impending passing should be afforded all the help we can provide. I'll tell you what I know about Floyd, but I don't think it's going to help you any."

Relief flooded my body and I barely contained myself from leaping out of the chair and yelling. "Thank you. You never know what might turn out to be important."

Big nodded. "Floyd had an affinity for sports betting and the wrong kind of women. He's most often a big loser in both cases. We loaned him money about two years ago, taking the title to his truck as collateral."

"How much did you loan him?" I asked, more out of curiosity than any perceived relevance.

"Ten thousand dollars. To be repaid over a six-month period." Big frowned. "Normally, we wouldn't do business with someone like Floyd. He couldn't keep a regular job and I couldn't see that situation improving. But he'd just signed on for roughneck work on an oil rig, and I knew the pay would cover the loan."

"Floyd didn't make his bets with you?"

"No. We got out of the bookie business several years back. Too much competition in New Orleans. It wasn't worth the administrative paperwork."

I nodded. "Do you know who he owed?"

"He didn't say and we don't ask. It's better that way."

"Did Floyd pay you back?"

"People *always* pay me back."

"You said that was two years ago…has he borrowed from you since?"

"No, but not from lack of trying. His last attempt was about four weeks ago."

"May I ask why you didn't do the deal? I mean, if he paid before?"

Big clasped his hands together on the desk, intertwining his fingers. "Despite the fact that we had no problem collecting from Mr. Guidry, every time I met with the man, it left me with a taste in my mouth that even whiskey couldn't eliminate. I didn't like his attitude or his standards, and he was completely without respect or manners. The aggravation wasn't worth the profit."

Feeling brave, I launched into my final question. "How do I know for sure that he paid you back? How do I know you didn't get what you could out of him and then kill him to cut your losses."

Big smiled. "You don't."

And that was that. Deciding I'd pressed my luck as far as it would reach, I rose and thanked him for his time. Gertie and Ida Belle followed suit, and Gertie dug two palm-size Scripture books out of her purse and left one for each of them on the desk. They looked at the books, then each other, clearly not certain what to make of the three of us.

"Thank you," I said. "I really appreciate your talking to us, especially given the sensitive nature of the information and your position."

Big gave me a nod. "I hope your friend gets her answers and finds some peace. I'll light a candle for her mother."

I noticed he didn't mention lighting a candle for Floyd.

We followed Little back downstairs, where he handed me a card. "If you ever need a loan, remember our services."

We made our way back to the car and I'd barely gotten my door closed before Ida Belle started in on Gertie. "Are you insane?" Ida Belle asked. "That guard pulled a gun on us just for being in the building, and then you come right out and imply that Big and Little killed Floyd."

"I didn't imply," Gertie argued, wearing a sheepish expression. "I asked."

Ida Belle rolled her eyes. "Right. Because that makes all the difference to a criminal. What happened to that promise you made not to talk?"

"I panicked. Sue me."

I shook my head. "You asked the guard if he knew Jesus Christ. That's not panic. That's surrender."

"Fine," Gertie said. "You two can keep ragging on me, but I'm going to get us the hell out of here before they change their minds about the information they gave us."

"Good idea," I said.

Gertie put the Cadillac in reverse and floored it, almost sending me to the floorboard, then she shoved the car into drive and took off so fast, the back tires showered the parking area with dirt and rocks. Ida Belle shook her head and clicked her seat belt in place. I decided that with the way she was driving, I'd rather be loose, just in case she put the whole car into the bayou.

By the time we hit the highway, Gertie had gotten the mad

out of her system and seemed to be back to normal.

"So, what do you think?" I asked.

"It seems to add up with our theory," Ida Belle said. "We figured Floyd was into things that weren't on the up-and-up. If he tried to borrow money a month ago, it was probably for whatever got him killed."

"Gambling, I suppose. Still, you'd think they'd want their money more than they'd want him dead, assuming he's always managed to pay in the past."

"Maybe the bookies disliked Floyd as much as Big did," Gertie suggested.

"That's possible," Ida Belle agreed. "If he was a constant problem, they might have chosen to cut their losses and make an example out of him at the same time."

I frowned. "Big was lying."

"What?"

"When?"

Gertie and Ida Belle both sounded off at once.

"When he said he didn't know why Floyd borrowed the money. I could see it in his eyes. He knew then why Floyd needed the cash, and I think he knew why Floyd needed the money a month ago. Big may be out of the bookie business, but the people in New Orleans are part of the same family, right?"

"I don't know how many families run books in New Orleans," Ida Belle said, "but the Heberts are definitely one of them."

"So if Floyd owed the Heberts, Big could have easily found out who and why."

"Probably so," Ida Belle agreed, "but why keep it a big secret? It doesn't really matter if he owed for football or ponies. It's all the same in the big scheme of things."

"Exactly. So why lie?"

Ida Belle frowned. "Yeah. Why lie?"

I shook my head. "I don't know, but something tells me that reason is important."

"Do you think they killed him?" Ida Belle asked. "Or had him killed?"

"I don't think Big had Floyd killed. He wouldn't have been so cocky about answering my questions if he could be connected to the murder."

"But you think he knows who did it and why?"

I nodded. "Yeah. I do."

"Then how do we find out?" Gertie said.

"If we could get into Floyd's house," Ida Belle said, "we might be able to find a clue."

"With the Feds watching it?" I said. "No chance. Unless…"

An idea began to form. A moronic, dangerous, almost-certain-to-fail idea.

"Tell us," Ida Belle said.

"The FBI will lock down the house and mark it off, but without a live witness inside, they'll only post a guard out front. Ally has to go to her house this evening to get some clothes for her date tonight."

"Date?" Gertie perked up. "What date?"

I waved a hand at her. "Later. Anyway, I want to take a look around her house and make sure nothing seems out of place— maybe try to figure out why Floyd was over there in the first place."

Ida Belle looked excited. "So we'll go to Ally's house with her, as protection and to inspect for security purposes."

"But we won't be done when she's ready to leave for her date," I said. "So we'll promise to lock up when we leave."

"Right," Ida Belle said. "Then we can sneak out back, take down that loose fence panel, and break into Floyd's house from the backyard."

I nodded. "It's risky."

"Very risky," Ida Belle agreed.

Gertie grinned. "Sounds right up our alley."

I'd switched my cell phone to silent mode during our visit to Big and Little and forgot to check it until I got home. Four missed calls from Carter. Crap. He probably wanted to warn me about the FBI and the change in his ability to control the investigation. I gave Ida Belle and Gertie a hasty explanation, then hurried off to the sheriff's department, figuring this conversation was one better had in person.

Deputy Breaux was manning the front desk at the department and he gave me a cautious hello when I walked in. Since he'd been in charge of getting me out of the building when the unfortunate toilet incident had occurred, he was probably afraid I'd do something else that he could be blamed for.

"Is Carter here?" I asked.

"Yes, ma'am. Let me call him." He picked up the phone and let Carter know I was here. Seconds later, he hung up the phone, looking relieved. "He said to go on back to his office."

"Thanks," I said and headed to the back of the building, then down to the end of the hallway where Carter's office was located. The door was closed, so I knocked lightly, then peeked inside. Carter stood by the window that looked out over the bayou. He turned around and waved me inside.

I took a seat in front of his desk and he sat on the edge of the desk, facing me. "I've been trying to get a hold of you."

"I know. I'm sorry. I was running errands with Ida Belle and Gertie. I thought it would get my mind off things. I didn't realize my phone was on silent."

He nodded but I wondered how much of my explanation he'd processed. In the time I'd known him, Carter had dealt with some serious issues, but I'd never seen him look this worried, and even worse, defeated.

"What's wrong?" I asked.

"It's that apparent, huh?"

"Well…yeah."

He took a deep breath and slowly blew it out. "There's been a development in Floyd's case. One I'm not happy about."

"Oh?"

"The FBI showed up this morning and took over the investigation."

I widened my eyes, doing my best to appear shocked. "The FBI? What…I mean, why…wow."

"I don't know why exactly. The Feds don't have to answer to local law enforcement, and in my experience, they take great pleasure in that. All I know is that they're taking over the investigation of Floyd's murder, and if I am deemed to be working on the case, they will arrest me."

"What in the world could the Feds want with Floyd?"

"Who knows? He wasn't exactly a model citizen and considering he was murdered, that only supports my theory that he was into all manner of illegal and nefarious things. Likely, they were watching him to build a case for something."

"And if they can figure out who murdered him, it might make their case stronger."

"I'm sure that's what they're hoping for."

"I don't suppose you had a chance to search Floyd's house?"

"A cursory look while the paramedics were preparing the body for transport. I didn't see anything out of the ordinary, but I didn't have a chance to look deeply."

"No bobcat?" I asked, trying to sound nonchalant. The last thing we needed to run into this evening was that angry animal with razor claws.

Carter frowned. "Now that I think of it, no sign of the bobcat or that Floyd was keeping a pet. It's more likely the cat lives in the swamp behind his house. Maybe he feeds it sometimes. It coming after you was probably a coincidence that he was happy to take advantage of."

"Some coincidence."

He reached down and took my hand in his. "I don't want you to worry about this. My case files contained only the barest of information and nothing about the Swamp Bar incident. They're not going to find out anything else from me."

"Thank you," I said. "Let's hope if they track Floyd that far, the Swamp Bar customers have the same tight lips you do."

"I doubt they'll go that direction. I think they already have a good idea who killed him. They just don't want me messing up their case with my inept, small-town investigative skills."

"Then that's their loss, right?"

He smiled and leaned over, brushing his lips lightly against mine. "When all this is over, you still owe me dinner."

"Don't you mean you owe me dinner?"

"Now you're a traditionalist?"

"Maybe." I squeezed his hand. "I'm sorry things got out of hand. If I'd never gone to the Swamp Bar…"

"Then it would have been something else." He released my hand and leaned back. "I spent a lot of time being aggravated that you wouldn't listen to my stellar advice—and it *is* stellar—but the bottom line is that if you always did what other people told you to do, even when it was for your own good, you wouldn't be you. That's something I have to learn to live with, even when I'm on the receiving end of your refusal to listen."

"That's an awfully big compromise to make just to hang out with me."

He shrugged. "I keep hoping my good sense and lawful nature will rub off on you."

I rose from my chair and despite the million reasons that all of this was a bad idea, couldn't keep myself from hugging him. Even though I wasn't the arsonist, hadn't killed anyone, and definitely didn't run the FBI, I felt responsible for the position he was in.

"This is all going to work out," I said as I wrapped my arms around him.

He hesitated only for a moment before squeezing me. "It has to."

I released him and left the building, more determined than ever to find Floyd's killer and get both our lives back to normal.

I couldn't wait to see what that looked like.

Chapter Seventeen

Ally held up two dresses. "Which one—the blue or the yellow?"

I looked at the two offerings, wondering why no matter how hard I tried, I couldn't seem to avoid girl stuff. "Uh, the most comfortable?"

Gertie rolled her eyes as she walked out of the closet and set a pair of sandals on the rug. "The blue. It brings out the color of your eyes and sets off your tan."

"The blue it is." Ally smiled and headed down the hall to the bathroom to change.

Ida Belle, Gertie, and I stood in the bedroom, trying to appear relaxed, but we were just waiting for her to leave so that we could get on with our investigation.

She popped back into the bedroom a minute later, and started stuffing clothes into a duffel bag. "Since I'm going to be staying with you a bit longer, I'm going to pack some more clothes."

"Smart move," I said. "Unless you want to do laundry every day."

"Gertie," Ally said, "can you hand me that shirt hanging just inside the closet?"

Gertie opened the closet and pulled out a green polo shirt that she handed to Ally. "What's up with this closet? It's got a door on the other end."

Ally rolled her eyes. "Another of Mama's great ideas. She had the wall between our closets removed. She said it was so we could easily borrow each other's clothes but in all our years in the same house, we never once shared a garment."

Gertie frowned. "So the closet opens into your mother's bedroom on the other side? That just sounds nosy to me."

"That's what I thought," Ally said. She zipped the bag and looked at me. "Do you mind taking this home with you when you leave?"

"Not at all."

She let out a breath and looked at the three of us. "It worries me that you're not leaving now. And you didn't even drive a car."

"There's three of us," I reassured her. "No one is foolish enough to return to the scene of a murder, especially when it's not even dark yet. We'll do a quick check of everything and then we'll lock it up and leave."

"And we need the exercise," Ida Belle said. "That's why we walked over in the first place."

She bit her lower lip. "I just don't know what you expect to find. Mama didn't have anything valuable. I mean, just the house and furniture and stuff, but no jewelry or art or anything else worth killing someone over."

"I'm sure you're right," Ida Belle agreed, "but it would make us feel better to know the house is secure. It's not like us to sit around doing nothing."

Ally smiled. "I'm lucky to have you as friends."

"Yes, well," Ida Belle said, looking a little flustered, "is David picking you up here?"

"No. Since I had to get clothes, I told him I'd meet him in front of the General Store."

"Make sure," Gertie said, "that he drives you home tonight

to Fortune's. Don't stop to pick up your car. Downtown will probably be vacant by the time you return."

I nodded. "I'll take you to work in the morning."

Ally shook her head. "I don't want to inconvenience you any more than I already have."

"Who's inconvenienced?" I asked. "It's a good excuse for me to have a chicken-fried steak and pancakes."

She smiled and slipped on the sandals Gertie had placed on the rug. "Okay. Well, if you guys think I look presentable, then I guess I'll head out."

"You look lovely," Gertie said. "David is a very lucky man."

Ally blushed and gave us a wave before leaving. I watched from the bedroom window, and as soon as she backed out of the driveway, gave Ida Belle and Gertie a thumbs-up.

"You two start up here," I said. "There's a lot more to check with all the storage furniture and closets. I'll start downstairs. Remember to try to lift every window. And if you see anything that looks odd, even if you can't figure out why, yell. Between the three of us, we ought to be able to figure things out."

Ida Belle and Gertie nodded, and I headed downstairs to start my search in the living room at the front of the house.

It wasn't a big room and fortunately, Ally's mother wasn't the collecting sort of woman. Two bookcases and a television cabinet made up all of the storage furniture in the room, and a small coat closet was the only other place to hide away things. Given that the bookcases were mostly made up of art objects and not books that had to be flipped through, I made quick work of that room and moved on to the formal dining room, which contained only buffet and table. The windows in both rooms were tightly fastened, and nothing appeared to have been tampered with.

I moved to the kitchen, first checking the plywood that covered the damaged section of the breakfast nook, but all the sheets were still nailed firmly in place and none of them showed any signs of being removed. The back door was locked but I noticed the dead bolt was broken, probably from when the firemen entered the house. The room had three windows, one boarded up, one window over the sink that was firmly latched, and one more window on the side wall at the opposite end of the kitchen from the fire. The latches appeared to be in place, but when I tugged on the window, it glided silently up.

I fingered the latches, but they didn't budge. I pushed the window back down and called out to Ida Belle and Gertie. Several seconds later, they hurried into the kitchen.

"Did you find something?" Gertie asked.

"Yes. But not what I wanted to find." I pointed to the window. "Does that look locked to you?"

They both stepped closer and inspected the window latches. Gertie nodded and Ida Belle said, "It looks fine to me."

"Try to open it," I said.

Ida Belle frowned and reached for the window. Her eyes widened when it slid easily. "What the hell?" she said, bending over to inspect the latches. "They've been cut off from the back!"

I nodded.

Gertie's eyes widened and some of the color left her face. "But there's no reason at all to do something like that unless…"

"Unless you want to sneak into someone's house without them knowing," I said.

"What is going on here?" Ida Belle asked. "Nothing about this makes sense."

I nodded. She was right. The arson, the creeper, Floyd's murder, Big and Little, the real estate agent…I had this feeling all of them were important somehow, but no matter how I arranged the pieces, they didn't make a picture. "Did you find anything upstairs?"

Gertie shook her head. "It's just as we thought. Ally's mother had modest tastes and wasn't much for clutter, which was to our benefit. She had a couple of nice jewelry pieces, but nice in a sentimental way for Ally. I can't imagine they'd bring more than a couple hundred dollars with a jeweler, even less at a pawn shop."

I looked at the window again and frowned. "Everything is so inconsistent. If someone wanted something inside this house, then why try to burn it down?"

Gertie shook her head. "And if they wanted something badly enough to rig the window, why haven't they taken whatever it is already?"

"Maybe they have," Ida Belle said.

A dark thought popped into my mind. "Or maybe what they wanted was no longer here."

Gertie sucked in a breath. "Ally?"

Ida Belle's expression turned grim. "It's the only thing that makes sense. It would explain the window and the creeper."

"But not the fire." I banged my hand on the kitchen counter, causing both of them to jump. "Damn it! I can't help feeling it's all right there in front of me, and I know I'm missing something."

Ida Belle placed her hand on my arm. "We're going to figure this out. Nothing is going to happen to Ally. Not on our watch."

A felt a sense of relief run through me as she spoke. No one I'd ever known backed up their word like Ida Belle. She was right. If someone wanted Ally, they'd have to go through the three of us. I almost felt sorry for anyone who tried.

Almost.

"The sun's going down," I said. "We should get ready to head over to Floyd's."

"I'll check the front," Gertie said and hurried off to the living room. A couple seconds later, she called out, "Houston, we have a problem."

Ida Belle and I hurried to the front to peer out of the blinds.

"Across the street three houses down," Gertie said. "That brown sedan doesn't belong to Beatrice or her daughter, but it's parked in front of her house."

I squinted, trying to get a better look at the car in the diminishing daylight. Two figures were in the front seat, and from the build of the shoulders, I was positive they were men.

"It's the FBI," I said and stepped back from the window.

"What?" Gertie stared at me. "Why are they watching Floyd's house? Surely they don't think the killer is going to return?"

"I'm sure they don't," I said, "but my guess is they've stationed a couple of Bureau Babies in the car as a cover-your-ass thing. I kinda figured they would."

Ida Belle nodded. "So those guys won't be the same two who went to see Carter this morning?"

"Not likely," I said. "Senior agents are usually in charge of an investigation. Juniors do the grunt work."

"Like sitting in a car staring at an empty house all night?" Gertie said. "Sounds riveting."

"We all have to start somewhere," I said.

Gertie raised one eyebrow. "I bet that's not how you started."

"Ah. Well, I was a bit of an overachiever."

Ida Belle snorted. "Like we didn't already know. You think

they're going to be there all night?"

"Probably, but it doesn't matter. They won't leave the car unless they see movement in the house. We just have to make sure the blinds are closed and don't direct your flashlight toward a window. As long as no one is on the bayou, we should be able to get in and out without anyone being the wiser."

Ida Belle nodded. "The fishermen should all be packed up and gone soon if they aren't already. I saw a couple of boats on the stretch behind Ally's house from her bedroom window, but unless someone's using a broad beam light, we should be able to avoid any traffic that might come down the bayou once it's dark."

"We've got about five minutes till sundown," Gertie said.

"Then let's get ready to do this," I said. I grabbed the purse I'd brought with me and pulled out three sets of gloves. Once we'd donned our gloves, I handed out flashlights. "I've got a hammer and a pry bar, in case Floyd got ambitious with the fence."

Gertie snorted. "More likely he propped it back up like it was before."

I pulled the strap for the bag over my shoulder. "Let's go see, shall we?"

We exited Ally's house through the back door, locking it behind us. That way, if anything went wrong, her house wasn't compromised. The barest sliver of moonlight lit the backyard and we hurried to the back fence and let ourselves through the iron gate. I scanned the bayou as we crept to Floyd's fence, but it was clear of any traffic. When we got to the fence panel that had fallen before, I gave it a gentle shove. It wobbled, so I shoved harder and the entire thing fell into Floyd's backyard.

"It's a good thing he never mows," Ida Belle said. "All the weeds helped cushion the sound of it falling."

I scanned the dimly lit backyard, looking for any sign of movement. "You guys see anything?"

Gertie shook her head. "No FBI agents. No bobcats."

Ida Belle snorted. "You wouldn't be able to see either of them unless they were standing in front of you under a spotlight. But no, I don't see anything."

"Follow me." I walked across the panel and started down the right side fence line, following it all the way to the house. I checked the back window, but it was locked, so I moved onto the porch and jiggled the doorknob. It was the cheap and old sort, so I pulled a screwdriver out of my bag and made quick work of it.

I inched the back door open and poked my head inside. The FBI had left a light on in the stairwell, and it cast a glow over the kitchen and living room, which were open to each other. It didn't take a second to see they'd also been through everything. I stepped inside, motioning Ida Belle and Gertie to follow me, and stared, disgusted, at the mess.

Every drawer in the kitchen had been pulled from its slot, the contents dumped on the kitchen counter or floor. Every container had been upended and items pulled out of all the cabinets, the broken remnants littering the floor.

"They do delicate work," Ida Belle said.

"Typical," I said. "And clumsy. When you search a house like you're driving a plow, you tend to miss things that are important."

"Have you had many dealings with the FBI?" Ida Belle asked.

"Not really. The, uh…serious aspects of my job only occur in other countries. But I talk to a cop at the range back home. He's always bitching about the FBI." I scanned the mess and sighed. "Let's see if we can find anything the FBI missed."

I started at one end of the kitchen counter, Gertie at the other. Ida Belle headed into the living room.

"They ripped the cushions on the couch and tore out all the stuffing," Ida Belle said. "What a mess."

I shook my head and started parsing through the mess on the counter—plastic forks and Styrofoam plates were scattered across the counter, and I pushed them toward the back in some semblance of a stack. Canned goods had been tossed onto the counter and the floor.

"Anything?" Gertie asked.

"He liked baked beans," I replied.

"And cigarettes," Gertie said. "There's four cartons in this cabinet."

"Did the man have any good habits?"

"People with good habits don't usually get capped," Gertie said. "I'm going to take a look at the dining room table."

I nodded. "I'll finish up here." I moved to the next section of counter, shoving cereal boxes to the side. My pulse ticked up a notch when I saw paperwork underneath. I picked the stack up and started flipping through it.

"You find something?" Ida Belle asked as she walked into the kitchen.

"Late notices, disconnect notices, insurance policy."

"Life insurance?"

I flipped back to the policy document. "No. Looks like homeowner's." I tossed the stack back on the cabinet. "All that does is tell us what we already know—that Floyd was broke and needed to put his hands on cash fast. What about the living room?"

Ida Belle held up a glass object. "Drug pipe. No drugs though."

"No money to buy them," I said. "I saw a couple of empty

shotgun shells in the sink. Do you think Floyd did his own refills?"

"Probably. Most of the hunters around here do. Is that important?"

"Not that I can see. I was just curious." I looked around the room and shook my head. "I've got to tell you, I'm at a loss. I don't have a single idea of what to do next. Not even a moronic, dangerous, almost-certain-to-fail one."

Ida Belle frowned. "Me either."

"Me three," Gertie said as she walked back into the kitchen.

Ida Belle glanced over at her. "If Gertie's out of harebrained ideas, then we're doomed."

Gertie leaned back against the kitchen counter. "I'm too depressed to argue."

"Hey," I said, "it was a long shot to begin with. We took a chance on it but it didn't pay off. Things could be a lot worse."

"Sure," Gertie said. "Like the FBI could come storming through the door, guns blazing, and arrest us all for breaking and entering."

The words had barely left her mouth when we heard a key turning in the front door lock.

Chapter Eighteen

Okay, so the FBI agents weren't exactly storming into the house, but it was enough to send us into a panicked flight for the back door. Gertie was closest but her reaction time wasn't as good as mine and Ida Belle's.

Ida Belle bolted around the counter with me right on her heels and practically shoved Gertie out the back door. As I reached back to smash the porch light with my hand, I heard someone shout at us to stop. I ran to the edge of the porch and leaped off, landing on Gertie, who'd already miscalculated the plunge.

Ida Belle and I each grabbed an arm and yanked her up from the ground, and we all took off at a dead run for the back fence. The moon had disappeared behind clouds, leaving only the tiniest sliver of light to illuminate our way, but that meant the FBI agents couldn't see us either. I increased my speed, hoping Ida Belle and Gertie were keeping at least 80 percent of my pace. Our only chance out of this was to lose them in the swamp.

As long as they didn't start shooting.

The words had no sooner flashed through my mind when the first gunshot sounded behind me. "Warning shot," I said as we ran. "The next one won't be."

I heard the FBI agents yelling behind us and knew they were in pursuit. I bolted across the fallen fence panel and set out into the swamp. The moon had reappeared, and a dim glow reflected off of the bayou, giving me a little light to operate by. Unfortunately, the FBI agents would have the same advantage.

I skirted the bayou and headed straight toward dense foliage, where I hoped I could lose them. One glance behind and I saw that Ida Belle and Gertie were keeping decent pace only twenty yards behind me. The agents hadn't yet breached the backyard. I focused on a hedge in front of me and pushed harder, my thighs burning with the effort.

When I was five feet away, the growl I'd hoped never to hear again echoed through the swamp, and I tried to put on the brakes. As I slid to a stop, the bobcat launched out of the bushes and ran directly for me. I whirled around and took off in the opposite direction, flying right by a stunned Ida Belle and Gertie. But I had a plan. Sort of. Maybe.

"Keep running," I told them as I passed.

I heard them continue behind me, and pulled out my flashlight, squinting to see Floyd's back fence in the moonlight. As soon as the FBI agents came around the back of the fence and into the swamp, I flicked on my flashlight and trained it on the ground in front of the bobcat, swirling it around on the swamp grass and praying that wildcats and domesticated cats shared some of the same affinities.

The bobcat immediately locked in on the beam of light and pounced. I moved the light away and he took off after it at a dead run…straight toward the FBI agents.

I heard one of them scream, a very girlie scream, but I didn't really have the time to enjoy it.

The bobcat let out a growl that sounded ten times bigger than the animal should be able to manage, and headed directly for the girlie screamer.

"It's a mountain lion! Run!"

The agents scrambled to turn around, slamming into each

other in the process, then ran back into Floyd's yard. I waited long enough to see the bobcat follow them past the fence line, then took off after Ida Belle and Gertie.

We'd identified an escape trail as our backup plan before we went to Ally's house, and left Gertie's car parked at the curb where the trail ended in a vacant lot. We figured if everything went right, we would stroll down the sidewalk to the car and drive home. If things went wrong, we could run for our lives, then drive home. Just once, I wished a backup plan could go unused.

Once I'd traveled about fifty yards down the trail, I slowed enough to listen, but I couldn't hear anyone or anything traveling behind me. I sped up again, but not at the death pace I'd had before, and a couple minutes later, I burst out of the swamp and into the vacant lot. Ida Belle and Gertie were hunched over beside the car, and as I approached, I could hear Gertie wheezing.

"I...may...die," Gertie huffed.

"You're not going to die," Ida Belle said, less winded than Gertie, but clearly spent. "Let's get out of here."

Gertie dug the keys out of her pocket and held them up. "I'm too exhausted and dizzy to drive."

I grabbed them and jumped into the driver's seat, then directed the Cadillac straight for my house. We were a sad lot, shuffling up the sidewalk to the front door. I had my arm under Gertie, helping keep her upright as we walked up the porch steps, then I leaned her against the side of the house while I unlocked the door. Once inside, we all collapsed on the living room furniture.

For several minutes, the only sounds in the living room were of the three of us breathing and the occasional mumble of "I'm going to die" from Gertie. When I'd recovered enough to consider moving, I went into the kitchen and fetched bottles of water for everyone. Ida Belle and Gertie gratefully took the water and I plopped back down on the couch and took a sip.

"Brain freeze!" Gertie yelled and clutched her forehead with one hand.

Ida Belle shook her head. "She does it every time."

Gertie lifted her hand about an inch off the armrest and gave Ida Belle a wobbly middle finger.

Ida Belle, who was in infinitely better shape and recovering much quicker than Gertie, sat up in her chair and looked over at me. "So what happened? I couldn't really hear much while I was running, but I thought I heard a scream."

I nodded and told them about my flashlight trick with the bobcat. By the time I was done, Ida Belle was doubled over laughing and Gertie was laughing so hard, she was back to gasping for air.

"I wish I could have seen it," Ida Belle said, wiping the tears from her eyes. "I bet the look on their faces was priceless."

"I couldn't really see that well," I said, "but based on the screaming, it probably would have made great video."

A knock on my door interrupted our giggling and I froze. "Crap. I bet the FBI called Carter."

Gertie, who was slumped over the side of her chair, waved a hand in dismissal. "I'm too tired to lie. Let him throw us in jail. Probably be the best sleep I've gotten in weeks."

I couldn't disagree but somehow, giving up our secrets that easily didn't feel right to me. I'd promised Carter I'd stay out of his investigation, and the fact that it was no longer his was a point the three of us used to justify our actions, but I had a feeling that Carter wouldn't see things the same way.

I got up from the couch and went over to open the door. Sure enough, Carter was standing there, but unlike all the other times he'd shown up after one of our master plans had fallen apart, this time he didn't look perturbed.

"Hi, everyone. Is Ally here?" he asked as he followed me into the living room. Ida Belle said hello and Gertie lifted one hand up before dropping it back into her lap.

"No," I said, "she's on a date with David."

"Really?" he said. "Good for her."

"Why?" I asked. "Is something wrong?"

"Not really. There was a bit of an, uh…situation at Floyd's house tonight, and I thought I'd check in on her. I had no reason to assume anything was wrong. I was just wanting to make myself feel better."

I plopped back down on the couch. "What kind of situation?"

"The two FBI agents assigned to watch Floyd's house said three people broke into it. The agents ran right into them when they went in to give everything a check."

"Did they catch the burglars?"

"No. They got out the back door and ran into the swamp. The agents chased after them but were intercepted."

"By what?"

"Floyd's friendly bobcat." Carter's mouth twitched and the grin he'd been holding in finally broke through. "They claim a mountain lion tried to eat them and chased them back into Floyd's house. They managed to get the door closed before the cat got in, then they called the sheriff's department for backup. They refused to leave Floyd's house until I arrived and escorted them to their car, where they will probably sit the rest of the night, refusing to leave, even if they have to pee."

We all laughed, and Carter looked even more pleased.

"They'll probably ask for transfers," Ida Belle said. "Then maybe they'll be out of your hair."

Carter nodded. "One can only hope. Well, I've got some things to do before I can clock out."

I hopped up from the couch and followed him to the front door. He stepped onto the porch and turned around to look at me. I knew that look.

I sighed. "Is this where you accuse me of breaking into Floyd's house?"

"Plausible deniability." He winked at me and left.

I shut the door and walked back into the living room.

Gertie gave a wistful sigh. "He may be the perfect man."

Ida Belle shook her head. "He's a man, so definitely not perfect. But I'll give you dangerously close."

I smiled. Good enough for me.

It was close to midnight when Ally returned home. Ida Belle and Gertie had stuck around, wanting to hear about the date firsthand. I had the fixings for nachos, so I'd made us a batch while Gertie whipped up some brownies. Then we put on an *X-Files* marathon because Gertie wanted me to see how real FBI agents should behave when faced with something out of the ordinary. The nachos and brownies were excellent, and I have to admit, I enjoyed the *X-Files*, although I quickly figured out that the real reason Gertie loved the show is because she thought Mulder was "smoking hot."

We were stuffed, happy, and relaxed by the time Ally let herself in the front door, carrying an armful of tulips. She called out a greeting and took a seat in the living room. Her expression was pleasant enough, but she didn't look like a woman who'd just been out with the man of her dreams.

"So how did it go?" I asked.

"All right," she said.

I glanced over at Ida Belle, who raised an eyebrow.

"Only all right?" I asked.

She frowned. "Yes. No. I'm not sure."

"Why don't you start from the beginning?" Ida Belle said. "You met at the General Store…"

"He brought me tulips," Ally said and lifted the flowers.

"And here I thought you'd gotten those for me," I joked.

"They're beautiful," Gertie said.

Ally nodded. "I've always loved them."

"Did he take you to dinner?" I asked.

She smiled. "He took me to Luigi's in New Orleans, which is my favorite Italian restaurant, and then we had pastries at Bernice's Bakery, another of my old haunts from when I lived in the city. They have the absolute best pastries."

Her smile slowly slipped away and she fingered the ribbon tied around the flowers.

"But?" I prompted.

She perked back up a bit. "He's nice and mannered and so cute. And God knows, there's a shortage of men who fit that description in the entire state, much less in Sinful."

"But?"

Her shoulders slumped. "Something doesn't work. I can't put my finger on why. On paper, he seems perfect."

"Hearts don't run on logic," Gertie said. "If the spark isn't there, it just isn't."

She sighed. "Maybe that's it. I don't know. Sometimes I think it's all me. That this is the worst time for me to attempt to date. Here I am living with Fortune, worried that someone will try to burn down my house again. Worried about the creeper. Worried about who killed Floyd. Maybe I shouldn't have agreed to go with so much else on my mind."

"It's all right, dear," Ida Belle said. "You can always try

again later on when things settle down. You'll have a better idea then whether or not it was the situation or David."

She nodded, but didn't look convinced. "Maybe you're right. I feel like such a bitch. Here's this great guy who wants to spend time with me, and I couldn't even muster up enough excitement about him to even agree to a second date."

"He asked you for another date?" I asked.

"Yeah. He wanted us to see a movie this weekend, but I told him I'd have to check my schedule first."

"Ouch," Gertie said. "The big blow-off."

"I know," Ally said, looking miserable. "I felt horrible when I said it, and *so* cliché. But I didn't want to come right out and say no, just in case I was feeling that way because of everything going on right now."

"He's a grown man," Ida Belle said. "Don't you be putting pressure on yourself about this. When you're ready to take on a relationship, you'll do it, and not one second before."

I nodded. "She's right. The last thing you need is more to deal with. If he asks again, tell him you want to put everything on hold until this mess with the fire is over and done with."

Ally smiled at us. "I love you guys. So let's change the subject—did you find anything at my house?"

I glanced over at Ida Belle, who frowned. The three of us had already agreed that Ally needed to know about the window, but none of us looked forward to telling her. "We found something," I said, and told her about the unlocked window.

Ally's eyes widened and her mouth flew open. "Oh my God. If it wasn't you guys telling me, I wouldn't even believe it. I've never even heard of something like this."

"I've never heard of it either," Ida Belle said. "It's most disconcerting."

I nodded. "Can you think of anyone who's been inside your

house lately—someone who would have been left alone long enough to tamper with the window locks?"

"No," she said. "Aside from Aunt Celia, I don't think anyone's been in the house since Mama moved."

"Repairman? Cable guy?" Ida Belle asked.

She shook her head. "After I got the power of attorney, I had all of Mama's accounts changed over to my name. I haven't changed any of the services and haven't needed any repairs."

"What about spare keys?" I asked.

"I keep a spare in one of my kitchen drawers."

"Does anyone else have one?"

"Only Aunt Celia. I changed the locks after Mama moved, because I wasn't sure who she might have given a key to. Couldn't someone have broken in the back door while I was gone?"

"Sure," I said. "Unfortunately, between the damage caused by the fire and the firemen, it would be hard to detect if the back door had been jimmied. Can you remember the last time you opened the windows?"

She scrunched her brow. "It's been too humid to open them for circulation. The last time must have been when I burned a piecrust. Yes, that's it. I opened all the kitchen windows to try to get the smoke out. That was about two weeks ago."

I nodded. "At least that narrows down the frame of time it could have happened in."

"Does that really help?" Ally asked.

She looked so upset that it made my heart clench. No one as nice as her should ever have this many bad things happening around them. It wasn't fair, and it pissed me off. "Don't worry. We'll have the construction crew replace the window and change all the locks on the house. I know a couple of things about hardware. I'll make sure we get you the best sets of locks money can buy."

"And I'll talk to Walter about a security system," Ida Belle said. "He had one installed at the General Store last month. He can give us a contact."

Ally sniffed and rubbed her nose with the back of her hand. "I don't know what I'd do without you guys looking out for me."

Suddenly, a thought hit me and I groaned. "We're not that efficient. I forgot your bag at your house."

"That's okay," Ally said. "I can get it tomorrow. Given the situation with the window, I can totally see how it would have slipped your mind."

I wanted to tell her about the FBI agents and the bobcat, because it was certain to cheer her up, but I wasn't certain Ida Belle and Gertie wanted more people knowing about it than already did. I glanced over at Ida Belle, who nodded.

I could barely contain myself. "That wasn't the reason I forgot it. In fact, I didn't really forget it at all as much as I couldn't risk going back to get it."

Ally stared at me for a moment, then looked over at Ida Belle and Gertie, who were already smiling. "Oh no. What did you do?"

I launched into the story about our futile break-in at Floyd's house and the chase through the swamp. Ally was already smiling, but when I got to the part about the flashlight and the bobcat, she started giggling so hard, her face turned red and her entire body shook.

"Oh my God," she said when I finished. "I would have paid a million dollars to see that."

"And then Carter came by," I said and filled her in on what happened with the agents and Carter's parting words to me.

"What a great ending to a weird day," Ally said. She rose from the chair. "I'm completely wiped out. I have the lunch and afternoon shift at Francine's tomorrow. If it's the last thing I do, I'm going to sleep in." She grinned. "Which probably means seven a.m."

She gave us all a wave and headed upstairs. Ida Belle got up and stretched. Gertie tried to get up but fell back into the chair.

"My knees," she cried. "My back. My ankles."

I rose from the couch, already feeling the tightening in my thighs, and extended a hand to help pull Gertie out of the chair. "I prescribe a hot bath for all of us."

Ida Belle nodded. "We're going to really be feeling this tomorrow."

"Tomorrow?" Gertie complained. "I'm feeling it now."

"Tomorrow you'll be comatose," Ida Belle said as they walked out the door.

I closed the door behind them and locked it, thinking about everything that had happened that day and what it all meant. I knew the solution to everything lay somewhere in the jumbled mess of information I had. Sometimes a flicker of a thought would spark in my mind but before I could lock on, it was gone as quickly as it had appeared.

I hoped the flicker would be stronger after a good night's sleep.

Assuming such a thing could be had in Sinful.

Chapter Nineteen

Ally was still sleeping when I woke up the next morning. I'd taken a shower and the world's longest bath the night before, so I pulled on shorts, T-shirt, and tennis shoes and crept out of the house, hoping Ally would get her late-morning sleeping in. She'd managed to hide the dark circles under her eyes for her date the night before, but I knew they were still there. She needed more rest before she hit exhaustion.

I left her a note and the keys to my Jeep, just in case I got caught up in town and didn't make it back in time to drive her to work, then headed outside and did some stretches to limber up my legs and back. Surprisingly, my thighs weren't nearly as tight as I'd expected them to be, so I set off on my jog around the neighborhood and past the park, but my uncontrollable curiosity had me changing my usual path and jogging by Ally's house.

The brown sedan was gone and no sign of the FBI remained. I wondered if the agents would be posted at the house again tonight or if they'd finally decided there was nothing in Floyd's house to return for. Granted, we hadn't gotten a chance to search upstairs, but it was a long shot we would have found anything useful anyway, especially with the way the FBI had tossed the house.

I made a wide sweep back around in the other direction, then circled the park and headed toward Main Street. It was almost eight o'clock and my stomach was sending me not-so-subtle reminders that I'd been up for an hour, not to mention exercising, and hadn't given it any fuel to run on.

The usual morning crowd was already seated at Francine's and the smell of homemade biscuits almost had me weeping by the time I took my seat in the corner. An older waitress everyone called Dixie came over to my table with a cup of coffee.

"Did your exercise this morning, did ya?" she asked, with one of the thickest Southern drawls I'd ever heard.

"Almost a good hour of it," I said.

She shook her head. "Then you must be near starving. What can I get you?"

"Hmmm," I said, taking a minute to consider. If I ordered what I really wanted, all that glorious exercise would be wasted, but by the same token, by virtue of all that exercise, if I ate something horrible for breakfast, it would be a wash.

"I'll have the chicken-fried steak and eggs," I said finally.

"Pancakes?"

"Not today," I said. It seemed like a reasonable compromise.

I settled back with my cup of coffee and glanced around the café. The real estate agent wasn't anywhere in sight and I wondered if he'd finally given up and headed somewhere else to find property. Sinful seemed like a long shot for commercial properties to begin with, but what did I know?

By the time Dixie returned with my breakfast, I was so hungry I barely managed to maintain some standards as I dug into the chicken-fried steak. Without pausing, I plowed through the entire plate of steak, eggs, and hash browns, pausing only to sip my coffee and breathe. I'd just polished off the last bite when Carter walked in.

He zeroed right in on me and strode across the café. "Almost done?" he asked as he stepped up to my table.

"You saved me from embarrassing myself by licking the plate."

He smiled, but I could tell it was forced. Something was wrong. I looked around him. "No FBI tail?"

He shook his head. "I got a message this morning that they had business elsewhere and would check in with me later. If you're done, would you mind coming over to the sheriff's department with me?"

"You're not going to put me in jail, are you?"

"Of course not, but I need to talk to you and I don't want anyone overhearing."

I pulled some money out of my pocket and left it on the table, then followed him out of the café and across the street to the sheriff's department. I gave Deputy Breaux a nod as we walked by, but instead of turning down the hallway to his office, Carter headed into the room where the back door was located and walked outside.

I followed him out the back door and down the steps of the small back porch wondering what in the world was going on. He walked around the edge of the porch and pointed at the back wall of the building.

"See that charred spot on the porch railing?"

I took another step forward and located the foot-long discolored spot on the weathered wooden railing. "Yeah, but I don't understand why—"

It hit me like a freight train and I whipped around to face him.

"Someone tried to set fire to the sheriff's department?"

Carter nodded.

"But that's insane!"

"Yeah, but it doesn't make it any less true."

I looked back at the porch railing, unable to get control of my shock. "How come it did so little damage?"

"I was here late last night, working on some paperwork up front with Myrtle. I went back to my office to get some information I needed to finish up a file and heard a noise out back. By the time I got out the back door, the side of the building was in flames. I jumped off the porch, grabbed the water hose, and managed to get it out before it spread to the porch or the siding on the second floor."

"Did you see the arsonist?"

"No. I assume he took off when he heard me coming."

I studied the building again. "You said the side of the building was in flames...you mean the brick?" The entire first floor of the sheriff's department was constructed from brick. The second-floor siding and the tiny porch were the only things constructed with wood.

"Yeah. Stupid, right? It's like he threw the gasoline on the wall and lit it up, but why would you do that if you want to burn a building down?"

I shook my head. "You'd think he would have tossed the gasoline on the porch, not the wall above it." I stared at the wall and frowned. It was so illogical that it seemed pointless. Only an idiot would think he could burn brick.

And then a thought flickered in the back of my mind, but this time, I latched onto it. At first, it seemed weak and stupid, but as the seconds ticked by it made more sense. An idiot. The gasoline splashed too high. I turned to Carter and said, "I know who the arsonist is."

"You're kidding."

I shook my head. "Remember you told me about the guy who burned his house down with his grill? Who was that?"

"Billy Vincent."

My pulse quickened. "Buckshot Billy. He wasn't trying to

soak the brick. He was trying to splash the gas on the porch but he has horrible aim. The night I went to the Swamp Bar, he hit me right in the face with an entire bucket of water. The bartender got onto him for aiming too high, which was apparently his norm. Just like here."

Carter stared at me, clearly uncertain what to think. "You're saying Billy is the arsonist."

"Yes."

"Why burn down Ally's house? Why the sheriff's department?"

"I don't know, but I'd be willing to bet it's not as random as it seems. Billy doesn't strike me as someone who makes his own decisions. Someone is pulling the strings."

Carter shook his head. "That's some thin evidence."

"I don't think it matters. My guess is if you question Billy, he'll tell you everything you want to know."

Carter stared at the back of the building once more, then looked back at me. "Then I guess we better go talk to Billy."

Carter made a couple of phone calls and found out that Billy had been living in his camp since the unfortunate incident with his house, so we headed to the dock for a ten-minute ride up the bayou to Billy's camp. A ragged-looking flat-bottom boat was tied to a post in front of what could only charitably be called a shack.

I tapped Carter on the shoulder and pointed to the porch. A plastic bucket and a gas can sat next to the steps. As soon as the thought had hit me, I'd known I was right about Billy being the arsonist, but I was happy to see confirmation staring at us before we even docked.

Carter looked down at the bucket and gas can as we walked

up the porch steps and shook his head. He knocked on a piece of plywood serving as a door and we heard movement inside. Several seconds later, the door swung open and a blurry-eyed Billy stared out at us.

"What's up?" He blinked a couple of times then stared at me. "Hey, you're Best Boobs."

"Yeah," I said. "I'm so glad you recognized me."

Carter looked over at me, his expression grim. If Billy was sitting in jail, there was a much bigger chance he might tell someone about Floyd chasing me out of the Swamp Bar, and all within hearing distance of the FBI.

"I need to talk to you," Carter said. "In an official capacity."

Billy gave him a blank stare.

"He means he's going to ask you questions as a deputy," I explained, "which means you need to tell the truth."

Billy's eyes widened. "Oh, yeah, of course!"

Carter pointed to the bucket and gasoline can. "Tell me about the fires you've been starting."

I don't know what I expected. Maybe for him to dash out the back door and us to pursue him into the swamp. Maybe for him to simply deny everything. Maybe for him to make up some ridiculous story that only a five-year-old would find plausible.

But he did the one thing I would never, ever have guessed.

He smiled. "What do you want to know?"

Carter blinked. "So you admit to starting the fires?"

"Sure. That's my new job. Came at just the right time, too. I need a new boat and truck, but the check from the insurance company isn't going to be enough for both."

"You mean the insurance money you'll collect for your house fire?" Carter asked.

Billy nodded. "Yeah. It wasn't worth a whole lot. It was old and small, and that guy from the insurance company said it was in a state of dis…disre…"

"Disrepair?" I offered.

"Yeah, that's it!"

No surprise there. If his camp and boat were any indication of his maintenance standards, the house was probably falling in around him.

"You said setting the fires was your new job," Carter continued. "Did someone pay you to set the fires?"

Billy looked confused. "It ain't really a job if you don't get paid."

"Who paid you to set fire to Ally's house?" Carter asked.

Billy stared down at the ground and shuffled his feet. "That one was an accident. I thought I read the address right, but I messed up the numbers like I sometimes do."

My pulse quickened as everything fell into place—the unprofessional nature of the fire, Floyd's alibi, and the home insurance policy he'd had out on his kitchen counter. "You were supposed to set Floyd's house on fire, not Ally's."

Billy looked up at us, wearing a sheepish expression. "Yeah. Floyd insisted it had to be done that night but he was going to settle up some outstanding tickets in New Orleans and figured he'd get tossed in the clink, so he asked me to do it."

Carter narrowed his eyes at Billy. "He just walked up to you and asked you to set his house on fire?"

"Nah, it wasn't exactly like that. We was shooting the shit over at the Swamp Bar. Floyd was saying as how he needed to get a hold of a lot of money fast. He tried to sell his house some time back to a weird guy with a funny accent, but the guy said it wouldn't work unless both houses were for sale."

"Was the weird guy a real estate agent?" I asked, figuring I already knew the answer. Aside from me, there was only one other person in Sinful that the locals would deem having a "funny accent."

"Yeah, I think that's what he said. Agent, or something like that."

"Floyd needed money?" Carter prompted.

Billy nodded. "So I told him about how I was getting a big check because I'd burned my house down."

"And Floyd offered to pay you to burn his house down?"

"Yep. On account of him maybe being in jail."

I glanced at Carter. Maybe, my butt. Floyd made sure he had an airtight alibi for when the fire occurred. It just hadn't gone exactly as he'd planned.

"What happened when he found out you set the wrong house on fire?" I asked.

"He was so mad. I thought he was going to throttle me right there. Said that was his last chance to get the money or they was going to kill him. Then he said because I was stupid, he was going to have to make a deal with the devil to get out of this mess."

Carter and I looked at each other. "The FBI," we both said.

It made perfect sense. Whoever Floyd owed had decided to either cut their losses or make an example of him, just as Ida Belle had suggested. The FBI had probably been trying to make a case against whomever he owed and offered him a deal to get out of the trouble.

"So the guys Floyd owed must have found out about his deal with the FBI," I said.

Carter nodded. "I said from the beginning that I thought they already knew who killed him. I guess I was right." Carter looked back at Billy. "What about the sheriff's department? Why that building?"

"That weird guy was in the bar when Floyd yelled at me about getting the houses wrong. He said he knew a guy who wanted to buy the sheriff's building, and that if you had the money to move into the old firehouse, everyone would be happy."

"He paid you to start the fire?" Carter asked.

"Not exactly. I mean, he said if something happened to make you move, then he could buy the building, and if that happened, there was something in it for me."

I glanced at Carter, and could see he was thinking what I was. I had no doubt the real estate agent was behind Billy's fire-starting project, but it would be hard to make a case against him since no money had exchanged hands.

"Who the hell is this guy?" Carter asked.

"He's a real estate agent," I said. "I talked to him in town one day and got a strange vibe from him, so I looked him up. He specializes in commercial properties. Ally said he tried to buy her house after her mother moved, but Ally wasn't interested in selling."

"I don't get it," Carter said. "Why that house?"

"I didn't get it at first, but I think I have an idea. Billy said Floyd tried to sell his house, but the guy wanted both of them. Then he figured if he could get you to move out, he'd buy the sheriff's department building. I think he wanted the building for the same reason you won't move—access to the bayou."

"You think his client wants water access?"

I nodded. "His list of clients was mostly importers. Sinful Bayou does eventually run into the Gulf, right?"

Carter's expression cleared. "And a location in Sinful is a lot cheaper than a location in New Orleans."

"Exactly. I offered him Marge's house and he said he needed something more remote but specified that it still had to have city services. The sheriff's department building sits a bit away from everything on Main Street, so it would be perfect."

"Unbelievable," Carter said.

I nodded. "Everything makes sense now. Except…"

"The creeper," Carter finished. He looked at Billy. "Have you been sneaking around Ms. uh, Boobs's house late at night?"

Billy's eyes widened. "No. I don't even know her real name, much less where she lives. Besides, I wouldn't spy on a lady. My momma raised me better than that."

"See," I said. "A man with standards."

Carter sighed. "I appreciate you being honest with us, Billy, but I'm going to have to take you down to the sheriff's department and book you."

"What? Why? I ain't done nothing wrong!" Billy's shock was completely genuine.

"You just admitted to setting two buildings on fire," Carter said.

"But I set my own house on fire and the insurance company said as long as I paid my premiums, I'd still get the check. I thought it was okay."

Carter closed his eyes and I wondered if he was weighing the option of arresting Billy against the option of shooting him in case a woman ever wanted to have his children and continue the bloodline.

"You didn't burn down your own house on purpose," Carter explained. "That's why you weren't in trouble. But it's illegal to burn down a building on purpose. That's arson."

"But Floyd didn't say nothing about no arson."

"I'm sure he didn't," Carter said, "but that doesn't change the facts. I have to arrest you. You can call a lawyer down at the sheriff's department, or I'll get the public defender's office to send someone."

A totally defeated Billy trudged out of the shack and down the porch steps. Carter grabbed the bucket and gasoline tank and we headed after him.

"All of this," Carter said, "because Floyd was a good-for-nothing petty criminal and Billy's an idiot."

"Not all of it," I said. "Billy's not the creeper, and I think the creeper is a bigger problem than we originally thought."

Carter stopped walking and looked at me. "What do you mean?"

I told him about our search of Ally's house yesterday and the rigged window. His worry was so apparent it might as well have been broadcast. He ran his free hand through his hair and blew out a breath. "That is so far beyond the scope of a Peeping Tom. It's stalking."

"I know."

He looked over at Billy, who was climbing in the sheriff's boat, then back at me. "Let me get him booked, then I want us to go over every single thing we know about the creeper. Can you stick around?"

"Of course."

He started off again for the boat and I fell in step behind him. A few days ago, I'd been convinced that nothing else in Sinful could surprise me.

I'd been wrong.

Chapter Twenty

It took Carter forty-five minutes to complete the booking paperwork, thirty to contact the public defender's office and explain the mess, and an hour to calm Billy down enough to stop wailing like banshee. I had my doubts the quieter sniveling would last for long, so I was beyond happy when Carter suggested we head to Francine's for a late lunch. Even at full capacity, it had to be more peaceful than the sheriff's department.

Besides, I'd been itching for the past two hours to call Ally and tell her we'd caught the arsonist. It was one worry she could scratch off her list. But Carter insisted that the conversation was one better had in person and that it would be better all the way around if he got Billy booked before the story spread through Sinful. I'd spent the entire time surfing the Internet and checking the clock every couple of minutes.

"I got an email from the FBI while I was talking to the public defender," Carter said as we exited the sheriff's department. "They arrested Floyd's killer."

"Who was it?"

"One of the Hebert family guys. Name of Marco Sabien."

"That's him! Billy said the weird guy in the bar who was looking for Floyd was named Marco. He was the one who took my shoe." I frowned. "Do you think I'm going to have a problem?"

"Doubtful. Someone popped him as they were transferring

him to lockup. Shot him as they were crossing the parking lot—Marco walking right in between two FBI agents."

"Holy crap!"

"It sounds like a big mess, but I doubt they pursue it any further. There's no point."

"Wow."

As we crossed the street, Gertie's ancient Cadillac pulled into a parking space in front of the café and Gertie and Ida Belle climbed out. They saw us and waited as we headed over.

"We caught the arsonist," I said, unable to hold in the good news any longer. "And the FBI got the guy who killed Floyd."

"What?"

"Who?"

They both spoke at once.

I smiled and Carter and I filled them in on the Marco situation first, then on the fire at the sheriff's department and my water bucket leap that turned out to be correct. When we were done, they both shook their heads.

"I always knew Billy would wind up in trouble," Gertie said. "He was always too gullible."

Ida Belle nodded. "Floyd and that real estate guy definitely took advantage of poor Billy. With any luck, a jury will see the boy's a dimwit and go easy on him."

"He's got no priors," Carter said, "and I'm sure some people would testify to his, uh, shortcomings in the mental department. It's possible he could get off with probation. It really depends on how much pressure Ally's insurance company puts on the prosecutor."

"I bet Ally is relieved," Gertie said.

"She doesn't know yet," I said. "We were just on our way to tell her and have some lunch."

"We were too," Gertie said. "Can we join you?"

Ida Belle elbowed Gertie in the ribs, and Gertie gave her a dirty look. "They probably have things to discuss alone," Ida Belle said and glared at Gertie.

Gertie glared back for a moment, then her eyes widened. "Oh, right. Never mind. You two go on about your business."

I shook my head. "Actually, I told Carter about the window at Ally's house and we were going to go over the facts on the creeper case. If you don't mind talking stalkers over lunch, you might be able to help."

"Of course we don't mind," Ida Belle said. "We'll do anything we can to help Ally."

"Ha!" Carter laughed. "Don't I know it? Farmer Frank is hounding me for that motorcycle owner. He wants to send a bill for the chicken coop. I don't suppose you can help me out with that?"

Ida Belle shrugged. "Don't have a clue."

Carter shook his head and we all headed into the café. The lunch rush was over, but the café was still half full. We managed to find a four-top in a back corner at least one table apart from the other patrons and took our seats. A couple seconds later, Francine popped out to take our drink order.

"Where's Ally?" I asked.

"She had to take off early," Francine said. "Her insurance adjuster called and needed to get inside her house. Lunch rush was almost over, so I figured I could cover until she got back."

Gertie looked confused. "I thought I saw her car parked out back when we were unloading some donation boxes for the church."

Francine nodded. "It wouldn't start. That cute new fireman took a look but said she probably needed a new battery. He gave her a lift. Y'all want sweet tea?"

We all nodded and Francine headed to the kitchen. "Oh

well," I said, feeling disappointed. "I guess we'll have to tell her when she's done with the insurance adjuster."

Ida Belle nodded. "So about the creeper…"

We started our discussion about the creeper, pausing only long enough to give Francine our food order. I covered the facts as I knew them, leaving out, of course, the unfortunate rock salt incident. I was taking that one to the grave. Carter filled in with the minimal information he had, then we all started throwing out ideas.

By the time our lunch arrived, we'd exhausted every conceivable possibility and weren't a bit closer to figuring out who the creeper was. The sad part was aside from a handful of people, the creeper could be anyone in Sinful, including the sleazy real estate agent whose cell phone was conveniently going straight to voice mail.

"Maybe it was Billy," Gertie said.

"He said he didn't know where I lived, and I think he was telling the truth." Billy was clearly a moron, but he didn't strike me as the type of guy who'd stalk a woman. Of course, given his limited mental capacity, he might not see it that way. I shook my head. "I just don't get the stalker vibe from him."

"What about Floyd?" Gertie asked. "I got all kinds of bad vibes from him."

"True," I said. "There's nothing I would put past Floyd."

"He had the easiest access to Ally's house," Ida Belle said.

Carter nodded. "Given that he was desperate for money, Floyd is the most likely explanation for the window. He might have thought he could lift cash or jewelry while the house was empty. Maybe he rigged the window so he could return later and see police reports or insurance documents about the fire. He *was* killed in her backyard. I have no doubt that whoever he owed money to had him killed, but he had to be on Ally's property for some other reason."

I frowned. "I suppose you're right. But it still feels like we're missing something."

"You haven't seen the creeper since Floyd was murdered," Gertie pointed out.

"Yeah. That's true." All the facts lined up and pointed to Floyd. It made as much sense as anything else, but with Floyd dead, we'd never know for certain, and that bothered me. "Wait a minute. Floyd can't be the creeper because the first night the creeper came to my house, Floyd was in jail."

Gertie's face fell. "That's right."

"Maybe it was Billy after all," Ida Belle said. "Once he realized he set fire to the wrong house, he may have followed Ally to your house to try to get information for Floyd. Or even to make sure she was all right. He's silly enough to do something like that."

"I suppose it's a possible," I agreed. "He could have come lurking around my house after the fire to see if he could overhear Ally and me talking about it. Maybe that first night it *was* Billy and after that it was Floyd."

"The simplest explanation is usually the right one," Ida Belle said.

"I don't know that it's simple," Carter said, "but it's the closest we can get to logical. I think I need to have another conversation with Billy."

I nodded. The explanation covered all the bases, but my mind still hadn't committed to our conclusion.

The bells above the café door jangled and a woman about Ida Belle and Gertie's age walked in and looked around. Ida Belle poked Gertie and nodded toward the door before lifting her hand to wave. "Cora," Ida Belle called out.

The woman looked around until she locked onto Ida Belle,

then smiled. She crossed the café to our table, where both Ida Belle and Gertie rose to give her a hug and they made quick introductions. Carter jumped up.

"Let me get you a chair," he said.

"No, that's fine," Cora said. "I'm meeting a friend for lunch."

"I thought you'd moved to Virginia to be near your daughter," Gertie said.

Cora nodded. "About ten years ago, but Stanley is at that awful fishing tournament in New Orleans. He comes back for it as many years as I let him get away with it. Anyway, this year, I figured I'd make the trip with him and visit a few people."

Ida Belle nodded. "Are you still in touch with Edith Leger?"

"I talked to her cousin sometime last year. She's in a nursing home in Houston, but her dementia is so bad, she can't remember anyone."

"That's too bad," Ida Belle said.

"It's awful," Cora said. "I hope the Lord sees fit to take me before I get in such condition."

"Her grandson is living here now," Gertie said. "I bet Edith would have liked that."

Cora frowned. "You mean David?"

"Yes," Gertie said. "She only had the one grandson, right?"

"Far as I know, but I'm afraid you're confused. David is in the military. He lives in the Philippines."

Ida Belle frowned. "Maybe he finished his time. He hasn't been here very long."

Cora looked even more confused. "That's simply not possible. He just got married last week. My grandniece was in the wedding. David only had enough leave to come back to the States for the wedding. They were leaving the next morning to go back to the base."

"He knew all her favorite things." I felt the blood rush out of my head and I jumped up from the table. "David, or whoever he really is, is the creeper."

I grabbed Ida Belle's arm. "He knew her favorite restaurant and bakery. He brought her tulips."

"Oh my God," Ida Belle said.

Gertie paled. "Oh no! Ally turned him down for another date."

"And she's with him now," I said. "That dead battery was a setup, and I'll bet anything the phone call wasn't from her insurance agent."

Carter jumped up from his chair and called dispatch to put out an APB for David and Ally. Cora stood frozen in place, the horror of what we were talking about apparently sinking in.

"Do you have any idea where he would take her?" Carter asked.

I tried to focus on every single word I'd exchanged with the fake David. "He said he was renting an apartment above the preacher's garage."

Carter shook his head. "He knows that would be the first place we'd look. I'll send Deputy Breaux over there to check it out, but I don't think that's our answer."

"Okay," I said, trying to force my mind to think like a stalker. "We have to consider what his plan is for her."

"Men who kidnap women usually only have one plan," Ida Belle said, her voice grim.

"Wouldn't he just leave town?" Gertie asked.

"Maybe," Ida Belle said, "but it's a long stretch of highway between Sinful and New Orleans, and not a lot of places to hide in between."

"Unless you go into the marsh," Carter pointed out.

"But if he's not the real David," I said, "that means he

might not know much about Sinful or its surroundings."

Gertie nodded. "Then he'd take her somewhere he knew."

"Like her house," I said. "With Floyd dead, no one is around to see anything unusual."

"And with the insurance story," Ida Belle said, "no one would go looking for her for hours."

I pulled out my cell phone and dialed Ally, but it went straight to voice mail. I looked at Carter. "We have to get to Ally's house, and don't even try to leave us behind or we'll just follow you."

"Let's go," Carter said and we all dashed out of the café, leaving a stunned Cora behind.

Chapter Twenty-One

Carter pulled out of Main Street and raced into Ally's neighborhood. "I can't pull up to her house," he said. "He'll be on watch and he might kill her if he sees me."

"Park down the block past Floyd's house," I said. "The road bends toward the swamp and he won't be able to see your truck from any of the windows."

Carter eased around the block and parked at the curb just in front of a huge hedge. He looked at us. "I allowed you this far, but I have to ask you to stay here. I can't be responsible for anything happening to you."

"But we can help," Gertie argued.

Carter shook his head. "You'd only be in my way. Please, stay here and if you see or hear anything, call for backup."

He jumped out of the truck and hurried behind the hedge that bordered Floyd's yard and the swamp. As he disappeared into the hedge, I turned around. "I don't have my gun on me."

Ida Belle stared. "You're kidding."

"I was running this morning and didn't think I'd need it. I haven't been home since."

"It's a flimsy excuse," Gertie said, "but I suppose I can loan you one of mine." She reached into the enormous handbag she was never without and pulled out a 1911 .45 ACP.

"Good Lord," I said as I took the pistol from her. "That's serious firepower."

She reached back into the bag and brought out a Glock. "I'll take the lighter one if you don't mind."

"Do you have any more guns in there?"

Gertie shook her head. "Just some Mace, a hunting knife, and a bag of prunes."

It was no wonder her back was always killing her. "Ida Belle?"

Ida Belle pulled her nine-millimeter from her waistband and chambered the first round. "I think we should head through the swamp and approach from the back," she said.

I nodded and we jumped out of the truck and dashed into the swamp.

"I wonder if that bobcat is around," Gertie said.

I'd been thinking the same thing. "Let's hope he sleeps during the day."

It took us only a couple of minutes to make it to Ally's back fence line. "What do we do now?" Gertie asked. "There's only the shed and a couple of bushes."

Ida Belle shook her head. "It's not enough cover. Anyone looking out a back window will see you."

I scanned the backyard, knowing that they were right, but searching for an alternative. Then I zeroed in on the row of trees on the side of Ally's house opposite Floyd's. "I have an idea," I said and pointed to the trees. I could use one of the trees to get over the fence and access the rigged window on the side of the kitchen.

"What do you want us to do?" Ida Belle asked.

"Break into Floyd's house and go upstairs. See if you can see into Ally's house. If you get a lock on their position, text it to me. And be careful that he doesn't see you."

They nodded and hurried off. I moved farther into the swamp and skirted the wrought iron fence, using a set of bushes for coverage. I ran down the side of the wooden fence, then shoved the pistol into my sports bra before leaping up into the cypress tree. I climbed quickly, careful to remain on the back side of the tree until I was higher than the windows.

My phone vibrated and I clung to the tree with one arm while checking the message.

Shadows moving through curtains in Ally's room.

I stuck the phone back in my pocket and as I started to swing around the tree, I heard movement below me. I looked down and saw Carter slide over the top of the fence from Ally's front yard and hurry down the side of the house, ducking below the windows. When he got to the rigged kitchen window, he pushed it up and eased himself over and into the house with barely any sound.

Impressive.

But I didn't have time to wax poetic on Carter's skills. And following him through the window put two of us in the same position downstairs. What we needed was coverage from another angle. I pulled out my phone and sent Ida Belle a text.

Stay put with sight line to bedroom. If you get a shot at David, take it.

A couple seconds later, the reply came.

Damn straight.

I moved up a couple more branches, then swung around the tree trunk and ran across a large branch that hovered over Ally's roof. I swung myself down below the branch until my feet connected with the roof, then dropped onto the roof without a sound and slipped across it to the corner over the master bathroom at the end of the hallway from Ally's room.

I leaned over the side of the house and pulled on the drainpipe. It felt sturdy, so I swung over the edge of the roof and shinnied down it until I was next to the bathroom window. I tapped the glass with my finger and smiled. It was that frosted plastic stuff. I pulled out my keys and dug into the frame of the plastic, sliding my key along the edge until I loosened one side of it. Then I slipped my fingers beneath and pulled the entire piece out of the flimsy metal frame.

I dropped it into the bushes below me and swung my legs around and into the window. I clutched the top of the frame to slow my drop, then slid silently into the bathtub. As I crept into the master bedroom, my phone vibrated.

Nice. Still two shadows in Ally's bedroom.

I texted back.

Carter is somewhere in house. Careful if you shoot.

I peeked into the hallway and saw a shadow move at the bottom of the stairs. Carter. If I took the hallway, we'd intersect, and then I'd have to explain how I got into the house. I was pretty sure I'd claimed to have studied gymnastics at some point, but somehow I didn't think it would cover what I'd just done.

Then I remembered Gertie and Ally's conversation about the weird closet. I hurried over to the closet and eased the door open. No light entered from the other side, so I knew it was closed. I slipped into the closet and pulled the handgun from my sports bra. I inched through the closet, praying that the hardwood wouldn't creak.

When I reached the door, I put my ear against it, hoping to gauge the situation.

"This is all your fault," the stalker said. "All you had to do was like me, but you turned me down. You think you're too good for me, don't you?"

"No," Ally said. Her voice cracked and my pulse shot through the roof. If I got my hands on that guy, he would never breathe again.

"Then why wouldn't you go out with me again? I did

everything right. I got the right flowers, took you to the right restaurant. Why wasn't that good enough?"

"I already told you. I have a lot on my mind. I can't focus on a relationship right now."

"That's what they all say. All you bitches are alike. A guy gives up everything to follow you and do you appreciate it? No. You push him away as if he doesn't matter. Well I matter!"

"Of course you matter," Ally said.

"Don't lie to me. You were carrying on with that trash that lived next door."

"No. I swear."

"Liar! Why would he be in your backyard late at night if he wasn't coming to see you? But I showed him. I cracked him good with that two-by-four. Cracked him so good he died."

The rest of the pieces of the puzzle fell into place, completing the picture. When Gertie had knocked Floyd's fence down, he'd yelled at us that he was tired of us lurking around his property. He must have seen David lurking around before. It was David who broke into Ally's house and rigged the window. Floyd must have seen him and went to Ally's house to get rid of his lurker once and for all. David thought he'd taken Floyd out, but all he'd done was make it easier for Marco to finish the job.

"I did it all for you, Ally," David said. "But did you appreciate it? No, you didn't!"

My heart sank as I heard him rage. Any thought of reasoning with him flew right out the window. He was clearly insane. I wrapped my hand around the doorknob and slowly twisted it open, then I inched the door open until I had a crack to see through. I was relieved to see that fake David had his back to me. Ally sat on the bed in front of him, her hands tied together in front of her with a scarf.

I clenched my teeth and fought the urge to blast him right

through the door, but I could risk the bullet going through him and hitting Ally. I leaned over a little and looked at the dresser mirror and my pulse spiked when I saw he had a pistol trained on her.

Based on his ranting, I was afraid I didn't have much time left. He was already over the edge and I didn't think he was coming back. Carter should be at least halfway up the stairs, if not on the landing. Unfortunately, the stalker had a clear view of the door, and with no way to determine his position in the room, Carter was at the same disadvantage I was.

Which left only one possibility, and it was a risky one.

I pulled out my phone and sent a text.

Going for it. Back me up as best you can.

A second later the reply came.

Kick his ass.

I slipped my phone back in my pocket and pushed the door open a tiny bit more—just enough to squeeze my hand out of it. Then I moved it up, trying to get Ally's attention. She was staring at David, but when my hand rose just above his shoulder, I saw her eyes widen. I held up one finger and shook it, hoping she'd get the message. She looked down just a bit and lifted her bound hands up to wipe her eyes, tapping her nose with one finger as she lifted her hands.

I pointed to the door, then held up three fingers. She gave me a barely imperceptible nod and I lowered the second finger. Taking a deep breath, I lowered the last one and simultaneously shoved the closet door open as hard as I could, right into the stalker's back. As soon as the door flew open, Ally shot out of the room. The impact jarred me so hard that I crumpled to my knees and lost my grip on my pistol. The stalker regained his balance and ran yelling after Ally.

I jumped up from the closet floor but before I could burst

out of the room, I heard three successive rounds go off and a huge thump.

"Thank God, Carter!" I heard Ally yell and then all I heard was sobbing.

Relief hit me so strongly, I almost sank to the floor again, but I couldn't afford the luxury of celebration. I had to make a decision. If I walked out of this bedroom, then I'd have to have a plausible means of having been there in the first place. I could sneak back out the bathroom window and pretend I was never there, but I had no way of letting Ally know to keep my role a secret.

My phone vibrated.

Cover in place. Ladder at master bedroom window.

I smiled and pushed the closet door open. I had no idea how they'd managed it but Ida Belle and Gertie had given me a feasible, if not insane, way to enter the house and accost a madman. I hurried out of the room and down the stairs, passing the stalker's lifeless body halfway down.

Carter, who was untying the scarf from Ally's hands, looked up in surprise. "What the hell? How did you get up there?"

"I crawled in the master bedroom window. I thought you might need help, but looks like you handled everything."

Ally gave me a strange look, then her expression cleared in understanding and she winked. I didn't know whether she thought I was protecting Carter's manhood or myself from the butt-chewing he was certain to give me if he knew the truth, but I didn't care. As long as the details never came out, I was safe from further scrutiny.

"You could have been killed," Carter said as he pulled the scarf from Ally's wrists. "And where did you get that gun?"

"It's one of the guns Gertie carries in her purse."

Carter looked at me in dismay. "*One* of the guns…that is so not what I wanted to hear."

I smiled and grabbed Ally in a hug. "I'm so glad you're safe. When I realized David was the stalker. I mean, not really David, but you know?"

Ally squeezed me tightly and whispered in my ear, "Thank you."

I released her and sniffed, silently forbidding myself to cry. A couple of seconds later, Ida Belle and Gertie pounded on the front door, and Carter opened it to let them in. They both rushed over to Ally and hugged her, exclaiming over everything that had happened and complimenting Carter on his shooting ability.

Ally turned to me, a confused look on her face. "You said he wasn't really David. What did you mean by that?"

"Whoever he is," Ida Belle said, "he's not David Leger. We ran into someone who knows the real David in town and the inconsistencies showed up immediately. Then Fortune remembered he'd known to bring you tulips and took you to your favorite restaurant…"

Carter nodded. "He's probably been following you for a while."

"But why use David's name?" Ally asked. "Why pretend to be someone with connections to Sinful?"

"I can only guess," I said, "that he knew the real David Leger at some point. He had too many of the details of David's childhood and family correct, including knowing that no family had lived here for some time."

Ida Belle nodded. "Having an old family connection got him instant credibility with the town, including you. We all saw him as Edith Leger's grandson, and that made him okay."

"That's so wrong," Ally said. "Bad enough you're terrorizing women, but to use someone else's identity to do it is even lower."

"Once we know who he was," Carter said, "I'll bet we find out this wasn't the first time he fixated on someone."

Ally nodded. "He said as much. Said we were all bitches that didn't like him. Do you think he's the one who tried to burn down my house?"

"No, but the arsonist is in jail," I said. "And the FBI got the guy who killed Floyd."

"What? Who?"

"It's a long story," I said, "and best told after a hot shower and over a beer. For now, all you need to know is that it's over."

Ally smiled and hugged me again. I looked over her shoulder and Ida Belle and Gertie both gave me a thumbs-up.

I sniffed again.

Epilogue

Saturday turned out to be the perfect ending to a bizarre week. The heat gave us a break and dropped into the low eighties. The humidity even dropped a little and a nice breeze blew off the bayou, creating the perfect environment for being outdoors.

Ally and I started off the day by having coffee sitting in lawn chairs on the bank of the bayou along with a nonstop discussion of everything that had happened. It was hard to believe so many things had transpired in only five days.

As soon as Carter ran the fake David's prints, he'd gotten a hit. His real name was Michael Fuller and he was originally from Lake Charles, as he'd told me. But that's where his truths ended. Michael had been in the Navy and served in the same unit as David Leger. When Carter contacted the real David and explained to him what had happened, David was dismayed that his identity had been used to harm Ally.

David told Carter that Michael had bunked in the same building as him, but he'd never trusted him. He seemed nice on the surface, but David always thought there was something strange about him. He didn't know the specifics, but said that Michael had been dishonorably discharged over a year ago, and rumor was that he'd harassed a female cadet. I had no doubt that rumor was true.

Michael grew fascinated by Sinful after David showed his bunkmates a picture album he'd brought with him, and used to ask David questions about the town. One of the pictures was a photo that a Sinful teen had taken and mailed to David one summer when he couldn't visit. He's listed the names of the teens on the back and a message "You're missing all the fun." David remembered Ally's name was one of the ones listed on the photo. While talking with Carter, David pulled out the album and discovered that the picture was missing. I figure Michael latched onto the picture and his obsession grew from there. He must have tracked Ally to New Orleans and stalked her for a while in order to know her favorite places.

When she moved back to Sinful, he probably panicked that she was now out of reach. After all, a strange man in a small town drew a lot of attention. I think the idea of impersonating David finally hit him and he put his plan in motion, figuring it was his ticket to instant acceptance since the real David had old connections with the town.

The whole thing was so twisted and mad. I was positive that I'd dealt with crazy and evil in my CIA work—Ahmad was a prime example. But I'd never interacted with it so closely and definitely not on a personal basis. It left me feeling so dirty that I didn't think a hundred showers could wash off the ick. I couldn't even imagine how Ally felt, having gone on a date with the guy. But it certainly explained why she wasn't attracted to him but couldn't put her finger on why. I think subconsciously our mind locks onto things that our consciousness doesn't register.

Ally took off mid-morning to meet a contractor in New Orleans. The insurance adjuster had deemed the kitchen a total loss, and she was off to choose new appliances. I offered to go with her, but she said she needed to do it alone, to remind herself that she could. She was so excited about picking out an oven that it was almost contagious. Almost. Then I reminded myself how much effort went into cooking and the moment passed.

I tinkered around the house for a while, then that afternoon, I grabbed a book and headed outside for the hammock. Merlin strolled out with me and crawled onto my stomach, purring so loudly I could hear it over the outgoing tide. I stroked his head and told him how smart he was. After all, he'd given me the idea for the flashlight-bobcat escape, and for that, I was eternally grateful. He gave me a look that said "I already knew all that" and went promptly to sleep.

I wasn't far behind.

I awakened that evening to the sound of a boat, but unlike the others that had traveled the bayou that day, this one cut speed and I heard the bottom scraping as it docked in my backyard. With Ally gone and Ida Belle and Gertie currently boatless, I figured there was only one person left who'd be visiting me by water. I opened one eye and sure enough, Carter was stepping out of his boat and into my backyard.

I opened both eyes and lifted a hand to wave.

"You're not going to throw that cat on me, are you?" he asked.

"There are enough legitimate things you can accuse me of. You need to let go of the handful of things I didn't actually do."

He grinned. "It makes my life easier to put it all in one bucket."

I hefted Merlin off of me and sat up. "Does it really?"

He nodded. "Then I don't have to think as hard. That leaves me free time for other things. Like boat rides. I thought you might want to take one with me. Unless, of course, it would interfere with your busy sleeping schedule."

"Hey, I'm just trying to catch up from all the loss the past week."

"I hear you. I thought the world ended this morning when I

rolled over and the clock read ten a.m. I don't think I've slept that late since high school." He extended his hand to me. "So, about that boat ride."

"I'm wearing shorts," I said as I took his hand and allowed him to tug me out of the hammock.

He pulled me up and close to him. "You look perfect. Just put on your shoes and let's go."

What the hell? If you have hammock hair and no makeup on and a smoking-hot guy says you look perfect, you're a fool to argue. I slipped on my sandals and walked to the boat, still holding his hand. He helped me inside, then shoved the boat off the bank and hopped inside.

He took off down the bayou at a moderate clip, waving at other boaters as we passed. It seemed as if everyone in Sinful were either on a boat or in their yard today. I leaned back in my seat and closed my eyes, enjoying the combination of the wind and setting sun on my face. When we got to the bay that the bayou ran into, he directed the boat to the right, rather than turning around and heading back to my house, as I'd expected him to do.

"Where are we going?" I asked.

"It's a surprise."

I watched as we approached a small island that sat off to one side of the bay. Carter drove his boat right up the sloped bank, and motioned for me to get out. "There's something I want to show you," he said. "I think you're going to like it."

He extended his hand to me and I climbed out of the boat, then we headed up the bank and onto a path that ran through a clump of cypress trees. I have to admit, walking down the path, holding Carter's hand, had my pulse ticking up a notch.

A couple minutes later, we stepped out of the trees, and my pulse went into overdrive. The tiny clearing was covered with low swamp grass, and it sat ten feet above the bay, like a little lockout on the tip of the island. The sun was setting directly in front of us, casting an orange glow over the water.

In the center of the clearing sat a table and two chairs. Plates with silver lids sat at each seat and a bottle of champagne chilled in a bucket next to the table. The smell wafting up from the table made my mouth water, and I couldn't stop staring at everything.

"You did all this for me?"

"I did it for us. I think I had it wrong before. I thought you might prefer this to a crowded restaurant in New Orleans."

I nodded. "The food smells incredible. I can't believe you cooked for me."

"Well, I'm smart enough not to ruin the evening with my own cooking, but I arranged for the perfect meal."

"Ally. She didn't really have to go to pick out ovens, did she?"

"No. She's been at my house all afternoon cooking and lamenting the fact that I have nothing suitable for preparing food."

I smiled as a warm, fuzzy feeling swept over me. All Ally's excitement had been about preparing this meal for Carter and me. It was the coolest feeling to know that someone cared about you so much they'd be excited about going to this much trouble for you.

Carter pulled the champagne out of the bucket and poured us each a glass. "To whatever the future may bring," he said.

Perfect. I clinked my glass against his and took a sip, then I put it down and did what I'd wanted to do since I first saw him walking up the bank at my house—I wrapped my arms around him and kissed us both senseless.

As my body pressed against his, all I could think was that I never wanted that moment to end.

The End

More adventures with Swamp Team 3 coming Fall 2014!

About the Author

Jana DeLeon grew up among the bayous and 'gators of southwest Louisiana. She's never stumbled across a mystery like one of her heroines but is still hopeful. She lives in Dallas, Texas with a menagerie of animals and not a single ghost.

Visit Jana at:

Website: http://janadeleon.com
Facebook: http://www.facebook.com/JanaDeLeonAuthor/
Twitter: @JanaDeLeon

For new release notification, to participate in a monthly $100 egift card drawing, and more, sign up for Jana's newsletter.

http://janadeleon.com/newsletter-sign-up/

Books by Jana DeLeon:

Rumble on the Bayou
Unlucky

The Ghost-in-Law Series:
Trouble in Mudbug
Mischief in Mudbug
Showdown in Mudbug
Resurrection in Mudbug
Missing in Mudbug
The Helena Diaries—Trouble in Mudbug (Novella)

The Miss Fortune Series:
Louisiana Longshot
Lethal Bayou Beauty
Swamp Sniper
Swamp Team 3

Made in the USA
Middletown, DE
09 February 2016